A HEART NOT EASILY BROKEN

M. J. KANE

A Butterfly Memoir Novel
Book 1

THE BUTTERFLY MEMOIRS

Butterflies symbolize change, evolution, the shedding of the old and bringing out the new. A memoir is a story, a narration told first hand, of someone's personal experiences.

Like butterflies in the spring that disappear into cocoons and emerge, completely changed, M.J.'s characters are no longer the same when their story ends.

CHAPTER 1

Ebony

"This is the last time I wear this dress."

"Oh, please, Ebony," Yasmine, my best friend and roommate, yelled in my ear.

The music pounding out of the nightclub's speakers made it nearly impossible to hear her.

"Stop fidgeting. You look uncomfortable," she added, winking at the bartender who handed us our drinks.

No matter how many times I adjusted the hem of my dress it was impossible to ignore the warm air tickling the backs of my thighs as people pushed past me in the crowded bar. It would take more fabric to keep my shapely derriere from involuntary exposure.

"Thanks." I slipped money into the bartender's tip jar, and he rewarded me with a gorgeous smile. "For the record, I *am* uncomfortable." I turned to face Yasmine.

"*Freakum* dresses are your thing, not mine."

Yasmine laughed. "True, everyone's not blessed with a body like mine." She ran a hand over her hips, striking a pose. "Besides, I love showing off mine."

I rolled my eyes and chuckled before sipping my margarita. Yasmine's light-skinned complexion, slender ballet dancer body, long legs, and B-cup breasts suited her personality. At times I wished my body was more like hers, though. It would make shopping for clothes a lot easier. As it was, I had been blessed with the shapely figure my Nana called *bootylicious*. According to her, and her photo albums, I looked just like her when she was my age, with caramel-colored skin, perfectly proportioned hips, a butt that drew major attention, and D-cup breasts, making it hard for a man to look me straight in the eye.

I groaned while making another wardrobe adjustment. The jaw-dropping cleavage of my dress threatened to give my *girls* their own airtime.

"I love my body, too," I said. "I'd just rather not show it to everyone."

Yasmine shook her head while my attention went back to the club patrons. A wide variety of men lined the dark walls, standing just out of range of the overhead lights, making it impossible to pick out their faces in the smoky room. No doubt, many were on the hunt, looking for an easy lay. It shouldn't be hard; one scan of the room revealed potential opportunities in every direction. Nearly every woman in the club wore a dress so tight it appeared to be a spray on, with skirts stopping just below their hips. I cringed. That sounded like my attire. Self-conscious, I tugged on the edges of my dress again.

The next time we go out, Yasmine is not selecting my outfit.

"That dress is going to get you some major action tonight. You'll be thanking me in the morning ... or afternoon." She laughed.

I rolled my eyes. "I don't have time to get into a real relationship right now. Finishing this last year of college is my focus. I've got to get that veterinarian job at the zoo; I've worked too hard to mess up now. Besides, I don't need a man to take care of me."

Yasmine smirked.

"Financially," I clarified. "Having a nice body to curl up with is a different story."

She laughed and held out her hand for a high-five. "That's my girl. Look around. I bet you'll find someone." Her attention went to a dark-skinned guy headed in our direction. "There's one right there."

He glanced over, smiled, and kept walking.

He was attractive all right, but not the physical type I preferred. I was attracted to men who were tall, had thick lips, and eyes that peered into the depths of my soul. A man with the body of a sex machine, yet had no problem working hard for a living and wasn't afraid to get his hands dirty.

One of the first things I noticed about a man was not his shoe size, but his hands. If they were too pretty and soft, the man didn't believe in hard work. If they were overly calloused with visible dirt under the nails and full of scrapes and bruises, those were signs that a man didn't take care of the little things, which meant the rest of him would be questionable. Now, a man with hands somewhere in between, calloused from work with no traces of dirt under his nails, those were signs of a hardworking man who could clean up nice. Everywhere.

I shook my head and sipped my drink. "He's not my type."

"Stop being picky. It's only going to be a summer fling."

"Even so, if I'm going to give a man my body and time, I should at least be able to hold an intelligent conversation. Everything doesn't have to happen between the sheets."

Yasmine shrugged. "Suit yourself." She resumed drinking her wine.

I scanned the crowd to find my other roommate. "Yaz, have you seen Kaity?"

"What?" Yasmine shouted back.

I leaned closer. "Kaity, have you seen her?" My voice cracked. Clubbing could be fun, but it wore out my vocal cords.

Yasmine pointed to the opposite end of the bar. "She's over there talking to some guy. Look at Miss Texas." Yasmine gestured to Kaitlyn with her plastic cup of wine. "She comes to the club to hang with us black girls and the guys go for her first." She shook her head. "I'm not mad at her, though. You work with what God gave you."

Kaity's choice of club attire made her stand out in a sea of women wearing barely-there dresses. Tonight, she'd opted to wear a form fitting dress, which stopped just above her knees. The olive satin fabric matched her green eyes, and she'd pinned her long blond hair away from her face.

Along with her outfit, Kaity's bubbly laugh and infectious smile attracted men like a magnet. Her large breasts on a slender frame didn't hurt either. Somehow, her country twang seemed to fascinate the men in Southern California.

Yasmine stared at me questioningly. "Why are you still here? This whole night is about you. How are you going to get laid if you just stand there?"

"I'm still looking."

My gaze centered on a man across the room who appeared to be watching me. A quick appraisal revealed a nice-looking guy with the appropriate build and a cute smile. He fidgeted with his drink more than I did with my dress. Every time our eyes connected, he looked away. Oh, well, if he couldn't man-up, it was his loss.

My search resumed just as the music blaring from the speakers ceased. The colorful strobe lights continued to twirl, painting the room with a blue, red, and yellow glow, while the house lights dimmed, cloaking the smoke-filled room in near darkness. Lights now centered on the stage as the club MC came on. After thanking everyone for coming out and making the obligatory remarks about the bar, he introduced the house band, *Diverse Nation*.

"Javan said his roommate is in this band," Yasmine said.

The club we were at came highly recommended by Javan, who of course was one of her hook ups. I never understood what she saw in him. The man was too GQ. Besides, he made me uncomfortable every time he came around.

I wondered what category Javan's roommate would fit.

Only one way to find out.

The band came onto the stage; their name suited

them. The different members represented every nationality, it seemed. My attention immediately went to the drummer.

He had dark mahogany skin, but it was impossible to judge his height, since he stood on a stage. His build was exactly what I liked — shoulders the width of a doorframe and muscles bulging through his T-shirt like the Incredible Hulk.

He took his place on stage, tapped his drumsticks together, and proceeded to drum out a rhythm, making the crowd go wild. Impressive. Within minutes, the dance floor filled with gyrating bodies, moved by the music.

I pointed to the drummer. "Is that Javan's roommate?"

She shrugged. "I've never met him."

"Come on, Yaz, let's dance," I said, draining the last of my drink.

"No thanks. Like I said, tonight is about you." She tipped her cup toward the sea of moving bodies. "Besides, girls in packs don't get picked up easily. Go shake what your momma gave you."

"So you're going to leave me all alone?" My hands rested on my hips while I tapped out a rhythm with my heel.

"Hey, my job is done. I picked out the dress, brought you here, and planted the seed of suggestion in your thick head. The rest is up to you, sister."

I searched the end of the bar, looking for Kaitlyn. Maybe she would join me on the dance floor. Unfortunately, she entertained the same man. I was on my own.

I rose to the challenge and made my way onto the crowded dance floor, through the myriad of swaying bodies — again, adjusting my dress's hem — with one goal in mind: meet the drummer.

After securing a spot near the front of the stage, I raised my hands and began to dance. For the first time in months, I forgot about books, the stress of my internship at the zoo, and work at the clinic. I closed my eyes and got lost in the music, letting it guide my body in sensual movements while telegraphing my desire, hoping the drummer would notice my body language.

The song ended, and I opened my eyes to cheer with the rest of the crowd. I was noticed all right. Various men in my immediate vicinity threw out catcalls and whistles, which were flattering, but the drummer paid me no attention. In fact, only one of the band members seemed to notice me.

One of the guitar players watched me intently. Astonished, I nearly stumbled in my heels. He was attractive but ... he was white, not what I was aiming for. My lips tilted in a small smile before I moved out of his line of sight, placing myself in front of dancers who'd moved closer to the stage, blocking my view of the drummer.

The next song played, and again, I tried to get lost in the music. My eyes closed, but it was impossible to find my groove again without feeling stalked. The hair on the back of my neck stood up. My gaze traveled the length of the stage, to the guitar player, who once again, watched me with a predatory gleam. When the song ended, I worked my way back to the bar.

Neither Yasmine nor Kaitlyn were there. They must have gone to the bathroom.

"What can I get you, miss?" the bartender asked, interrupting my thoughts.

After the MC announced the band was taking a brief intermission, music blasted from the speakers again.

"Margarita, extra shot of tequila, please." The bartender nodded and went to fill my order.

"Did you get a load of the blond guitar player? He's hot!"

My attention turned to a busty brunette who'd taken up residence in the seat next to me. I recognized her as being one of the women who'd been dancing next to me. She adjusted her boobs, primping while talking to her friend.

"He doesn't know it yet, but I'm going home with him tonight," she continued. Her friend giggled.

Good luck. She had a better chance than I did of finding a man tonight.

"Here you go." The bartender placed a napkin in front of me with my drink.

"I've got this," a deep voice said close to my ear, making me jump. It was incredibly sexy despite the fact it scared me. It also sent a warm tingle down my spine. Intrigued, I turned and found myself face-to-face with the guitar player. The same one my barstool neighbor wanted to go home with.

Any sort of coherent words failed me.

"Sorry, I didn't mean to scare you." Two dimples rested on either side of firm lips when he smiled.

Wow. The man looked good from the dance floor, but up close, his presence demanded my full attention. He was tall, probably a good six-two to my five-foot-five. His build reminded me of a well-built basketball player. The low lights of the club reflected off damp blond hair with dark undertones. His confident smile cocked to the side, revealing pearly white teeth. The blue shirt he wore complimented the color of his eyes, sparkling like waves of the ocean while hinting at mischief. Baggy shorts and a pair of clean black Converse completed his attire.

He turned to the bartender. "Joe, put her drink on my tab. I'll have the usual." The bartender nodded before walking away. The blond focused his gaze back on me, watching before he spoke again. "You're not going to thank me?"

I raised my eyebrows at his comment. "I didn't ask you to pay for my drink." I couldn't stand a man who expected me to be ecstatic because he bought me a drink. I was capable of doing that myself.

Humor flashed in his eyes. "Excuse me for being a gentleman. Unfortunately, it's too late for you to pay. Guess you're stuck." He reached for his beer when the bartender returned, twisted off the cap, and took a huge swig.

Stuck? Is that what he thought? Passing the drink over to the brunette, saying it came from him, then ordering my own sounded like a good idea. But at ten dollars a drink, I'd be a fool not to accept a freebie.

Instead of saying thanks, I said, "Don't let this dress fool you. If you expect me to sleep with you because you bought me a drink, forget it." My focus left him and resumed searching the crowd for my friends.

I turned back around in time to catch blue eyes exploring the length of my body.

"That was not my intention." His eyes now focused above the deep cleavage of my dress. "Since we've gotten that out of the way, maybe you'll answer this question."

I narrowed my eyes. "What?"

13

He chuckled. "What's your name?" He extended a hand. "I'm Brian."

My focus immediately went to his hand. Large palm, slightly calloused, sporting a deep tan, his nails were a little rough, fingers sporting a few cuts, but they were clean. I glanced back up at his face. This white man was hitting on me. I was flattered knowing he watched me dance, but buying me a drink and asking my name? What did he expect to happen next?

He waited patiently, his hand suspended in midair.

"Ebony." I accepted his handshake.

"Ebony. That's a beautiful name."

The tingle going up my spine from the way it rolled off his tongue, and the sensation of our connected hands, kept my lips from moving. This was unreal. I didn't expect any kind of spark from him.

I studied his eyes; lust and desire weren't visible, but there was something else. Something made him hold my hand longer than necessary. I squirmed involuntarily before being the first to turn away.

"Meeting like this is not the best way to get to know someone." He released my hand before leaning down to talk to me without yelling quite as loud.

My body tingled at the warm caress of his breath near my ear again. The scent of his musky cologne mixed with sweat from standing under the stage lights was alluring, the heat from his body inviting.

I stared up at him, expecting him to burst out in laughter any second. "You're kidding, right?"

"Why would I be joking?" He took another swig of beer, his gaze steady on mine.

I laughed lightly while raising my hand to break his line of sight, wiggling my fingers.

He studied it briefly. "I don't see a ring. Are you married or in a relationship?"

I glanced over my shoulder for a moment, wondering which corner of the club my roommates were hiding in while laughing at the practical joke they'd sprung on me.

"Are you color blind?"

"No."

"The lights in here are low, but you can't say you didn't notice. I'm black, that doesn't bother you?"

A deep line creased Brian's brow. "Why should it?" He appraised me for a moment. "Does it bother you?"

"No," I said a little too forcefully. I'd left myself open for that remark.

"So what's your point?" He angled himself to look directly in my eyes.

I assessed him again. His cerulean eyes were sharp, studying me as much as I studied him. Sun-bleached hair set off his bronzed skin, a clear sign of time spent surfing, no doubt. Long legs led to a narrow waist and broad shoulders. I could only imagine what he would look like naked. *Wait, why did I think that way?*

"You're not my type, and I'm not yours." I put my cup to my lips and gulped. Forgetting about the extra shot of tequila, I nearly choked.

Brian angled his head, apparently musing over my statement. "You have no idea what my type is."

"What about her?" I nodded at the brunette who sat behind me.

She'd gone quiet the moment Brian came to the bar. I risked a glance over my shoulder and saw her lips were in a tight line as she glared at me. She didn't bother to look away. If looks could kill, the coroner would have picked me up off the floor a long time ago. Fortunately, the music was too loud for her to hear our conversation.

When I turned back, Brian's stare continued to be intense. The room felt as if it had shrunk to the size of a shoebox.

"If I wanted her, I wouldn't be talking to you."

Disbelief had me laughing. Of all the brothers in the club, none had approached me. Yet, this man spied me from the stage and made his way over. I had to admit, he was bold.

"I want to get to know you. We could —" Annoyance flashed on his face when he acknowledged the hand on his shoulder.

I scoffed, nearly spitting out my drink. The drummer, the object of my suggestive dancing — and oh, my God, that body — stood next to Brian. He didn't give me the time of day.

"Yo, man, the next set starts in five."

Brian nodded. "Sorry. I want to continue this discussion, but they need me back on stage. Why don't you meet me in VIP when I'm done? It's less crowded. Plus it's away from the speakers, so you can hear yourself think."

As if to prove his point, a waitress carrying a large tray full of empty cups bumped into his elbow. He managed to hold his beer without spilling a drop. "Tell security the Bass Man sent you. You'll get in with no problem."

"The Bass Man?"

"Yeah, I play bass guitar. You'd be surprised how many women try to get in there." He nodded to the roped-off corner of the room with oversized plush sofas under focused track lights. A few women were already lounging in the area. A man the size of Chewbacca and thankfully, a lot less hairy and dressed in black, stood, his arms crossed while wearing dark shades. He mean-mugged the crowd, discouraging them from walking his way. My eyes must have bulged, because Brian chuckled. His laugh was as deep as his voice.

"He won't bite," he said with a wickedly charming grin. "'Til then, Ebony." He toasted me with his bottle, drained the remnants of his beer before disappearing into the crowd, and then reappeared on the stage.

"Who was he?" Yasmine sat on the barstool Brian had left empty.

Well, well, my roommates found their way back. "As if you didn't know."

"Uh, no," Kaitlyn replied in her country twang.

I eyed them suspiciously. "A guy from the band."

"Really?" Kaitlyn stood on tiptoes to peer over the crowd. "He's hot."

I couldn't disagree.

"Did you get his number?" Yasmine asked when she finished her own study of his anatomy.

"No, but I got an invite to VIP."

Two sets of eyebrows rose.

"So, are you going?" Yasmine studied me, no doubt wondering if tonight's mission had been a success.

I stared at the stage as the music began to play, watching Brian in action. He looked in my direction and smiled.

"I haven't decided yet."

CHAPTER 2

Brian

"Hey, Brian, we're done over here. Is there anything else?" My cousin Dylan waved for my attention.

I cut off the weed whacker to appraise Dylan and Peter's work, inhaling the smell of freshly cut grass. They did a good job clearing the yard of all the clippings. The decision to hire my young cousins for the summer had paid off. Letting them handle the grunt work left me time to handle the finer details, like trimming the edges of my clients' professionally landscaped flowerbeds.

I loved to work, but after spending the weekend playing late-night gigs with my band, sleeping in on Monday would have been my preference, except my bills made it impossible.

Besides, laziness was not in my nature.

"No, we're done. Take the bags to the curb." I wiped the back of my gloved hand over my brow to keep the sweat dripping down from stinging my eyes.

Dylan nodded before passing the message to his brother.

I removed the weed whacker's carrying strap from around my neck, placed it in the bed of the truck, and then reached into the semi-melted ice in the cooler to retrieve a bottle of Gatorade. The liquid saturated my parched mouth.

"Heads up." I tossed them both a bottle.

They murmured their thanks before leaning against the tailgate.

"Man, it's hot," Peter said. "How many yards have we done today?"

Dylan laughed. "This is the fifth one, bro."

Peter turned to me for confirmation. I nodded and threw my empty bottle into the truck bed, adding to last week's collection of bottles to be recycled.

"Man, how did I forget that?" Peter mumbled.

"Because your mind is still stuck on three jobs ago," Dylan teased.

Peter continued to have a look of awe on his face. I chuckled. If he got this flustered at the sight of three grown women lounging topless poolside, he was going to be dumbstruck when attending his first frat party in college.

I remembered my time spent in college. Somehow, I managed to discover my independence without screwing up too much along the way. Hot women always found their way into my dorm room once they learned I was in a band. A year after joining *Diverse Nation*, I got over the hype and focused on my craft instead. Being a member taught me discipline and kept me grounded with my eyes on the prize when it came to my career.

Music was my life. Cutting grass made it possible to pay the bills until my career took off.

I walked the yard one last time, surveying our work. The hedges trimmed, grass cut evenly, and clippings set curbside. Mrs. Dillard would be pleased.

"Finish loading up," I instructed while walking up the long stone path that led to a partially covered over-hang and rang the doorbell. The narrow strip of shade didn't do much to ward off the sun's oppressive heat. My gaze went to the flowerbed near the front door. There were a few weeds growing among her flowers.

I smiled down at the older woman as the door opened. She was in her late sixties and believed in looking her best at all times. Mrs. Dillard lived next door to my parents. She'd been my first paying customer. She'd advertised my services at the monthly homeowner association meetings until nearly every neighbor became my customer. As a thank you, I offered her a lifetime of free yard maintenance. She refused, insisting she pay a discounted rate instead.

"Mrs. Dillard, you look young as ever." I flashed the smile that used to earn me milk and cookies.

She laughed. "Brian, you are such a flirt. If I were thirty years younger ..."

I shook my head. "Yeah, but then Mr. Dillard wouldn't want me to come back around."

"True, oh, well." She stepped out onto her porch to survey the yard. "A great job as always, thank you."

"You're welcome." Unable to resist, I asked, "When are you going to let me weed your garden? It would be free of charge."

"Never. I love to have my hands in the dirt. You handle the rest of the yard. I'll handle my weeds."

"Yes, ma'am." I accepted the check. "Thank you. We'll see you in two weeks."

Sweaty bare feet hanging out the passenger side window greeted me when I reached the truck.

"Peter, I am not going to be held responsible by Aunt Gina if your foot gets cut by road debris."

"Sorry," he muttered, sliding his feet back inside. "It's hot as h-e-double-hockey sticks out here. My feet were on fire in those boots."

Now that his feet were inside, it made sense he'd hung them outside. Telling him to climb into the bed of the truck didn't sound like a bad idea.

"Aunt Gina's not around. You can drop your choir-boy act, and say hell. It'll be our secret."

"Yeah, right. My mom probably has my boots bugged. She'd come home and slap me upside the head after listening to the recording."

I cracked up. "Do you plan to let loose when you move into your dorm?" I concentrated on backing out of the driveway.

"Hell, yeah."

Dylan and I both chuckled. My attention turned to my parents' house next door. The yard would not need maintenance for another week. Unfortunately, my mother wasn't home. What I wouldn't give to snag a piece of homemade apple pie she always had on hand.

From time to time, I missed home and my four obnoxious sisters. There were plenty of good times shared in my childhood home; birthdays, holidays, and just flat out fun. My father made sure that as the only boy in a household full of women, we spent a lot of time together. My mom and sisters taught me how to treat a woman while my dad taught me how to be a man. Work hard, and never, ever take no for an answer. Words I lived by on a daily basis.

We'd reached the front of the subdivision when my cell rang. I jotted down notes before snapping the phone shut. "It looks like we've got one more job."

Groans erupted from my passengers.

"Hey, you want to get paid, right?" I glanced over my shoulder while punching the address into Google Maps. "This is how it's done. You guys want money for dates; I need money for my girl, too."

"What girl?" Peter blurted.

Dylan cackled from the back seat.

"I have a girl. Unlike you guys, my girl isn't high maintenance. She loves it when I hold her, and it doesn't take much for me to make her sing." I grinned so hard my face felt like it would split in two.

Dylan pretended to puke.

"Dude," Peter said, "you seriously need to find a girlfriend. I can't stand listening to you talk about your guitar like it's a real woman."

"Yeah, man, you need help," Dylan chimed in.

"No, what I need is a new guitar. That will take my playing to a whole new level."

Peter snickered. "Maybe, but your love life is gonna suck."

I laughed, ignoring the ribbing. These young guys just didn't understand. There was more to life than chasing after women.

Twenty minutes later, we arrived at the new customer's address. There were no cars in the driveway. According to the woman who called, her roommate was on her way and would be responsible for payment. The guys waited in the truck while I surveyed the property, walking the length of the lawn, tossing small rocks to the yard's edge. The last thing I needed was to pay for a customer's broken windshield caused by a rock thrown by the lawnmower.

The two-story house had a decent sized yard. There were a few large shade trees in the front. A quick assessment showed the roots shouldn't get in the way of the lawnmower blades. My height allowed me to peer over the high wooden gate of the backyard. It was less than half the size of the front. We'd be able to knock it out in no time.

Peter and Dylan were out of the truck when I returned, so we went over the game plan. We'd just wrapped up when a car pulled into the driveway. I exhaled deeply before turning back to fill the weed whacker with gasoline. Our drive would not be a waste of time.

I heard the slam of a car door, followed by the opening of another. Light footsteps crunched on loose gravel in the driveway as my customer approached. I turned to introduce myself in full customer-service mode.

I paused, thankful my customer's eyes focused elsewhere, and quickly shut my mouth. It was Ebony, the woman from the club.

Her attention appeared to be on something in her purse as she walked my way, so she hadn't seen me yet.

She was not dressed as she was Saturday night. Her hair wasn't flowing over her shoulders, tempting my fingers to get lost in its waves. Her legs were not bare, nor did she wear a skin tight, short dress, showing off shapely calf muscles. Instead, she wore a baggy shirt over pants with some kind of printed design, something like standard medical wear. She wore her hair in a ponytail, and her feet were in tennis shoes. She struggled to balance an armful of books of various sizes and a book bag over her shoulder.

Ebony was still sexy as hell.

"I'm glad you haven't got started yet. My roommate called me at the last minute and told me you were coming. I don't have any cash on me. Do you take checks or —" Her voice faltered when she saw me. "Brian? What are you doing here?"

I caught a hint of fire in her eyes and something else. Maybe guilt for not meeting me in VIP?

"I'm here to cut your grass." I screwed the top back on the gas can, fighting the urge to laugh at the irony of the situation.

Play it cool. I was not about to let her know how disappointed I'd been sitting alone. What happened a few nights ago had nothing to do with the money she was about to put in my pocket.

"I thought you were a musician."

I pulled goggles and gloves out of the driver's side door pocket. "I am, but it doesn't pay the bills just yet. This is my day job."

Ebony's gaze traveled to the truck and my cousins before settling back on me.

"This is my business," I added, watching her thin eyebrows arch.

Since I hadn't questioned her about the VIP incident, she seemed to relax. The sound of a lawnmower cranking up broke the awkward silence.

"Well, I'll get out of your way." She backed away

from the truck and headed for her house.

It dawned on me I didn't answer her question regarding the form of payment. At least it would give me something to talk about when we were done.

Saturday night, Ebony disappeared like Cinderella, without leaving a hint of a glass slipper. Now, barely two days later, I found where she lived. What were the chances? This was fate.

I took the opportunity to appreciate every inch of her hidden under baggy clothes. The image of her in the black form-fitting dress revealing every curvy inch of her body had haunted my dreams.

Outside the club, in natural light, Ebony did not disappoint. Her almond shaped eyes were a rich shade of brown, dark and mysterious. She wore no makeup on her caramel skin, and her lips were naked, with no hint of gloss.

I chuckled when she finally got her front door unlocked. It appeared she'd run into some trouble with her key. *Flustered perhaps?*

I hoped so. With a little luck, I just might have a chance to get her to talk to me about more than grass.

CHAPTER 3

Ebony

"**D**amn it." I pushed the door shut with my foot, nearly dropping the books balanced in my arms. A quick peek out the living room blinds showed Brian staring at the closed front door with a smug look.

Of all the people in southern California who cut grass, how in the world did he end up at my home? Where did Yasmine find this guy? Did she know Brian?

My roommates had given me a hard time for not accepting his VIP offer. After Saturday night, this smelled of a set up. And now this. First, Yasmine calls at the last minute, knowing I'm on the way home and tells me to expect someone to be there cutting the grass, and then coincidently forgets the guy's name. Yeah, right.

Annoyed, I pulled my phone out of my purse and called first Yasmine and then Kaitlyn. Of course,

Yasmine's phone went to voicemail. Kaitlyn's did too. It would be a waste of time to leave a message, but when they got home, there would be hell to pay. I appreciated their interest in my love life, but it was exactly that. Mine. After Saturday night's attempt to set me up, they agreed to stay out of it.

The sound of a lawnmower gliding past the living room window caught my eye. One of the guys rolled the mower across the grass. At least the yard would receive the attention it needed. I headed for the kitchen; it was my turn to cook dinner. Tonight's menu would consist of frozen lasagna and salad. Thank goodness for bagged salad, because I was in no mood to cut up any vegetables. Even though school was not in session, my goal was to stay on top of my game. Dr. Jacobs, my mentor and one of the head veterinarians on staff at the Los Angeles Zoo, had allowed me to borrow several books from his personal library. He appreciated my hard work and offered to give me a heads-up on classes I'd be taking in the fall. I was anxious to get started.

Before I started dinner, I needed to take a shower and wash off the odors of the animal clinic where I worked as a veterinarian's assistant. Juggling both jobs was a lot of work, but the rewards were well worth it.

I closed my eyes and groaned. Oh, no, I reeked. No wonder Brian grinned like an idiot when he thought I wasn't looking. It wasn't as if he could talk. His shirt clung to his body, saturated with sweat as though he had run through my neighbor's sprinklers.

I grabbed my things and headed upstairs.

Unable to resist, I stacked the books on my desk and pulled out one that caught my attention the most. It dealt with the daily care of orangutans. The topic interested me most because of the zoo's recent addition. Baby Nala was born a few days ago, but sadly, her mother had died. It was now up to the zoo's staff to provide the care she needed to keep her healthy until she matured enough to join the other orangutans in the zoo exhibit. As an intern, I would be one of the select few tasked with this job. It promised to be a rewarding experience.

After a quick review, I set down the book. The lasagna had another forty-five minutes to cook. I walked to my window to check on the guys' progress. They were nearly finished. It wouldn't be long before Brian would be looking for payment.

Crap. He never answered my question. If he didn't accept checks, he would have to follow me to the ATM.

I stripped down and reached in the shower to adjust the water temperature. Body wash in hand, I stepped into the steaming water.

The stench of work swirled down the drain, replaced by the scent of melons while the water caressed my body like a summer rain. I pulled off my ponytail holder, letting the water run down my face while washing my hair. The next time Brian smelled me, I wanted it to be something soft and sweet, not animalistic.

Hold on, why did it matter how I smelled? Irritated by the thought, I scrubbed a little harder.

My thoughts went back to Friday night. Brian smelled nice at the club. His rough, callused palm felt nice too. No wonder. He did more than strum a guitar all day. I admired that.

Getting out of the shower, I toweled off. Even though Brian was five times sweatier than when we'd met, it somehow made him more attractive. When I realized it was him standing at the truck, I assumed he would demand to know why I avoided his invitation. Instead, he'd been cordial, making the surprise easier on both of us. He was definitely about his business.

Oiled up, smelling good, my damp hair in a bun, and wearing a pair of cotton shorts and a tank top, I headed back down to the kitchen. The lasagna should be nearing completion and so should Brian.

The buzzing sound of yard equipment drew my attention to the bay window. Somehow, they'd gotten over the locked gate. Oops, I'd forgotten to take the chain off before hopping in the shower. He was resourceful, too.

Brian stood with his weed whacker, swinging it in a controlled arc along the fence. My eyes widened; he was shirtless. The man had an incredibly strong looking back. His shorts hung loosely from his hips, exposing the top of his underwear from the weight of the sweat-stained shirt stuffed under his belt. *Hmm, boxers or briefs?* Sweat ran in heavy rivulets down his shoulder blades, trickling to the already damp shorts.

None of that compared to the way he looked when he turned around to speak to one of the guys working with him. His long torso, free of body fat, sported a light sprinkling of blond hair between his pecs. His abdomen showed every cut of muscle I'd seen in high school biology textbooks. His abs were tight, his belly button nearly nonexistent.

Brian's bronzed skin reminded me of a Greek statue, a testament of many hours spent working outside. His backward baseball cap hid the thick blond curls I'd seen at the club. The damp ringlets hung below its rim, accentuating his square facial structure and the shape of his nose. His blue eyes seemed to glow from deep within his skin.

Brian was unbelievably sexy.

One of the younger guys stepped into my line of sight, blocking my admiration of his anatomy. I bit my lip in irritation until Brian extended an arm. My eyes widened at the sight of tattoos over well-defined muscle. Intricate dark rings banded both biceps. How did I miss that? Oh yeah, his abs had distracted me. Curious, I stepped closer to the blinds, parting them. Damn, I couldn't see the entire design. What was it?

At that moment, Brian faced the window. He remained expressionless for a moment before he squinted, then smiled.

Busted.

My face felt hot. I took a moment to clear the expression on my face before grabbing three cold bottles of water out of the refrigerator and walking outside.

I surveyed the yard while offering him a bottle. "It looks good."

"It sure does," Brian said.

I glanced at him. He didn't hide his examination of me. His gaze started at my bare legs and slowly traveled up. His expression made his thoughts apparent. I started to open my mouth and comment, until our eyes met. His blue eyes held mine, sending a warm tingle along my skin, reminding me of the way I'd felt when he held my hand.

"Thanks for the water," he said, then whistled for the other workers.

Try as I might, it was impossible to keep my eyes off his body when his back was to me. I took the opportunity to peek at his tattoos again. Standing this close, I could make out a little more of the intricate design. To truly see it, I would have to get close, so close I could ...

I looked up to find his lips tilted in a lopsided grin.

Damn, busted again.

Not wanting him to think I was impressed, I forced my face to stay blank. "How much is it going to cost?"

Laugher danced in those gorgeous blue eyes. Brian took long draws of water, apparently in no rush to answer my question. I forced my eyes to stay on his and ignored the fact that sweat should not look so good.

He raised an eyebrow. "I haven't decided yet."

I frowned. "What do you mean? You've been here for nearly an hour."

He shrugged, pulled a rag from his pocket, wiped his face, and then dragged the thing down his chest. I automatically followed the movement before snapping my eyes back to his. A slow grin spread across his face. "It depends."

"On what?"

"On how honest you're going to be with me."

I clamped my jaw tight while crossing my arms, fighting the irritation building. Brian apparently thought he could do or say anything to get his way. He did it when buying me a drink at the club. He'd done it when assuming I'd meet him in VIP. Now this.

My lack of a sex life and unexplained physical attraction to him made my irritability worse.

"Honest about what?" I ground out.

Brian's eyes flashed with humor again as he finished off the last of his water. "Why didn't you meet me the other night? I looked for you, waited around thinking maybe you got stuck in the bathroom." He crossed his arms, taking a wide stance. "Nothing. No note, no message left with security. You just disappeared."

Realization hit me. "You're going to charge me more because I didn't hook up with you?"

"Hey, don't put words in my mouth. I haven't decided what to charge. That's not the same thing."

"Okay, so what you really mean is if you like my answer, I'll get a discount. If you don't, then you're going to screw me."

Brian's mischievous smile caused me to suck my teeth. Bad choice of words.

"Overcharging my customers is not good for business." He chuckled. "Besides, offering a discount would be an incentive for you to answer the question and not avoid it the same way you avoided me." He paused to unhook the weed whacker's strap from around his neck and set it on the ground. He rolled his neck and shoulders, then crossed his arms and resumed his wide-legged stance.

I glanced down and noticed the slight bow in his muscular legs. Damn, he looked good.

"Brian." I forced myself to stare at the men bagging lawn clippings. "I went home."

"Why didn't you stick around? You could have left your number if you needed to leave."

Brian regarded me intently while waiting for my reply. His scrutiny made me nervous.

I took a deep breath and held it for a few seconds before blowing it out. "Why do you care? Plenty of women were ready to jump at the opportunity to be with you. Why are you interested in me?"

"Why not? I've seen most of those women before." He laughed as I twisted my mouth. "That didn't come out right. What I mean is they are all the same. None of them have caught my attention like you do."

My mind went back to the buffet of women available at the bar, the brunette who gave me the evil eye, red heads, a few blondes, women of every size, shape, and race.

"So you saw me wearing a tight dress and figured you'd get me in bed as a trophy. You know, sex with a black woman?" I rolled my eyes. "I'm an educated black woman with a good head on my shoulders, not some *ho* from the hood. If that's what you want, then I suggest you go take a ride down—"

Brian's dimples popped as his lips pulled back in a hearty laugh. He shook his head. "I knew there was something about you I liked."

Confused, I stared at him. Was he serious?

"You're feisty and don't hold back, I like that. And yes, the color of your skin did have something to do with it."

I pointed a finger at him. "See, that's what I thought." I moved to march back inside, steam practically blowing from my ears.

"No, I'm pretty sure you're thinking the wrong thing. Your skin is beautiful. And by the way, I've dated black women before."

That comment put the brakes on my exit.

"But like I said, the color of your skin is not why I want to take you out." His head cocked to the side as if remembering something. "Wait a minute, you're avoiding my question. Why did you stand me up?"

"Stand you up? We weren't on a date. You assumed I'd come running because you bought me a drink. Was I supposed to be impressed?"

A roguish grin appeared as he shrugged. "Honestly,

I'm glad you didn't. It makes you more interesting."

I tilted my head, appraising him. "Interesting, yeah, right. Would I have been this interesting if we never saw each other again?"

He shrugged. "Maybe, maybe not, I guess we'll never know. What I do know is we're here now. It's a second chance to get to know you. I already know your name, where you live ..." He wagged his eyebrows in an attempt to make me laugh, I supposed.

It didn't work. My internal alarm began to chime. If he didn't like my answer, would he start stalking me?

He raised a hand to tick off fingers. "You're educated, you have a smart mouth, and you're not supposed to be attracted to me." He creased his eyebrows in thought. "That's not enough, I've got more questions."

Vexed beyond belief, I threw my hands up in surrender.

"Okay, fine. If it will save money, I'll play along. What's the question?"

He grinned in victory while I closed my eyes and massaged the bridge of my nose.

"Do you have a problem going out with me because I'm white?" he asked, straight to the point.

"What?" My eyes flew open. It was the last thing I expected him to ask.

His hands went up in defense. "Hey, you're the one who made a big deal about it. Me? I see a sexy woman who's got more to offer than just her looks and a body that's ... well, there's a lot more going on. I'm curious. So what do you say?"

That was unexpected. It took several tries before I could open my mouth. "No, I don't have a problem with you being white."

One of Brian's dark-blond eyebrows rose as if he didn't believe me.

"It's true. One of my best friends and roommate is white," I said in defense.

"Good. Since race isn't a problem, go out with me to-morrow night."

CHAPTER 4

Ebony

I slapped a square of steaming lasagna on Yasmine's plate.

Yasmine watched it slide onto the table when I dropped the plate in front of her. "Whoa, Ebony, what's wrong with you?"

"You guys promised to stay out of my love life."

Her eyes were small slits when she looked up at me. "Yeah, so what's your point?"

My attention went to Kaitlyn. "Oh, don't try to play innocent, you were in on it, too," I said, stomping toward the refrigerator.

"In on what?" Kaitlyn's hazel eyes widened. "I didn't do nothin'."

I rolled my eyes in exasperation and slammed the refrigerator door, salad dressing in hand. "Both of you set this up."

Kaitlyn's eyebrows scrunched together. "Set what up?"

I studied her perplexed expression. Kaitlyn wasn't good at lying, which could only mean one thing. Yasmine was the true source of my irritation.

"Brian." I turned to face her. "You lied. You do know him. I came home to find him standing in our yard. You're the one who set this up." I grabbed my plate from the counter and intentionally dragged my chair from the table, hoping the scraping noise irritated my roommates.

"Excuse me?" Yasmine's well-trimmed eyebrows arched. "The only Brian I know is a guy I dated a year ago. He's a male dancer."

I ground my teeth. Between Yasmine and Brian, my dentist would make a lot of money.

"Yes, you do," I reminded her with a thin amount of patience. "You called him to cut the grass. You know, the same Brian I met at the club."

Kaitlyn held up a hand. "Hold up. You mean the white guy? The one you dissed, was here?"

"I chose to ignore his invitation. It's not the same thing."

Yasmine sat up straighter, all hints of her irritation disappeared. "Wait a minute, how did he find out where you lived?"

"Because you called him." I fought the urge to yell my response.

"No, the number I called belonged to Javan's roommate," Yasmine said.

Both women were silent, watching me as the pieces clicked together.

My mouth dropped open. "Oh. My. God."

"What?" Kaitlyn focused on me.

"This is unbelievable. Brian is Javan's roommate. I thought the drummer was his roommate." I laughed in disbelief.

Yasmine's eyebrows narrowed in confusion. "Did I miss something?"

My anger deflated. "I'm sorry, you guys."

Yasmine picked up a generous helping with her fork. "All's forgiven as long as this lasagna isn't burnt."

Kaitlyn's food remained untouched. "Are you gonna tell us what happened, or what?"

Aware of their questioning faces, I leaned forward to rest my elbows on the table. "Well, you got the gist of it. Brian—"

"The one you dissed," Kaitlyn said.

"Yes, him. It turns out Brian does more than play in a band. He owns a lawn-care business and cuts grass during the day."

"Hmm, on a first-name basis and the man has two jobs. Impressive."

I flicked my gaze to Yasmine.

She shrugged. "What?"

"Anyway, he started flirting with me." I paused, remembering the mischievous gleam in his eyes. "Don't get me wrong, the man is fine, just not my type."

"Because he's white?" Kaitlyn asked.

"No." Brian's gloriously half-naked, sweaty skin and devilish blue eyes were committed to memory. "He's just not ..." I waved a hand over my body. "I like a man with a lot of muscle."

Yasmine smirked. "That's the excuse you're using?"

"Okay, I appreciate a good-looking man of any race. But when it comes to dating, I can't imagine being in an interracial relationship. First, there's the whole, we-don't-have-anything-in-common thing, followed by the look-at-them-staring-at-us thing. And let's not forget the, bring-a-white-boy-home-to-meet-your-family thing. And oh my God, there's the —"

Yasmine put her hand in the air. "Okay, we get it; you have a problem with dating a white guy." She shook her head. "Ebony, let's be real. Your family lives three thousand miles away. Besides, you're not trying to marry the man; you're trying to get your freak on. If black is what you need, wait till it's dark, and turn off the damn light."

Kaitlyn nearly choked on a mouthful of food, while I howled in laughter. Yasmine joined in. We laughed until tears streamed from our eyes. No matter what the situation, Yasmine kept it real.

"Is this based on personal experiences?" I asked when able to speak again.

"Yeah, and hello? Black father, white mother." Yasmine smirked. "Besides, I've been there, done a hell of a lot of that. Black, white, Hispanic, Asian ..." She counted off each with her fingers.

"How could I forget? You're an equal opportunity lover," I mocked.

"Smart ass." She smiled. "Think about it. You mix black with any race and you get a whole lot of beautiful. Vanessa Williams, Halle Berry, Shemar Moore ....mmm, he's yummy. Vin Diesel —"

"Oh, don't forget Tiger Woods," Kaitlyn added enthusiastically.

We both shot her a questioning glance.

"Okay ... he's got a whole lot of everybody in him. Too much, though, because he is not cute," Yasmine stated.

"But he gets paid," Kaitlyn pointed out.

"She's got a point there," I agreed.

We all laughed.

"Back to the story. You guys recognized each other ..." Yasmine prompted.

"We recognized each other, all right. He was nonchalant and all business. Until I went to give him some water, then he changed on me."

Yasmine laughed.

Kaitlyn's eyebrows narrowed. "Whaddya mean?"

"Well, Brian stopped being professional and accused me of standing him up. He wanted to know why I didn't meet him and insisted on an honest answer." I stared down at my plate, pushing pieces of broken lasagna around with my fork. "So I told him he wasn't my type."

"You are never going to get laid," Yasmine muttered.

"He didn't seem to care," I said, shooting her the evil eye. "He asked me out. Well, dared me is a more accurate description."

Kaitlyn laughed. "He dared you to go out with him?"

"We're going to meet tomorrow night at the Santa Monica Pier for dinner."

"See, Kaitlyn, that's why Ebony never plays Truth or Dare. She's a sucker every time," Yasmine said.

I laughed. "Don't get excited. It's more like a business transaction than a date."

They looked at me with raised eyebrows.

"I agreed to go out with him if he cut the grass for free." I jogged my eyebrows.

Both women were all grins as they gave me high-fives.

Yasmine beamed. "See, that's what I'm talking

about. I knew you'd pick up on my lessons one day."

***

The Santa Monica Pier was the perfect location for a first date. Couples strolled along, holding hands, or cuddled up on benches facing the ocean. Several of my past dates were here. But this wasn't a date.

A business transaction. A dare in response to his dare.

When Brian suggested a date instead of payment for services rendered, I'd been speechless. Apparently, he felt getting to know me was worth it. The thought was flattering.

Brian resented the idea of going Dutch, but it was one of my stipulations. After all, he'd bought me a drink and fallen for the free-grass ploy. Besides, this wouldn't go any further. My plan was to answer his questions to stave off his curiosity, and then go home. The next time we needed yard maintenance, I would be sure to have cash on hand. If not, I'd find another company to use. Although I had to admit, it'd be disappointing not to see him half-dressed in my yard again.

I reached for my cell phone to check the time. Brian was fifteen minutes late. There were no missed calls or messages. We'd exchanged phone numbers in case either of us needed to cancel. He never called, so I figured we were still on.

The idea of meeting Brian wasn't so bad. After the day I had at work, a break from the norm would be nice. The closer I got to graduating, the fiercer the competition for the coveted veterinarian technician position became. I had earned the opportunity to move up from being a volunteer to an intern once I graduated U.C.L.A.

Moving from intern to vet tech would put me one step closer to my career goal.

I began working as a volunteer during my second year in college. After five years of working at the zoo, I was privy to everything that went on. The routines, all the secrets, and who was screwing who. Animals weren't the only ones in heat.

I stared at my menu. Instead of food, the image of Dr. Jacobs and Lily — the newest volunteer who was barely legal — in an unimaginable compromising position in the supply closet came to mind. I'd excused myself and made a quick exit from the building. Dr. Jacobs found me a short time later in the orangutan habitat. He pulled me to the side and promised to make me a shoo-in for the full-time position upon graduation if I kept my mouth shut. The idea disgusted me.

After nearly eight years of working my ass off, I didn't give a damn where Dr. Jacobs stuck his private parts, as long as he didn't think I was the one holding his balls. I made my position clear; I didn't need his help, nor did I plan to gossip about his personal affairs. He didn't seem satisfied when I didn't accept his offer. I had a feeling he would be watching my every step. So much for having a mentor.

The delicious aroma of melting cheese and pepperoni awakened hunger pains. Where was Brian?

Fed up with waiting, I dialed his number and got sent straight to voicemail.

Could he be standing me up? Was this retaliation for not hooking up at the club?

Maybe something I said caused him to change his mind.

I wiped a hand across my forehead. It felt as if fate

branded the word *IDIOT* there for the whole world to see.

This definitely had to do with the club. I'm the one who fell for it.

There were no other reasons for me to hang around. I mused over my dinner choices — chicken noodle soup or McDonald's — and signaled the waitress, paid for my drink, and headed out of the pizza parlor. I'd nearly reached the parking lot when I heard my name called.

"Ebony, I'm sorry," Brian shouted as he jogged toward me.

I stopped and waited for him to join me. Either I was under-dressed or he was seriously over-dressed. He wore a black vest over black shirt, silver tie, and black slacks. Black-and-white Converse completed his ensemble. My eyebrows went up in surprise. Not only did he clean up nice, he had a weird sense of style.

"Ebony, I can explain. Just let me catch my breath." He bent over and rested his hands on his knees. His cheeks were flushed red.

I didn't know how to react. A part of me wanted to rejoice because he hadn't stood me up, while another part wanted to fuss for the lack of communication.

I crossed my arms. "This better be good."

"I promise you it is. I was on my way here when I got a call from another musician. He had a gig scheduled tonight but got sick." He paused and wiped sweat from his brow. "I'm sorry. I've got to take this job." His eyes beseeched me in a heartfelt apology, begging me to understand. Brian's smile was apologetic, and his voice sounded genuine.

I knew exactly what it meant to make ends meet.

"I understand the need to get your hustle on, Brian.

You should have called, and I would have understood. We could have canceled."

Brian dug into his pocket and displayed the screen of his phone. "My battery died after that call, and your number is in my phone. My cousin broke my car charger, and I didn't have time to get a new one or charge my battery before I left the house. All I could do was pray you'd still be here."

Beads of sweat dotted Brian's brow. He'd apparently run the entire length of the parking lot to find me. His blue-eyed gaze continued to beg for my forgiveness. Softening, I uncrossed my arms.

"I don't want to cancel. Please, let me make it up to you."

I pursed my lips. "Fine, maybe some other time."

"No, I mean tonight. You've already driven out here. Come with me. This should only take an hour, hour and a half tops. Then I'll take you out for steak, my treat." Brian flashed his baby blues and killer smile.

I was a sucker for dimples.

Besides, steak was a step up from pizza and a lot better than a can of soup. How could I say no to that?

CHAPTER 5

Brian

I t was six-thirty. If I drove fast enough, we would get to the gig with a few minutes to spare.

Ebony hadn't spoken since we pulled out of the parking lot.

Getting her to go out with me had been a challenge. Running late nearly blew the opportunity.

The condition of my work truck made a bad first impression. I didn't consider this detail before insisting she go with me to the dance. Mentally, I slapped myself for being an idiot and not accepting her attempt to reschedule. My pride wouldn't allow me to let her walk away from me again.

Discovering where she lived was a coincidence. The reward of spending time with her was worth more than the fifty dollars I would have charged. Besides, she would only play this game once. Tonight was make-it-

or-break-it time.

While merging into traffic, I grabbed an empty bottle of Gatorade as it rolled from underneath my seat. The recently purchased pine-scented air freshener swung wildly beneath the rearview mirror.

Maintaining a clean truck had never been a top priority. The cab's only occupants were my cousins — when they worked — my guitar, and me. Most of my dates were either at the woman's house or we'd meet somewhere. When a woman was worth my time, I would pick her up. Only then would I spend time cleaning my truck. The amount of food wrappers, empty bottles, and junk mail attested to the fact I hadn't taken a woman out in a while.

I inhaled deeply, testing the air. It didn't smell too bad. Maybe the pine fragrance would mask the odor of gasoline, grass, sweat, and foot funk. The odors no longer bothered me.

Even though Ebony hadn't complained, it wasn't hard to miss the wrinkling of her nose. I rolled down the windows, grabbed the half-eaten bag of chips and empty water bottle off the middle console, and tossed them into the seat behind me.

If we went out again, I would definitely get my truck detailed.

Traffic came to a stop, so I stole a peek at her. The fading light of the setting sun glinted off her auburn hair. She wore it down again. Long spiral curls graced the slender curve of her neck, resting on bare shoulders.

She wore make-up. A hint of color matched her brown shirt, accentuating her eyes. Her lips were shiny from some kind of gloss and looked delicious.

I cleared my throat to get her attention. "You look

good."

Ebony tilted her head in my direction. "You've got to be kidding me. I dressed for dinner at a pizza parlor on a Tuesday night. Now you're dragging me to a dance. You're dressed up, and I'm dressed for the movies. Everyone will look at me and wonder why I'm there."

"Where we're going, nobody's going to notice."

"Yeah, right. How do you not notice the only woman at a dance who's not dressed up?" She crossed her arms and turned her attention to the car next to us.

I didn't care what she had on. Over the past few days I'd seen Ebony dressed for a night at the club, work, and around the house; all fit her body perfectly. Each time felt as though I was seeing a different side of her personality. And each time she'd been more beautiful.

"I'm wearing Capris, a tank top, and flats," Ebony continued, sulking. "I am seriously underdressed. Why did I let you talk me into this?" She paused, putting a finger to plump lips. "Oh, yeah, a dare."

My chuckle earned me a glowering stare. "Look, it's not the kind of dance you're thinking about. It's at a senior-citizen retirement home. Everybody's probably got cataracts."

Ebony's burst of laughter was infectious and made me smile. I enjoyed the sound of her laugh.

"Brian, are you serious?"

"As a heart attack ... wait a minute, that was not a good reference since we're going to an old-folks home. But yes, after an hour, everybody will probably be ready for bed."

"So let me get this straight," she said when her laughter subsided. "You play in a band at a nightclub, own your own business cutting grass, and you play at senior-citizen homes during the week?"

I nodded. "Well, not every week."

"And I thought I stayed busy." She angled her head and studied me. "What made you decide to be a musician?"

My attention returned to the road when the car in front of us moved. "My grandfather gave me a guitar for Christmas when I was seven, and that pretty much sealed the deal. I learned as many instruments as I could. When I graduated high school, I went to U.C.L.A. to get a bachelor's in music."

"What do you play?"

"Bass guitar for the band. But I played the double bass in high school. I also play the piano, which was my mother's doing."

"Wow. Playing an instrument is something I've never been able to do."

"It takes a lot of work and years of dedication. I don't plan to work in nightclubs for the rest of my life. The big money will come from working in the studio or going on tours." When we stopped at another red light, I studied Google Maps. We were almost there. "It'll happen one day. Right now my focus is on getting a newer guitar. I own two guitars, but it's time to step it up a notch. I've saved for three months for the one I want. After tonight I'll only be $150 away." I tossed her a look. "If I'd gotten paid yesterday, it would have been one hundred."

Her eyes widened. "So it's my fault you didn't get paid? You're the one who decided to go with it. I thought you were going to say no."

I laughed. "I made the right decision. When this is done, I plan to show you a good time."

Ebony's smirk didn't hide the laughter in her eyes. "We'll see."

***

It didn't take long for me to find the band's rhythm. By the end of the night, we would exchange business cards and stay in touch for future work. One thing about the music business; networking was key. The more people you know, the more opportunities you got to play, the more money you made.

I unhooked the guitar strap from my shoulder as we paused for a ten-minute break. Ebony sat alone at a vacant table in the back of the room. She watched a crowd of elderly people gathered around the punch bowl, a look of amusement on her face.

I approached the table, veering out of the path of a woman in a wheelchair. "Hey, are you okay?"

She reached down to the floor beside her seat. "Yes. Here." She handed me a bottle of orange juice. "I managed to grab a few of these before they were all gone. It seems orange juice is a prized commodity around here." She grinned. "There are two more if you're really thirsty."

"Thanks." I appreciated her thoughtfulness. "I want to apologize again for changing our plans. I'm sure you'd rather be somewhere else right now."

Ebony studied the room. "Honestly, I've never been asked to dance or out on a date so many times before. Not even at the club." Her finely arched eyebrows rose. "There might be some life left in these old players." Laugh lines crinkled around her eyes.

Ebony was truly a rare find. A woman who could laugh at the change of circumstances instead of thinking everything revolved around her. Mark one in the plus column.

I scoped out the competition. "Are you serious?"

She motioned with her head toward an old man staring me down. "Harry over there has offered to put me in his will and give me half of next month's Social Security check if I let him see me naked."

I choked; juice dribbled out of my mouth. Harry appeared to be at least seventy. He grinned when Ebony looked his way. He had abnormally white teeth for someone his age. His plaid suit appeared to be thirty years old. He'd perched his Kangol hat over a knee, revealing the shiny skin of his bald head under bright lights. His hands rested on a cane between his legs. His eyes were all over Ebony.

When I turned back, she handed me a napkin and her smile widened. "Don't worry, I told him if he couldn't cut my grass for free then he didn't have a chance."

I chuckled while wiping my mouth. She had a great sense of humor. "You can add dessert to the steak deal." I promised.

"Good, because sugar-free cookies and Jell-O may be good for my figure, but they are not satisfying." Ebony reached for the empty juice container and set it on the table. "You guys are really good. Watching you play is … interesting. I like the way you hold your guitar." She bit her lip. Her eyes flashed something that could have been sexual. She attempted to play off embarrassment by looking at Harry. It didn't hide the rosy hue under her caramel cheeks. though.

Call me crazy, but I could have sworn she envied my guitar.

"You were paying attention."

"I'm an observant person. You're confident when you play. I like confidence."

I raised an eyebrow. Confidence was my middle name.

"Don't let it go to your head. Cutting my grass and taking me out to dinner is not going to get you in my pants."

I chuckled. Taking her to bed wasn't my goal for the evening, but it felt like an issued challenge.

"Well, if —" Someone smacked me on the ass, interrupting my witty reply.

I looked over my shoulder and discovered a woman leaning on a walker. The pink flower pinned to her shoulder hung lazily over sagging boobs. The woman appeared to be as old as my great aunt.

"You can get into my pants anytime, blondie."

I stood speechless. Ebony's muffled laughter floated from behind me.

The facilities director hustled over from serving refreshments to thwart the elderly woman's second attempt to swat my behind. "Mrs. Johansson!"

Unfortunately, it didn't stop the toothless grin Mrs. Johansson flashed me.

The director placed a gentle hand on the woman's back and attempted to turn my admirer in the opposite direction. "I'm sorry," she said.

"Uh ... no problem." My cheeks burned. "I'm going to head back now." The guys had congregated around the instruments.

Ebony nodded and attempted to hide her grin behind her hands.

The gig ended a short time later as some of the partygoers headed to bed. The spry ones put on music and continued to dance.

I was putting my guitar in its case when Ebony's playful laughter caught my attention. She no longer sat at the table. Instead, she danced with good old Harry.

The old timer's attempts to tear up the dance floor with my date amused me. The old guy could move. Ebony laughed again as he spun her around then attempted to dip her. Try as he might, his body wouldn't comply. So instead he settled on pulling her closer, sliding his hands lower on her waist.

Watching Ebony dance mesmerized me. Even though she wasn't dancing like that night in the club, it was impossible not to appreciate those God-given curves. What I wouldn't do to be able to hold her in my arms.

I shook my head. I was jealous of a seventy-year-old man because his hands were on my girl.

Date. Get a grip. She's my date, not my girl.

My attention went back to the guys who were in deep conversation. I shook hands, asked questions, and collected my portion of tonight's performance fee. We exchanged business cards and talked about various work opportunities we'd heard of. Eventually, my focus turned back to Ebony. The first song had ended. They were now on to song number two. Ebony looked my way. Our eyes connected, and she mouthed a silent plea for help. A survey of the situation revealed good old Harry trying his best to round second base with my date. His large wrinkled hands were on her ass. Her very fine, shapely ass.

The sly bastard.

Ebony grabbed his wrists, pried his hands off, and pulled them back to her waist. Harry put them back. Irritation flashed in her eyes, though she kept a smile on her lips.

I dismissed myself to go to her aid.

"Excuse me, may I have this dance?"

Harry stared me down. Despite his age, he was still an imposing figure. We were nearly the same height, and he looked me dead in the eye.

"Do you want to dance with this fella?" he asked Ebony, his gaze never leaving mine.

"Yes, this is my date," Ebony said smoothly, though irritation still shown in her eyes.

"*Humph.* Just remember what I told you." Harry released her and hobbled back to the table where he'd been sitting to retrieve his cane.

Clearly relieved, Ebony slipped into my arms. Our bodies connected as if we'd danced a million times; every part of her fit perfectly against me. Her intoxicating perfume hinted at something sweet and forbidden, a line I'd willingly cross if given the chance. I'd gotten a whiff of her fragrance in the car before rolling down the windows. But now I was up close and personal. There was no doubt about it, I wanted her.

The only time we'd been this close had been the night we met at the bar. In her flat shoes, her head stopped at my shoulder. Ebony tilted her head up. Her almond shaped eyes were liquid pools of chocolate, pulling me in hard. I zeroed in on luscious lips curved into a sexy smile that made my heart stop. Damn, they would be perfect for kissing.

Her hand felt soft and delicate in mine. Her curvaceous body, the inspiration for last night's erotic dream, pressed against me. God help me, it was impossible to ignore the softness of her breasts when she brushed against my chest.

I drew in a deep breath and held it for a few seconds in an effort to control the increased beating of my heart. I didn't want her to know how much she turned me on.

Ebony's warm body against mine was the most exquisite form of torture.

My focus went to the old couple dancing on the other side of the room and the empty punch bowl. Even Harry, as he gave me the evil eye, anything to prevent the hard-on threatening to betray my thoughts.

"He said I reminded him of his first wife."

Her melodic voice captured my attention.

"The man's got good taste."

"Yeah, well, if he groped my butt one more time ... Men, no matter how old, will always try to feel you up."

I chuckled. "The only difference is old men tend to get away with it. Young guys like me risk losing a limb or facing jail time."

Ebony looked up again, studying me.

"I can't offer you Social Security money, but I can buy you dinner without requiring you get naked." I smiled while Ebony giggled. "Let's go eat."

CHAPTER 6

Ebony

S ince our plans had changed, Brian insisted he pay for dinner. I studied the menu. At these prices, I would need to sleep with him in order to be even again. That was not an option.

I studied my surroundings after the server took our order. Dark floors complimented the hardwood tables. Pictures depicting forest landscapes were on the walls. Animal heads and antique farming tools mounted on the walls added to the rustic cabin theme. Nearly every seat in the restaurant was taken, which could mean one thing; they served good food.

A server walked by with a tray weighed down by steaming plates. Shrimp rested on rice next to cubed potatoes and steak covered with onions and bell pepper. My mouth watered while my stomach growled at the delicious aroma.

"The next time we go out, we'll eat first." The deep timbre of Brian's voice took my mind away from hunger pains.

"Who said there would be a next time?"

A lopsided grin spread on his handsome face as he reached for his cup of water. "Call it wishful thinking."

"Anyway, this isn't exactly a date."

Brian chuckled. "That's not what you told Harry."

"I said you were my date so he would let go of me." I allowed a half smile.

Brian laughed loudly. "It definitely worked."

Another server delivered a tray to the patrons sitting across from us. I contemplated the events of the evening. Over the past few hours, Brian had entertained me with live music, we'd slow danced, and a seventy-year-old man made a move on me. Most dates were boring, but not this one.

An outburst of cheers and clapping disturbed the ambiance as servers walked by singing happy birthday. I studied Brian as he watched the show. He'd ditched the tie and vest in his truck before loosening the top three buttons of his shirt. His chiseled features — deep blue eyes under thick eyebrows, cocky smile, and curly blond hair — were heart stoppingly handsome.

My gaze followed the movement of his Adam's apple down the opening of his shirt. It had been impossible to ignore his hard body as we danced. His rough fingers were strong and sure on my body. His eyes drew me deep into the sea of blue. My initial reaction was to press myself against him because it felt … secure. How could being in his arms have felt right? I barely knew the man.

Brian's attention turned back to me. He smiled.

"What are you thinking?"

I straightened in the booth, glad he couldn't read my thoughts. "Javan is your roommate? You guys are nothing alike."

"Are you one of his *friends*?" He made air quotation marks, his expression curious and eyebrows creased.

"Do you mean am I sleeping with him? No, he's dating my roommate, Yasmine. She's the one who called you."

Relief seemed to dawn on his face. "I've never met her, but tell her I said thanks."

"So, how did you two become roommates?" I reached for my cup of water.

"We met in college, lived in the same dorm room, and graduated the same year. We decided to rent a house together." He shrugged. "Economically, it works for both of us."

"Do you guys get along? I don't know Javan, but … he makes me nervous."

Brian's brow creased. "Nervous? How?"

"I only run into him when he picks Yasmine up. I'll answer the door, and it's as if he's mentally undressing me." Goose bumps sprouted along my skin at the thought.

Brian looked away. "Javan plays games with people. He studied to be a shrink and likes to experiment. In college, his favorite past time was finding out how many women he could manipulate." He shook his head, a look of disappointment on his face. "I figured he'd stop once we graduated, but apparently he hasn't. Just ignore him, and he'll move on to somebody else."

I hoped he'd do it soon. Telling Yasmine about her new man was the last thing I wanted to do.

"That's enough about him. Tell me about you."

"What do you want to know?"

"You've got roommates. How did you meet?"

"Same as you, in college. I have two roommates. Kaitlyn and I lived in the same dorm room. Yasmine lived off campus. We bonded like sisters." I paused. "You'd like Kaitlyn. I'll introduce you sometime."

He appeared baffled. "You want me to meet your roommate? Thanks, but no thanks."

"Are you sure? She's very pretty, blond hair, green eyes, and big boobs. You didn't notice at the club? Every guy in the room gravitated toward her."

Brian remained quiet, his eyes steady on mine. "Are you insecure?"

I sat back. "Excuse me?"

"I'm asking because you don't seem to understand. I like you. Are you telling me about her because she's white?"

My back went up in defense. "No, I'm not insecure. You seem like a nice guy, and Kaitlyn would like you. Besides, you guys might have some things in common."

Brian's eyebrows lifted. "Ebony, you don't know me. How can you say we could have something in common?"

"Well, you're both single."

His gaze stayed on mine as he drank from his beer. "You and I are both single. I bet we have some things in common, too." He sipped again. "We're approaching this relationship differently."

I scoffed. "We don't have a relationship."

He sat quietly, watching the remnants of his beer as he swirled it around. "When you look at me, what do you see?"

I preoccupied myself with the ring on my napkin. "A white man—"

"Obviously," he said before I finished my thought.

I forced myself to look at him. "A *man* who is not my type."

Brian nodded, drained the last of his beer, and sat back. When he spoke again, his eyes focused on mine. "You know what I see?" His gaze traveled to my mouth and lingered.

Damn, when was the last time any man looked at me that way?

"The first time I saw you, your curves were what got my attention." He smiled. "A man would have to be Stevie Wonder not to notice you."

"You and every man there," I mumbled, crossed my arms, and focused on a picture across the restaurant. I couldn't hide the heat in my cheeks though.

"I'm not finished."

The commanding tone of his voice drew my attention.

"At the bar, up close, your eyes revealed more than just a pretty face and hot body. You're intelligent and witty. I like that. I want to know *you*, Ebony." He paused to lick his lips. "Once I do … I want you in my bed."

My eyes widened in shock.

"Let me get this straight. You want to sleep with me, but you want to get to know me first?" I shook my head. "Is this supposed to be some line to get me naked?"

His dazzling blue gaze was mischievous. "No, it's putting my cards on the table."

"You know, no matter what race, all men are alike." I sat back, irritation in my voice and heat in between my legs. Damn. The man was good.

"We all have dicks, but that's where I draw the line." He grinned.

I bit my lip to keep from laughing and shot him a look filled with daggers instead.

Brian's smile faded. "Ebony, what bothers you most? The color of my skin or the fact I want to sleep with you?"

"Both."

"Is there something wrong with me wanting you? Everything doesn't have to be about skin color."

"Maybe not for you, but back home, people voice their disapproval of interracial dating."

"Where are you from?"

"North Carolina."

"That explains a few things. Look, you're in California, home of legalized weed. An interracial couple is nothing."

I couldn't quite argue with that.

I shook my head instead. "Look, Brian, no matter where you go, people still look at interracial couples differently."

"That's their problem. What you need to understand is this; I couldn't care less about the color of our skin. I like you, I'm attracted to you, and I want to know you. Let go of your inhibitions and take a chance." His voice went cocky. "Besides, if all I wanted was sex, you would have been in my bed the night we met."

Laughter shot out of me. "How do you figure that? I left."

Brian continued as though I hadn't spoken. "If I wanted sex ..." His voice deepened as he placed his elbows on the table and leaned toward me. His blue gaze caught me, leaving me speechless. "I could have you to-night."

My body felt as if it would burst into flames. It was hard to dispute his comment.

I struggled to regain my senses. "You are another cocky, arrogant son of a bitch."

"Cocky, hell yeah," He shrugged and sat back again. "Arrogant about a few things. The word you're looking for is confident. You like confidence, remember?" He flashed a devilish smile as the server returned with our meal.

The image of Brian standing half-naked and sweaty in my yard forced its way into my mind. Annoyed, I pushed at the rice pilaf on my plate. He was definitely confident. Knowing what he wanted turned me on. But that didn't mean I would land in his bed.

We sat in silence. Brian cut his steak while I tried to ignore the stares coming at us from across the room.

If I were honest, I liked Brian. Personality wise, he was different from other guys I'd dated. He seemed to be honest and straightforward about what he wanted out of life. But seeing him again beyond tonight? What would be the cost?

I forced a forkful of food into my mouth. It was hard to ignore the table of women who watched me. You would think I had stolen one of their boyfriends.

"When was the last time you went on a date?" Brian asked as he cut into his baked potato.

"Since this is not officially a date, I guess Harry would be it."

Brian let loose a big laugh. "Damn, my feelings just got hurt. Are you sure you don't want to reconsider? That way you can change your status from dating an older man to a young one."

"Ha, ha, very funny." I continued to pick at my food. "Men try to ask me out all the time. I tend to avoid their invitations."

Brian looked past me. "You definitely have the eye of those men over in the corner." He nodded in their direction.

I followed his gaze. He was right; I did have their attention, but they scrutinized both of us. When I turned, Brian stared back at them as intently as they stared at us. I cleared my throat, drawing his gaze.

"The problem is men assume I'm a model, a video dancer, or a stripper. A man once offered me money for a private show," I said in disgust. "My goal is to get my education. Unfortunately, no one sees beyond my body."

"I do." All laughter had left his voice.

I broke his gaze and played with my rice. No man had ever said that. Not even Patrick.

"What made you come to California to go to school? It's a long way from home." He turned his attention back to the plate, cutting his steak.

"U.C.L.A. They are a good school, plus they're near one of the best schools for veterinary medicine." I sampled my rice.

"I went there, too. What did you take?"

"Biology." Pride filled me as I watched his eyebrows shoot up in surprise. "I graduated with a bachelor's degree and am working on my veterinary degree. This fall will be my final year."

"I'm impressed. How long have you been in school?"

"Seven years. I start my final classes this fall."

"Damn." He laughed. "I did my four years and got

out. Enough was enough." He reached for his water, sipped. "That's when the band formed. We were all music majors and started playing our freshmen year. We've been together ever since."

"When did you graduate?"

"Five years ago."

I did a quick calculation. "We were there at the same time. You graduated a year ahead of me."

Brian looked up from his plate. "Small world, huh?"

"It seems like it."

"I admire your dedication. It takes discipline to stay in school that long."

His statement made me view him differently. Most guys thought my work was a waste of time.

"What made you decide to become a vet?" He grabbed his fork and dove into his baked potato with gusto. The man was serious about his food.

"My father manages an animal rescue and adoption center. I spent my weekends and summers helping him. My first paying job was working at the local animal hospital, cleaning cages and walking dogs." I shrugged. "That's when I decided what to do with the rest of my life."

"What are your plans after graduation?" He listened in rapt attention.

"What I really want is to work full-time at the Los Angeles Zoo. I intern there now, so my foot is in the door. They're going to have a few permanent spots to fill next year. I want one of them to be mine." Hiding the determination in my voice was impossible.

"Hmm, passionate about what you want out of life. What are you doing to make it happen?"

I picked up my knife and sliced through my steak

like butter. "I worked my butt off for the internship. I also work part-time as a veterinary assistant in an exotic animal hospital. Anything I could do to build my résumé, believe me, I've done it."

"What about grades?"

My attention diverted from my food. Most guys would have begun talking about themselves by now.

"I maintained a three-point-nine GPA for the last five years."

"Now I'm really impressed." He smiled his approval.

Hearing Brian's praise was refreshing and unnerving. No one besides my family and friends ever took my passion for my profession seriously. He knew nothing about me, yet seemed genuinely pleased.

I cut another piece of my steak; it was the best I'd ever eaten. Then again, maybe it was the company that made it better. "My turn."

"Ask away."

"What type of women have you dated? What's different about me? And you have to be honest."

Brian wiped his mouth with his napkin and sat back, a look of satisfaction on his face. His plate was empty.

"I have no problem with honesty." He paused. "I haven't dated in a year."

I eyed him suspiciously. "Women at the club practically threw themselves at you."

He shrugged, nonchalant. "If you mean dated as in having a steady relationship, then it's been a year. If you mean when I last had sex, then two weeks would be right."

Hearing him say the word again made me warm in all the right places.

"Ah, you're one of those types." I nodded in understanding while trying not to imagine him naked.

"What type?"

"A guy with a phone full of numbers for girls to hook up with."

Brian shrugged. "I used to, but right now I've got other things taking up my time."

"You mean you don't have anyone you spend time with? No friends-with-benefits? I don't believe you."

Oh crap, the words just flew out of my mouth. What was I thinking? Who he did in his spare time was none of my business.

"No, the position is empty. Are you interested?" A sly grin appeared on his face.

I laughed. "I've never understood how people can have sex with someone and not be in a relationship of any kind. Yasmine does it all the time. Why is everything about sex? What about friendship or love? You have to relate to a person in order to truly enjoy sex."

Brian laughed. "Ebony, when you break it down, everything is about sex. It's human nature."

"No, it isn't," I protested. "Not for me."

"So what you're saying is you're not interested in hooking up from time to time; you're looking for a permanent relationship."

Uh-oh, this conversation had strayed way off track. My efforts to dig out of it only made it worse.

"Well, no. I'm not looking for anything. What I meant to say is ..."

His eyebrows knitted together. "Then answer this. Why am I not your type?"

How in the hell did I answer without sounding like an idiot? I glanced up and saw Brian patiently waiting for a reply.

"I have a certain preference, that's all."

"Uh huh. Is it racial or physical?" Before I could answer, he said, "I saw you checking Derrick out. He's engaged by the way."

"Who's Derrick?"

"He's the drummer. So it's safe to assume since he's built like a linebacker, that's what you want."

I wanted to open my mouth, but couldn't.

Brian cocked his head to the side. "Hmm, no response. I must be right. Unless," he held up a finger, "it's about me being white. What's the matter, you don't think I could please you in bed?"

I could not answer any of his questions. Any reply would leave me sounding like a jackass or racist; I was neither.

"Brian, I'm not like that. If I went to bed with you, it would be because I like you. I'm not basing anything on stereotypes or ignorant thinking. When I sleep with a man, I have certain requirements."

One of his eyebrows lifted. "What requirements?"

"Monogamy. No long-term commitment required, just … I don't want to wonder if you're with someone else when you're not with me."

"I can handle that." Brian's expression had gone serious.

Oh, man. I felt my eyes widen and skin flush.

"But since you've made it obvious sex is not an option, I'm willing to settle on being friends," he added.

Our server walked by and placed the check on the table. I reached for my purse just as Brian dug into his wallet.

"You don't have to —"

"I've got this. You can pay for dinner the next time

we go out if it makes you happy."

I scoffed. "Who said there would be a next time?"

Brian placed his credit card on the tray with the bill and handed it to our server. He waited until he walked away to reply. "Because, Ebony, you like me. We can be friends and still go out. We'll just leave out sex."

We stared at each other. His smile was halfcocked, eyes intent on mine. Even though he didn't speak, the unspoken words, *for now*, echoed in my head.

CHAPTER 7

Brian

*B*eep. Beep. Beep.

I growled and slapped the alarm clock. The image of Ebony naked dissipated. So much for my fantasy.

I rolled out of bed, grabbed the remote, and turned on the morning news. Damn, another forest fire. The smoke mixed with smog would wreak havoc on my bronchitis, which in turn hurt my wallet. At least there was an alternate stream of revenue.

Taking the day off was not in my vocabulary. I had too much stored up energy. Since there was no woman in my bed, it was time to get moving.

I showered, then grabbed my day planner to re-schedule my customers. Two hundred dollars was now out of reach. I spied the huge red circle on my calendar. Rent was due this week. At least I had earned my part.

Times like this made me wish my father was like Javan's. Doctor Simmons was a psychiatrist who sent money anytime his son asked for it. He'd been doing it since we were in college. It had been cool when Javan helped me out when my funds ran low. It was one reason why I rented a house with him. His father would always have his back. We were adults now, careers established, and Javan made good money. It was way past time for him to quit relying on his father.

My attention went to the next red circle; the deadline for purchasing my guitar neared. The money I spent on the date with Ebony set me back, but it was well worth it. Just thinking of her made me smile. Yeah, I'd definitely do it again.

In the meantime, I needed to make money. Several people had asked for private guitar lessons, but my busy schedule didn't allow time for teaching. The smog alert for the next few days gave me time to spare.

After scheduling two students for lessons in the evening, I grabbed my guitar and sheet music to work on the song I composed for the band.

An hour later my roommate knocked on my door. I put the guitar pick in between my teeth and made a notation on my sheet music. "What's up?"

Javan leaned against the doorjamb. "You got a minute?"

"Sure." I set the guitar in its stand and reached for my bottle of water.

"Did Yasmine Phillips call you about her yard?"

"Yeah, on Monday. She wasn't there, but her roommate was."

"Oh, yeah? Which one?"

"Ebony."

Javan whistled. "Man, did you check her out? She is fine. I mean, with her body ... I'd love to hit that. Yasmine's my girl, but we're not exclusive. She isn't looking for a commitment, just a good time, you know what I mean?" He paused, eyebrows furrowed in thought. "Hmm ... if Ebony is like that ..." His eyes lit up. "Damn, that would be one helluva threesome."

It took everything to control my mouth. I could understand why Ebony felt uncomfortable around him. He wouldn't care that she's an intelligent woman, because he'd be unable to see past her shapely behind.

"She's not a *ho*, J." I twisted the cap back on the empty bottle with a vengeance and pitched it into the garbage.

We had occasional testosterone-based disagreements, but we always worked through them. But when it came to the treatment of women, we'd long since agreed to disagree.

Javan believed women were good for three things: satisfying his sexual needs, cooking, and bearing his children. Nothing more, nothing less.

The only thing similar about us was our height. Both six-two, though he had a good twenty pounds of muscle on me. Women loved his dark brown skin, hazel eyes, and shoulder-length dreads. He visited the barbershop weekly to keep his goatee trimmed and kept a Jamaican beautician on call to keep his hair done just right. Of course, she was also one of his hook-ups.

When it came to clothes, Javan was strictly GQ, everything top of the line. He was so stuck on himself it surprised me we got along.

If Ebony's roommate liked casual sex, she and Javan were a perfect match.

The pretty boy façade was not me. I worked outside, not in an air-conditioned office. I sweated and got dirty, but still took pride in my appearance. My style of dress was casual, laid back. My closet housed jeans, shorts, pullovers, and polo-styled shirts. I kept my face clean-shaven, most of the time, no beard or goatee. Sometimes I let my hair grow until it curled at the nape of my neck. Ladies loved running their fingers through it.

Javan looked at me with raised eyebrows. "What do you know about Ebony?"

"I took her out Tuesday. She's nothing like one of your girls, J. Don't even think about it."

He stared at me silently, meeting my hard gaze with one of his own.

"She's off limits."

"You've got a thing for her. So it's like that?"

"With her, it's definitely like that."

He inclined his head. "Didn't you get over dating black women after what happened with, what's her name?" He snapped his fingers.

"Trina," I said sourly.

"Trina, yeah." He shook his head. "So you're ready to try again. You've got balls, man." He held out a knuckled hand to bump fists. "Just watch your back this time."

"Believe me, I will. There's something about her. I can't put my finger on it, but it'll be different with her. I can feel it."

"Good luck. So, do you have your half of the rent?"

I reached into my nightstand and pulled out a wad of twenties bound together in a rubber band. "Here, count it."

"I trust you." He stuffed the roll into his sports jacket

pocket. "What do you have planned this evening?"

I glanced at the clock. "I have an hour left of practice before heading out for a private lesson. Tonight's band practice. How about you?"

"Damn, you always have that guitar in your hand. Is it in bed when you ..." He made an obscene gesture with his hand.

I chuckled. "You're an idiot."

He lifted his hands. "Hey, I wonder sometimes."

"It takes work to make the big bucks." I reached for the guitar.

He shook his head. "To each his own. Tonight I'll be in bed with Yasmine, an insatiable woman while you ..." Javan pointed at my guitar and laughed before disappearing down the hallway.

"Whatever, man." I grinned and got back to work.

CHAPTER 8

Ebony

The forest fire subsided, leaving the air breathable enough for families to spend Saturday outdoors.

I loved days like this. My usual work assignment kept me behind the scenes cleaning cages or assisting the veterinarians with routine checkups. Today, I worked in the children's petting zoo. Watching children run along the gated area, their faces lit up with excitement, reminded me of my love for animals when I was younger.

The petting zoo offered tame animals that were free to roam during the day. At night, they were housed in stalls. My responsibilities included keeping the troughs full of food and water, and making sure the walking areas were free of waste. The job wasn't glamorous, but I wouldn't trade it for anything.

I held my breath, scooped up a large pile of dung, and walked it across the yard to the compost pile.

"I don't wanna touch it!"

"Cody, stop being a baby."

"I'm not a baby!"

A little boy stood, his arms crossed and bottom lip poked out. He appeared to be at least six years old. He directed his hazel eyes at an older girl with long blond ponytails. She returned his pouty stare with a glare.

I set my shovel down. "Hi, my name is Ebony. What's going on?"

"Cody's being a scaredy cat. He won't touch the goat," said the blue-eyed girl.

"I'm not a scaredy cat," he whined. "It's gonna bite me."

"See?" Cody's sister threw her hands up in exasperation.

I smiled warmly, keeping the laugh inside. "The goats don't bite. I'll show you how to touch them, okay?"

He nodded, wiping at the corners of his eyes.

I held his hand and walked over to a goat in the pen.

"This is Delilah. She's very friendly and won't bite."

His eyes widened, filled with disbelief.

"I promise it's okay. Start petting her here." I demonstrated by running my hand over her rump. "Don't pull her tail, though. When you're ready, you can rub here." I ran my hand over her back.

Cody joined in with his free hand, hesitant at first, while gripping my hand tightly. He relaxed and an excited smile spread across his face.

His sister, on the other hand, stood with her arms crossed, refusing to touch the animal. "Touching is for babies."

"You know, you're right. Why don't you try this?" I released Cody's hand and pulled hay from the trough. To her delight, Delilah ate from my hand. "What's your name?"

"Hannah."

I squatted and held out a bunch of hay. "Here, Hannah, hold it steady so she'll come to you."

Hannah followed my instructions, but her hand trembled. Delilah turned to consume it.

"Wow," Hannah said in a small voice.

"Uncle Brian, Uncle Brian, look at me!" Cody yelled, jumping with excitement.

I laughed at his enthusiasm and followed his line of sight. My mouth fell open in surprise.

Brian walked toward me with a confident swag. "Looks like we meet again." He stood with his hands in his pockets and a sexy half-smile on his face. A red T-shirt, shorts, and sandals fit him perfectly. "What are the chances?"

Even though he'd cleaned up nice the evening we went out, he was just as attractive now. I wiped my hands on my pants and stood. "Uncle Brian, huh?"

"Yeah, these are my sister Lisa's kids. They wanted to come to the zoo. Their parents needed a day to themselves so," he shrugged, "I volunteered."

Giggles erupted from the kids as they exchanged glances but stopped when he cleared his throat.

"Really." For some reason I found that excuse hard to believe. "Cody, keep rubbing her that way. You'll be fine." I grabbed my shovel and moved toward a newly released pile of dung as I shot him a look over my shoulder.

Brian followed closely, wrinkling his nose. "Wow, this looks fun."

"Shoveling crap? It comes in all forms." I threw the dung into a pile.

"Ouch!" He chuckled. "Okay, the truth is I hoped to run into you."

I faced him, stabbed the shovel into the ground, and leaned on it. "It's a big place, Brian. Your chances were slim. I'm usually behind the scenes."

"Guess today was my lucky day."

When it came to finding me, Brian never seemed to run out of luck.

I couldn't help but smile. "Okay … Now what?"

"What are you doing tomorrow?"

I shook my head. "Brian, I'm not going out with you."

"I didn't ask you out. I just want to know what you have planned." He tried his best to be charming and innocent at the same time.

"Am I supposed to believe that?" I forced my smile to stay hidden.

"I swear my intentions are pure. If you're free, I'm going to the amusement park at the pier. It would be fun to ride the Ferris wheel, grab a funnel cake … talk while watching the tide come in. It'll be nothing more than just two friends meeting to hang out."

I eyed him skeptically. "And it wouldn't be considered a date?"

"Not if we meet there."

"We did that last week, and you considered it a date."

"That was at night. This is during the day."

I laughed at his reasoning. He seemed to make a

habit of making things work to his advantage.

"It sounds nice, but I don't think so. I need to study."

Even though school wasn't starting for two months, I had borrowed books to read. Between my friends talking me into going out, spending the evening with Brian, and work, I hadn't studied in days.

The glow in Brian's eyes fizzled. And great, now I felt guilty. Although he seemed disappointed, his smile remained genuine.

"That's too bad. Well, if you change your mind, I'm going around three o'clock. You've got my number. Text me, and I'll meet you at the gate." He looked over his shoulder. "Hannah, Cody, let's go. There's a lot to see before we eat lunch."

Cody ran to his side. "Can we eat at McDonald's?"

Brian ruffled his hair. "Sure thing, kid. Did you guys thank Ebony?"

Both blond heads turned. "Thank you," they sang in unison.

"You're welcome. Have a good time." I waved at them as they left the petting area.

They'd walked a few feet when Hannah's voice floated over. "You were right, she's very pretty."

"I did what you said, Uncle Brian, can I still get cotton candy?"

I shook my head and laughed. Sneaky bastard.

Brian peered back over his shoulder, a sheepish grin on his face as he grabbed Cody in a headlock. "Kids, gotta love 'em."

"You talk too much, Cody," Hannah said.

CHAPTER 9

Ebony

My Sunday morning routine started with yoga, followed by breakfast and a shower. My body loose and mind free, I was prepared to study. Dr. Jacobs hadn't asked for his books back since our run-in. But it didn't mean he wouldn't change his mind. His books held invaluable information, which would make my last year in school easy. Especially since he'd been generous enough to give me copies of his notes on each chapter.

Determined to make the best use of my time, I settled in at my desk to read.

Forty-five minutes later, I realized I'd read the same page five times. I closed the book, rubbed my eyes, and massaged my neck. Ten minutes later, I tried again.

No matter how hard I tried, I couldn't concentrate on the words on the page.

I went downstairs to grab a bottle of water from the kitchen. The house was empty. Both Yasmine and Kaitlyn were on dates, which left me home alone. Water in hand, I walked onto the back patio and surveyed the lawn. Brian and his crew did a great job. Thinking of that day brought back the memory of watching him hard at work without a shirt. Tiny shivers ran along my skin. Whether or not he cut our grass again, the image would remain imprinted on my mind for months.

I shielded my eyes and peered up at the cloudless sky. Another typical California day. The heat was bearable, nowhere as intense as it was back home. It was the perfect day to be outside doing something fun.

Like riding the Ferris wheel with a friend.

Brian's invitation tempted me. His confident eyes and picture-perfect smile were hard to forget. Hanging out with him for the day would be more fun than sitting around the house continuing to read a book I could not focus on.

A day spent with no strings, no commitment, no expectations, and no sex. Just two adults enjoying each other's company in a public setting. After all, in order to become friends, you needed to spend time together.

He'd be there. I'd show up. That was it.

I headed upstairs, grabbed my phone, and sent him a text message. Deciding what to wear should not have been hard, yet I found myself unable to decide on shorts or jeans. I didn't want to wear the same thing twice.

Five minutes passed with no reply. Could he have changed his mind about going? Or worse, found someone else willing to jump at the opportunity to spend the afternoon with him? Maybe I shouldn't have waited to decide.

I grabbed my phone and flopped onto the bed, unable to ignore a pang of disappointment. I was about to send a message to cancel when my phone chimed.

glad u changed ur mind. c u there.

An unexpected feeling of warmth spread through me from head to toe.

CHAPTER 10

Brian

C No, I wasn't dreaming. She was actually here.

When Ebony refused my invitation, I scrapped the idea of going to the pier and dedicated the day to practice. My phone had been set on vibrate in order to avoid distractions. I didn't see her message until I stopped to take a break.

And now, I waited with tickets in hand, unable to shake the nervous feeling in my stomach. I hadn't felt like this the night we went out. But today was different. It wasn't coercion that brought her here. She wanted to see me.

I surveyed the crowd as groups walked by on their way inside the park for a day of fun.

And then, there she was.

How did she do it? Never had I seen a woman manage to be so beautiful, so sexy, and fun at the same time.

A deep purple shirt stopped at her midriff, drawing my eyes to the sexy flat plane of her caramel skin. Black fitted shorts hugged her hips and stopped mid-thigh like a second skin. Long, shapely legs ended in sandals with strings wrapping up her sexy calves. She wore her auburn hair away from her neck and face leaving her throat visible. I could imagine my mouth there, kissing her, whispering in her ear as my hands ran around the smooth expanse of her exposed flesh. My fingers ached, longing to slide along her narrow waist.

And then our eyes met. Her eyes seemed to sparkle as luscious lips pulled up in a sexy smile.

God, I wanted to kiss her.

"You look good," I blurted the moment she got close enough to hear.

"Thanks." She tucked her hands into the pockets of her shorts. "So do you."

I looked down at my clothes. They were nothing special. "I try." I nodded toward the entrance. "Ready for some fun?"

We headed into the park, taking in the sights, in no hurry to decide what to ride first. The lines were long, which allowed plenty of time to chat about our jobs, likes, and dislikes.

Several hours later we had ridden nearly every ride in the park. It was time to take a break. We found a stand selling funnel cakes. Our snack in hand, we searched out a spot on the boardwalk to enjoy the sweet treat.

"Oh, man, I can't remember the last time I ate one of these." She licked the powdered sugar off her fingertips. "I take that back, it was my senior year in high school.

My sister took me and my twin to the fair to celebrate our birthday."

"You have a twin?"

Ebony nodded. "Yes, my brother, Trevon. He lives in Atlanta and co-manages an Applebee's. My sister, Lashana, and her husband, live in Charlotte along with their daughter and my parents." Her eyes lit up at the mention of her family. "My niece, Mia, is the most beautiful thing I've ever seen."

"Do you and your brother look alike?"

"Oh, God, no. We're fraternal twins." A mischievous expression lit her eyes. "I always tell people he's my younger brother."

I laughed. "Your younger brother?"

"We are, except I'm the oldest. I was born five minutes before him, so we call him the baby." She laughed. "It pisses him off all the time."

"Are you close to your family?" I bit my cake, savoring the powdered sugar and melted chocolate chips. I'd given up using my fork and went straight at it with my fingers.

Ebony giggled. "You've got sugar on your nose. I'll get it."

My hands were full holding the plate and the funnel cake.

I focused on her tantalizing lips as she leaned closer, concentrating on the cleanup. As great as the funnel cake smelled with its various toppings, nothing compared to her exotic perfume. She wore the same fragrance as the night we'd danced. It was sensual and sexy, yet sweet at the same time. It reminded me of caramel and cream. I wondered if her skin would taste the same way.

"Thanks," I said when she pulled back.

"You're welcome."

Our eyes held before she cleared her throat and looked away.

"My family is pretty tight. Trevon and I are close, but not just because we're twins. It's because ..." She giggled. "I'm a tomboy at heart. Dressing up used to be a pain as much as playing with dolls. My sister did all the girly stuff. I used to run away from her to play with Tre and his friends."

"You were a tomboy?" I licked chocolate off my fingers. It was hard to imagine her running away from the dress she'd worn the night we met. "You're kidding right? There's nothing about you that says tomboy." I allowed my eyes to linger on her legs. When I looked back up, Ebony's cheeks sported a pink glow.

"I hated dresses. My favorite outfit was a pair of jeans and a T-shirt."

I could imagine Ebony in pigtails and jeans.

"My mom hated it though. Lashana did everything feminine. Fingernails always painted, hair always done. She never left the house without looking perfect." Ebony shook her head. "For fun, she'd tell my mother Tre's friends were making me play hospital, and I was the patient. Mom freaked out about me playing with a bunch of boys. She would make me stay inside all day with Lashana."

I howled with laughter.

Ebony's expression feigned irritation.

"What did you play?"

"Fashion show." Her button-shaped nose wrinkled at the memory. I continued to laugh, but toned it down.

"That annoyed the hell out of me. My brother would

be outside playing *Star Wars*, while I got stuck inside wearing a stinking dress."

"Let me guess, you wanted to be Queen Amidala."

"Nope. I was the doctor who worked on the Wookie." She grinned.

"An animal lover all the way, huh?"

"Oh yeah." She cut her way through strawberries and whipped cream with a fork.

"When did you turn into a sexy vixen?"

Ebony rolled her eyes. "I'm still a tomboy. I just know how to attract the opposite sex."

I allowed myself to appreciate the voluptuous curves of her body. Yeah, she definitely knew how to attract.

"Did you have a lot of boyfriends in school?"

"A few, but not like my sister. Every guy in school wanted her. She's prettier than me."

"That's not possible."

Ebony's gaze turned to me. "You're kidding, right?"

Was she serious? "Ebony, you are a beautiful woman. It doesn't matter what you wear by the way, because I've seen you as sexy as you want to be and in your work clothes."

"Brian, you have a great sense of humor."

To my surprise, she wasn't being sarcastic. Was it possible she was actually insecure? With a body built for sin, how could she not know how attractive she was?

"Did you look into the mirror before you left home?"

She squirmed. "Of course I did."

"Then you should know why men look at you the way they do." I hoped she knew my words were coming from my heart.

Ebony broke the connection.

"You're the first guy who hasn't asked to see a picture of my sister." A half-laugh followed.

What kind of man would ask to see a picture of her sister?

"They were assholes."

A bashful smile spread across her lovely face.

"How many assholes have you dated?"

"I broke up with the last one six months ago."

"Why?" I prompted.

"Both of us had hectic schedules. We rarely saw each other except for ..." She laughed. "You know."

Man, did I. If I had the chance, I'd spend every waking moment naked with her body wrapped around me.

"After a few months, we realized we didn't want the same things. He ended up wanting something I couldn't give him. The last I heard, he had gotten engaged."

"Wow." Lucky me.

"The messed up part was, my mom found out I dated a doctor and damn near started planning the wedding."

"How long did you date?"

"Eight months. If you count time spent getting to know each other and didn't involve sex ... four months." She sighed. "In my mom's eyes, he made the perfect match. Smart, handsome, career-oriented, educated ... black."

I sat the remnants of my funnel cake aside and wiped my hands on a napkin. "What do you want, Ebony?"

Her eyebrows furrowed as her gaze shifted to her plate. "What do you mean?"

"What do you want? Good looking, intelligent, educated. Easy. But does he have to be black?"

Shocked, her eyes widened as her attention came back to me. She studied me for a moment, obviously processing the question before looking away. "When my family says 'a young black man is what you need' ..."

"Ebony." I waited to get her full attention. "Is that what you want? Can't you have those things regardless of what package it comes in?"

Could you find it with me? The words burned in the back of my throat. I did my best to communicate it with my eyes.

"I don't know," she said softly, but her gaze didn't falter.

At least she didn't say *no*. Her saying *"I don't know"* was more like saying, *"I'm open to trying something new."* I could work with that.

We sat in silence while she finished her funnel cake. When she was done, I decided to lighten the mood.

"Have you ever been rollerblading?"

She laughed. "Not since high school."

I stood and extended my hand. "Come on, let's give it a try."

She hesitated. "Are you serious?"

"Yes."

"I will probably fall flat on my ass," she warned as she stood.

I made a show of looking at her lovely ass. "I think you'll be okay. Besides, I'll catch you."

Ebony choked out a laugh.

"Come on, we'll wear knee pads and helmets. It'll be fun."

Twenty minutes later, we found a skate rental shop, padded up, and were ready to go. She asked the cashier to take a picture of us with her cell phone. She called it the *before* picture. For some reason, she felt we'd end up covered in grass stains and bloodied knees.

I had my fair share of sports related injuries over the years. I'd done everything from rollerblading to trick bicycle riding. My true passion was surfing.

Staring out into the distance, I wondered if she would be willing to give it a try. Maybe not, but the idea of her in a bikini sent my imagination running wild.

We reached the boardwalk and struggled to find an area where skaters and bicycle riders weren't clogging up the space. It took a few minutes for Ebony to gain her balance. After many attempts, she laughed, a look of pure happiness on her face.

"Let me help." I slipped a hand around her bare waist. Her skin was unbelievably soft. The scent of strawberries and whipped cream from her funnel cake mixed with her perfume made it hard to keep my focus.

"Don't let me fall, Brian."

"If you fall, I'll protect you."

She didn't seem reassured, but she took my hand and held on tight. "Believe me; if I go down, I'm taking you with me."

"Deal."

Once she found her balance, I moved in front of her. Ebony kept her knees bent and skates pointed straight while I pulled her along, skating backward doing all the work until she got comfortable.

We started slowly, navigating our way down the boardwalk staying out of the way of the more experienced skaters, bike riders, and skate boarders. I continued to glance over my shoulder, making sure our path was clear.

The happiness on Ebony's face was a memory I

would never forget. Her eyes were full of laughter. She smiled the entire time, and never once did she loosen the grip on my hands. No matter how hard her grip, the connection was what I savored.

We traveled a good distance away from the skate shop. I mentioned it to Ebony, and she looked over her shoulder.

A dog ran by chasing a Frisbee. The dog's sudden appearance surprised Ebony who instantly moved her feet. Our skates tangled. Everything moved in slow motion as I started to fall, allowing me to live up to my promise to protect her body.

"Oh, no, Brian, are you okay?"

Sprawled out on my back, I closed my eyes, taking a moment to evaluate the situation. I could still feel my toes and fingers. My head was okay, thanks to the helmet.

My butt, on the other hand, was a problem.

An unexpected weight rested on my chest. I opened my eyes to the most beautiful sight: Ebony on top of me, staring into my eyes. Strange, I hadn't noticed the light flecks of gold in her brown irises. Her lips were inches away from mine. My first thought was to feign unconsciousness so she'd perform CPR.

"I'm sorry!" She fiddled with the straps of my helmet while I groaned. "That dog ran by … oh, man. Where does it hurt?"

She sat up, straddled me, felt the back of my head, and then ran her fingers over my chest. Since her hand came away free of blood, I assumed I wouldn't die today. She shifted her weight and ran her hands down my legs. The pain was worth having her hands on me. The feeling ignited my body. It wouldn't be long before the growing bulge in my pants became visible.

"Why don't they make butt pads?" I struggled to sit up. "I'm okay."

Ebony aided me in the movement, genuine worry in her eyes. In the end, we were sitting facing each other.

"Are you sure nothing's broken?"

"Yeah." I massaged my neck and rolled my shoulders. I would pay for this in the morning.

Ebony removed her helmet. Her hair was a mess, but it looked good. She reached to release the curly locks from the ponytail holder, allowing them to settle on her shoulders.

Once our eyes met, she bit her lip. Her eyebrows shot up as she stifled a laugh. I grinned, which caused her laughter to burst out and me to join in. We looked like idiots.

Ebony wiped tears from the corners of her eyes. She was beautiful. Unable to resist, I ran my fingers through the free strands of her hair. She didn't pull away. I indulged, brushing my fingers along her cheek, and tucked the hair behind her ear.

It felt like silk. As my fingers grazed her cheek again, her laughter slowed. Her eyes focused on me with just a hint of a question. Her lips parted, sending what I hoped was a silent invitation.

I was aware of the people veering around us as they rushed by. The sound of the ocean, laughter, and dogs barking were no longer the focus of my attention though. Nothing else mattered. No longer thinking, I did what came naturally. My finger rested beneath her jaw as I leaned in to kiss her.

I pressed my lips lightly against hers, inviting her to return the kiss, silently praying for permission for more. Her body tensed beneath my fingertips, so I stopped myself from taking more. But it was too late; I'd crossed the line.

After a day spent talking, laughing, and getting to know each other, it all came down to this kiss.

Ebony didn't pull away, so I kissed her again.

I was about to give up hope and deal with the consequences when her lips came to life.

For a moment, I thought I imagined it. But then she did it again. The warm slide as her lips pressed harder against mine.

I didn't hesitate. I opened my mouth wider, slipping the tip of my tongue in and tasted … strawberries. Her hand came up and slid into the hair at the nape of my neck. If it were up to me, the kiss would never end. But this was neither the time nor the place to explore the softness of her lips.

Ebony moaned when I pulled away.

"We'd better get up before we get run over," I whispered, my voice thick with longing.

She said nothing, only nodded. I stood first and pulled her back to her feet. We rolled over to the nearest bench and removed our skates.

After wanting to kiss Ebony hours earlier, I had no idea I would be able to do it. She hadn't said a word, and I didn't know what to expect next. So I stood, holding my skates, and extended a hand. She took it willingly, and a smile played over her lips. Curiosity filled her eyes.

We strolled back to the skate shop hand in hand.

CHAPTER 11

Brian

The day had been long. With thirty minutes until Ebony was supposed to call, I checked the volume of the ringer on my cell phone for the tenth time. A driver's blaring horn alerted me that the traffic light had turned green. I grimaced and set my cell phone in the cup holder.

Dealing with Peter and Dylan had put me behind schedule. My cousins were anxious to impress some girls they'd just met. Not wanting to disrupt their savings, they hit me up for money. I didn't have a problem helping out if there was a dire need. However, after hearing their plans, I refused to give in. Both wanted fifty dollars. They were crazy.

When the dust settled, I'd given them twenty-five dollars apiece along with suggestions on how to go out without spending a lot of cash and still have fun.

"Be creative," I'd told them. "Do something most guys wouldn't do. If they really like you, it won't matter how much money you spend. If not, chalk it up to a lesson learned." They didn't like hearing it, but I knew from experience.

On the highway heading for home, I winced while rolling my shoulders. My back still ached from the tumble onto the concrete with Ebony. The memory of our afternoon at the beach and the kiss we shared put a smile on my face. That opportunity was worth falling on my ass. When the evening ended, we walked to her car and kissed again. She'd been a willing participant, exploring my mouth as eagerly as I'd explored hers. We promised to talk the next day.

That had been a week ago.

The start of the week found us both busy. Ebony's schedule at the zoo changed to longer work hours and interfered with her part-time job.

After being unable to work for two days and falling behind with my customers, my phone rang off the hook. On top of that, I had practice. *Diverse Nation* played three nights a week, and every show was different.

The minute traffic stopped again, I grabbed my phone. We were playing phone tag, leaving voicemails or sending text messages when we found the time. I listened to the last message she'd left again. Her sexiness even came through the phone.

She said she'd call after seven. Come hell or high water I would be available.

My phone rang. A check of the caller ID made me smile.

"Hi, Mom."

"Are you home yet?"

"No, and before you ask, I haven't eaten dinner yet, but ..." I glanced at the restaurants on the strip. "I'm pulling in for some barbeque now." No matter how old I got, she would always view me as her little boy. Then again, out of five kids, I was the youngest and the only boy.

"That's better than eating a hamburger. What you need to do is find a young woman to take care of you. When do you plan to settle down? I want more grand-kids running around my house."

"Whoa." I laughed. "First of all, I've got some things to accomplish before I'm ready for a commitment. Second, you've already got five grandkids."

"And I love all of them. But you and Bridget owe me. I don't know what your sister's problem is. But you, my son, need a wife. You should come home from a hard day at work and have a homemade meal on the table, not fast-food."

"Mom, I'm capable of taking care of myself. Besides ..." I put the truck in park and climbed out. "I can't afford a wife or kids right now. That's a long way off."

She sighed, her disappointment obvious through the phone. "Well, at least you need someone to keep you happy. I hate that things didn't work out with you and the last young lady you were seeing."

"Yeah, well ... life goes on."

"Are you seeing someone now?"

Damn, she was in full nosey-mom mode.

"I'm working on it," I mumbled while studying the restaurant menu. "Look, Mom, I've got to go; it's almost my turn to place my order."

"Okay. Don't forget about the Fourth of July barbecue at the house. What can you bring?"

"Beer, as always." She knew not to ask me to cook.

"Don't forget soda, juice boxes for the kids —"

"And ice," we said in unison.

"I got it, Mom. Gotta go."

"Okay. Why don't you bring the young lady you're seeing?"

"Who said I was seeing anybody?"

"I know my son. You're too handsome to be sitting around all alone. If she's important, you will. Don't forget, next Saturday. Your dad's firing up the grill at twelve. Everyone should start arriving no later than two."

"I'll be there."

My mother always seemed to know what went on in my life. Sometimes I wondered if she were psychic.

I placed my order and then sat at a vacant table to wait. Inviting Ebony to go with me to meet my family wasn't such a bad idea. My family would welcome her with open arms. Race had never been an issue in the Young household. Besides, Ebony wouldn't be the first black woman to come home with me.

Soon, I was back in my truck and heading for my house. The delicious aroma of my meal made my mouth water. I'd reached my driveway when my phone rang. It was seven o'clock on the dot.

"Hey, beautiful."

"Brian, I was beginning to believe we'd never talk again," Ebony said.

"Me, too. I'm all yours." I climbed out of the truck, dinner in hand.

"And you've got me."

Hearing her voice made me want to kiss her again.

"How was your day?"

"Same old thing, sick dogs and picky cats. Personally, I prefer the zoo. The animals there are more interesting."

"I'll bet." I pictured her scraping goat dung with a shovel.

"How was yours?" she asked.

"Long, hot —" Her laugh made me pause. "What's so funny?"

"Nothing, just ... never mind. Go ahead. Long and ..." She continued to giggle.

"Tiring." Then it dawned on me. "Where is your head?"

Another round of sexy laughter bubbled through the phone. After putting my key in the front door, I paused. The urge to see her again made me consider climbing back in my truck with my plate and going to her place.

"You don't want to know."

It was too late. It's amazing how a few kisses could push your thoughts, wants, and desires to a whole new level.

"All right, change of subject. What are you doing right now?" She stopped laughing, but I could hear the smile in her voice.

"I just got home with a steaming plate of ribs."

"Ribs?"

"Yeah, collard greens and mac-n-cheese, too."

"Soul food? You're eating soul food?" She laughed her disbelief.

"The minute I get inside I am. Why?"

"That's like me saying I'm eating a big bowl of mac-n-cheese for dinner. The only people I know who do that are white."

I shook my head. "There you go with the race thing again."

"Come on, Brian, you know I'm right. Do you see black people in Kraft commercials eating bowls of mac-n-cheese as the main course? Of course not, because we eat it as a side dish with ribs."

Her laugh was contagious. She had a point.

All too soon, her laughter slowed. "I miss you, Brian."

"What?"

Ebony hesitated. "I miss you." The words were no longer a whisper.

I stopped in the foyer. If I drove fast enough, I could be at her place in twenty minutes.

"I miss you, too."

"Are you busy Friday? I mean, do you have plans? I don't have to work either job, so I figured, you know, if you're free, maybe we could ..." She paused. "I know you've got to go to the club Friday night. I would love to come see you play, but I've got to report to the zoo early in the morning, so I can't stay out late. What I'm saying is I want to see you."

She'd finally stopped rambling.

"Did you just ask me out on an actual date?"

Nervous laughter came through the phone. "Yes."

"Friday's good, although I have mandatory practice from three to six —"

"Oh."

"We don't go on until eleven. Why don't I pick you up around two? You can go with me. Afterward we could grab something to eat and do whatever you want. I'll be yours until ten."

"I'd like that."

CHAPTER 12

Ebony

I t was one o'clock, and I didn't know what to wear. Brian would be here in an hour. I hadn't done my hair and make-up yet. The only thing I'd done was shower.

"Yasmine!"

"Oh no, who died?" She rushed across the hall and took one glance at the clothes strewn across my bed. Her hands went to her hips. "Fashion emergency?"

I nodded, biting my lip.

"Is this a date?"

"Yes."

Her eyebrows went up in surprise. "Okay, *hmm*, what kind? First date? Meeting for drinks?"

My eyebrows furrowed. "Not exactly. I'm meeting band members, and then we're going on a date."

"Hold up, band members? Are you seeing the guitar

player, Javan's roommate?"

My cheeks felt hot. "I guess I am."

"Holy shit! And you haven't said anything? I thought we were friends." She feigned disappointment.

"Yaz, you know you're my girl. I didn't say anything because it just sort of happened." I plopped down on the piles of clothes on my bed. "I met him Sunday, and we had fun. And by the end of the evening, we kissed."

Yasmine stood wide-eyed, her mouth hanging open.

"And it was ..." I didn't know how to describe it. Warm and sweet sounded like kissing a childhood boyfriend. Hot and passionate didn't cut it either, though I'm sure if we'd kissed long enough, we'd have ended up there. "Perfect," I decided.

Yasmine laughed while she sorted through my mountain of clothes. "Different is what you mean. Not saying white men can't kiss, it's just with a brother, there's more lips to suck on, you know?"

"Yasmine!"

"What? You know I'm right. But it's all about technique. I've kissed some guys whose lips were the size of tires. I felt like I was being licked by a dog." Yasmine shivered in mock disgust.

I cracked up. "That is so wrong."

"I've also kissed guys whose lips were smaller than mine, but man, did they have technique." Her eyes closed as if having a flashback. "David could suck the hell out of—"

"Enough!" I laughed, throwing my hands up. "I get the point. Besides, I like Brian's ... technique and plan to explore it some more tonight. First, I need the perfect outfit."

"You called the right one. So, what does he like?"

"Huh?"

She sighed. "What does he like? You know, what has he commented on? What has his roving eye looked at when he's not staring at you?"

"Um, his attention is always on me. Plus, he says I look good in anything, even my work clothes."

"What the hell?" She rubbed her eyes. "Okay, he's one of those."

"One of what?"

"A man who's always giving compliments to suck up."

I loved Brian's compliments. He never gave the impression of trying to get something in return. His facial expressions made it obvious that what he said came from the heart.

"All right, what has he seen you in?" She eyed the clothes pile. "Jeans?"

"Not exactly, Capri's, yes."

"Dress?"

"That skin tight number the night we met."

"Told you it would work." She gave me a smug smile. "Shorts?"

"Yes, on Sunday, the day we kissed."

"*Hmm*, how about this?"

I turned to see what she held. "Perfect."

"Now for hair and make-up."

At exactly two o'clock, the doorbell rang.

"I'll get it," Yasmine yelled from downstairs.

I finished tying the strings of my wedge heels around my legs and made sure I sprayed perfume in all the right places. I took a deep breath and stood in front of the mirror. Yasmine had a hidden talent for dressing people.

"Well hello, Brian, right? I'm Yasmine. It's nice to meet you."

I could hear Yasmine's voice floating up the steps.

"Hi, Yasmine. I'm here to pick up Ebony," he replied.

God, I loved to hear him say my name.

"Come in. She'll be down in a minute." The door closed. "Take care of my girl."

"I will."

When I heard her coming up the steps, I counted to ten and composed myself.

She stopped at my doorway and winked. "He's a keeper. Nice lips." She laughed and disappeared into her room.

Brian's back was to me when I walked down the stairs. He appeared relaxed with his thumbs hooked in the pockets of his jeans. He had the same black sneakers and a deep blue shirt that was the same shade as his eyes. Blue was fast becoming my favorite color. His blond curls with dark undertones were shorter than when I'd last seen him.

"Hi," I said upon reaching the bottom step.

He turned and his eyes traveled over my outfit. "Damn."

I wore a floral print halter-top accented with red lace trim that molded to my waist and breasts. The tan background complimented my skin and the floor-length skirt fit like a glove. A long sexy slit ran from the hem to the middle of my thigh and gave him an eyeful every time I moved my leg.

"You look ..." He cleared his throat. "Amazing."

He did too. Besides cutting his hair, he'd grown a sexy five o'clock shadow. I couldn't decide whether to stare at his mouth or his eyes.

I closed the distance between us without saying a word. My heels didn't bring us eye-to-eye, but I was close enough. I took his face between my hands, slid my fingertips into his hair, and drew his head down until his lips met mine. After talking about the kiss we'd shared, I was anxious to do it again.

Without hesitation, Brian's mouth opened. Enjoying the firmness of his lips, I slipped my tongue in between. His hands came out of his pockets, around my waist, and pulled me close.

My breath caught. I pressed against him, willing myself to mold to the shape of his body. There was no denying the attraction either of us felt. After days of not seeing each other, we definitely had the same thing in mind.

"Um, excuse me. I kinda need to get through here. It's the only way to the kitchen."

We stopped kissing, but neither of us released our hold. I couldn't believe I was in the living room with Brian, damn near ready to make out. I slipped my hands out of his hair and satisfied my need to touch him by running a hand over his chest. "Sorry," I told Kaitlyn. "Brian, this is my other roommate, Kaitlyn."

She glanced from me to Brian. Her arms were loaded down with grocery bags.

"Hi. I'd love to stay and chat, but I've been standin' here for forever waitin' for y'all lovebirds to come up for air. This stuff is heavy."

"Let me help you," Brian let go of me and reached for the bags.

"No, I've got this. Do ya mind grabbin' the box out of the trunk?"

"Sure."

We watched him disappear out the front door.

"Holy crap!" she whispered. "That's the guy from the club?"

I grinned, slipped a few bags from her hands, and headed for the kitchen.

"He's hot! Does he have a brother?"

I laughed. "Kaity, didn't you just find a man?"

"Yeah, so?" She put the remaining bags down before punching my shoulder. "And you've been holdin' out."

"I know, I know. Yasmine already fussed. I'll fill you guys in with the details when I get home."

"After a kiss like that you're plannin' on comin' home?" She shook her head. "You show up tonight, and I'm calling the crazy police to turn you in."

***

The band practiced at one of the members' houses. Fortunately, the garage had an air conditioning unit installed, so it was quite comfortable.

To my surprise, I wasn't the only female there. I sat against a wall on an old bench seat, which appeared to have come from a truck. Jessica, the fiancée of the band's drummer, sat beside me. Brian and I shared a private laugh when he introduced me. Besides knowing Derrick was engaged, looking back at him now, I was glad Brian ended up being the one I met.

Just like the night at the retirement home, watching Brian play was erotic. Since we'd kissed, I found myself paying more attention to the way he held his mouth and the seductive slide of his fingers up and down the neck of his guitar. My imagination ran wild, causing the lingering heat from our kiss to build. It was impossible to keep from squirming in my seat.

"Here, one of these helps." Jessica handed me a bottle of ice-cold water. She laughed at my confused expression and pointed to the row of ladies sitting near us. All toasted me with their bottles. "We all get turned on while watching them play. It's always a good night whenever we leave a rehearsal or performance."

"Thanks." I'm sure my cheeks flushed pink.

I turned my attention back to the action, watching Brian study the sheet music and interact with the group. He was in full music mode, intent on what he was doing. His curly locks lay plastered to his damp forehead. He'd told me it was a mental and physical workout every time he played. I truly admired him.

He also claimed to get the best sleep on the nights they performed at the club. Of course, it wasn't clear whether he'd expended energy any other way before going to sleep. But after watching him play, I couldn't imagine him going to bed alone.

I suddenly hated the idea of going to work in the morning. Tonight would have been the perfect opportunity to sleep with him.

Our friendship had changed the moment we kissed, but that didn't mean we had to jump straight into cut-buddy status, did it? Oh, hell, who was I kidding? I was horny, and being anywhere in the vicinity of Brian made me want to jump him.

This stupid bottle of water did nothing to cool down the fire that simmered inside me for the past few months. Not even a trip to Antarctica would work. At this rate, I'd probably melt the polar icecap.

"You know, I've never seen Brian this focused before. I mean, he's always prepared, but tonight is different," Jessica said, drawing my attention away from my thoughts of sex. "It's because you're here."

I laughed. "I'm sure he's showed off for plenty of girls before." I took another swig of water. Nope, this definitely wasn't working.

She shook her head. "No, I'm sure it's you. He's never brought anyone here before."

***

Dinner went by fast and neither of us wanted the night to end. At least, I didn't want it to end like this.

We sat in his truck in my driveway. I was grateful he'd taken the time to clean it. There was no trash or funky odors coming from the seats. Not that I would have cared. I was more interested in the action going on between us than what it smelled like. The console between us made it impossible for me to feel his body as we kissed. I made due with the gentle grip of his hand while he tilted my mouth to meet his.

"What's on your mind?" Brian pulled back and watched me.

I blew out a deep breath, then rested my head against the headrest. "For the first time in my life, I'm not looking forward to work in the morning."

"Why, is there something wrong?"

He had no idea. "No, work is fine. I'd just rather be with you tonight."

And still be with him in the morning, tomorrow afternoon...

"I wish you could be there too, but I understand. You have to do the things you love. Besides, it won't be the last night we play."

I eyed him. He honestly didn't have a clue about the true meaning of my statement. Maybe it was for the best. If he knew what I really meant, he'd probably have me naked and in bed in no time.

"What time do you go in?"

"Five a.m.," I groaned.

"I'll probably be getting in bed by then."

Alone, I hope. "Can I ask you a question?"

Brian stopped running his hand through the ends of my hair. "Anything."

"Jessica told me something, and well, it's hard to believe. She said tonight was the first time you've brought a date to practice. Is that true?"

He chuckled and glanced out the window. I saw a slight red hue appear in his cheeks. "Leave it to Jessica. Yes, it's true."

I studied him in surprise. "Why? I mean, don't you take girls to your shows to impress them? You'd definitely be able to get laid."

Brian's head fell back against the headrest as he laughed. "I used to in high school and during my first two years of college." He turned to face me. "I'm older now with goals and no time for games. When I invite a woman, correction, when I invite you to share an important part of my life, it means something."

"Oh."

"Which reminds me, do you have plans for the Fourth of July?"

I had a hard time wrapping my head around his last statement and barely let out an audible, "No,"

"Good. I'd like to spend the day with you. There's a barbeque at my parents' house. It's nothing major. We get together every holiday. I usually don't invite anyone, but I want you to come with me."

Somehow, I managed to find my voice. "You want

me to meet your family?"

"Yes, and I want them to meet you."

I tried to hide my discomfort. A flood of *what if* scenarios ran through my head.

What if they don't like me because I'm black? What if I'm not pretty enough? What if nobody talks to me? *What if ...*

"Hey." He reached over and pulled my face back to meet his. "Don't worry. I promise you'll fit right in." He chuckled. "Believe me, the last thing they'll be interested in is the color of your skin."

Oh great, now I was really nervous.

Brian leaned over and kissed me. His cologne was all-male and ignited primal urges in me, making it impossible to think. I moaned against his mouth.

"Is that a yes?" he asked when our lips parted.

I looked into my private blue ocean that was his eyes. It was impossible to say no to him.

CHAPTER 13

Brian

I focused on the road as Ebony turned to me; she'd been asking questions from the moment I picked her up.

"Let me get this right." Nervousness was in her voice. "You have four sisters, right?"

"Yes."

"And you're the youngest?"

I glanced over to see her expression. Priceless. "Yes."

She stared out of the windshield, probably contemplating another question.

I reached for her hand. "Don't worry, they're going to —"

"Love me. You keep saying that. But, Brian, you have four older sisters. I only have one, and she's extremely protective of my brother and me. I'm the same with women my brother likes."

We were ten minutes away from my parents' house. There was nothing else to say to reassure her, so I changed the subject. "How's work? You're helping take care of a monkey, right?"

"It's an orangutan. If you're going to change the subject, at least know what you're talking about." She shook her head in disapproval.

"See, it worked. How's it going?"

She dove into detail about her daily work routine. Listening to her speak passionately about something she enjoyed made my day. Her enthusiasm reminded me of the way I felt about music. Women I'd dated before only talked about what they expected from me. It was refreshing to be with a woman with goals.

"Oh, God, we're almost there, aren't we?" Ebony said when we slowed down to turn into my parents' subdivision.

"Breathe, Ebony. Just breathe."

"Easier said than done. You're not the black girl coming to the party," she muttered. "They do know I'm black, right?"

I shook my head in exasperation. "Ebony, let's not do this now."

"That would be a *no*." She pulled her hand away and put her head into her hands.

I ignored the comment and parked at the curb in front of my parents' home. Ebony stayed rooted to her seat when I opened her car door. She stared at me with mixed emotions.

"Do you trust me?"

"Is that a rhetorical question?"

I leaned in to kiss her. "You look beautiful by the way. Come on so we can get this over with and you can relax."

We walked up the winding walkway holding hands. Various cars sat in the driveway. The intoxicating aroma of the charcoal floated in the air. The sound of music and children's voices drifted from the backyard.

At the door, I shifted the box of beer under my arm. Ebony gripped the cake she'd baked for the occasion tightly to her chest.

"Ready?" I asked.

"It doesn't seem like I have a choice." She plastered on a grin and squeezed my hand.

I tested the front door and found it unlocked. "Hello?" No response. We walked through the foyer, through the living room to the kitchen. Evidence of the meal's preparations sat on the kitchen counters and table. Bags of chips, dips, desserts, and covered dishes made my mouth water. I sat the beer down.

I heard my father's voice through the opened sliding-glass door, as he told another one of his corny jokes. Laughter erupted as we reached the doorway. Cody and Hannah ran around the backyard while everyone else's attention focused on the center of the yard where my father stood. I squeezed Ebony's hand.

"So this is where the party's at," I said.

Startled by my voice, my family turned.

My mother got out of her seat. "Brian!" She came over to hug me and kissed my cheek.

A chorus of *hellos* came in response as all eyes left me to focus on my date.

"Hey, everybody," I said. "I'd like you to meet Ebony Campbell. Ebony, this is my mother, Laura, and my father, Winfred."

My mother shook her hand. Dad stayed at the grill,

but smiled warmly and waved a pair of tongs.

"I made a cake," Ebony said, holding it out to my mother.

"Oh, thank you. I'll just put it in the kitchen." Mom took the plate inside.

"This is my sister, Lisa." I waved a hand at my niece and nephew. "Her children, Cody and Hannah, are the ones tearing up the yard. And this crazy girl is Bridget."

Both came to shake her hand. Ebony's voice remained warm despite the fact she squeezed the heck out of my hand.

Lisa sat back down, but Bridget remained next to me, a wicked gleam in her eyes.

"Where is everyone?" I scanned the yard again. "I saw cars out front. Where are all the bodies?"

"Andrea and Caroline went to the store to grab a few things. Tim and Randall are working so they'll be late," Bridget informed me while studying Ebony.

"Andrea and Caroline are my other sisters. Tim and Randall are their husbands," I said, turning to Ebony to fill her in.

"Jackson is on the way with Josh and Sara. They went to pick up some fireworks. Aunt Gina and her boys should be here soon."

I groaned. "Tell me Dad isn't going to be in charge of lighting them again this year."

"After last year's fiasco? Hell no." Bridget leaned around me and spoke to Ebony directly. "Last year, Dad burned down the gazebo. He shot off a rocket that went sideways instead of up in the air, and poof," she demonstrated with her hands, "instant fire."

"Oh, no." Ebony covered her mouth to conceal her laughter.

"Fortunately, Tim and Randall are both firefighters. They got it quickly under control." I pointed to the gazebo's remains. "He's supposed to rebuild it, but Mom refuses to let him start until after tonight's fireworks."

Bridget's contagious laughter kept Ebony from being able to contain her own.

"Hey, are you kids talking about me over there?" my father bellowed.

"No," Bridget and I said in unison.

"I might be getting older, but I'm not deaf. Brian, bring your lady friend over here."

I winked at Ebony as we walked over to the stainless-steel giant we'd chipped in to buy him on Father's Day. The savory smell of hot dogs, steak, and chicken permeated the air.

"Dinner looks great, Dad."

"This grill and I are a match made in heaven." He took a moment to flip a row of steaks. "The kitchen is for the women. But this ..." He pointed with pride to the grill. "This is man's work. It's like the caveman days of cooking over a pit fire."

"Winfred, cavemen didn't know how to make fire," Mom said.

Everyone laughed.

"Look, woman, go grab me a beer," Dad said. He glanced at Ebony. "So, you're dating my son, huh?"

My heart dropped to my knees. I should have seen this coming. My dad had no problem getting to the point. We hadn't been here for more than ten minutes, and he'd already jumped to the wrong conclusion. Even though the sexual attraction was there, the only thing we'd done was kiss. I wanted more, damn, I really wanted more. But I didn't want to push and risk the chance she'd decide we were doing too much. Bringing her to meet my family was more than I thought would ever happen. The last thing I needed my father to do was —

"Yes, sir, I am his girlfriend." She squeezed my hand.

Holy. Shit. My heart started beating again. I studied Ebony to make sure I heard her correctly. Her smile said it all.

"How did you guys meet?" Mom reappeared with a beer.

"She picked me up at the bar," I joked.

"Brian!" Ebony poked me in the ribs with her elbow.

Bridget laughed. "And he's the only thing you could find? Girl, I have to take you out sometime and show you where to find a real man."

"Ignore her. She's got a few screws loose," I warned.

Ebony giggled. "I like her."

Annoyed, I decided to mess with my sister. "So, Bridget, what happened to the last guy you dated? What was his name, Raul? Wasn't he like twelve years younger than you?"

Bridget's gaze shot over to our mother who eyed her questioningly. "His name was Francisco, and he was not twelve years younger." She held her head high. "He was five years younger. I broke up with him a few months ago because we couldn't agree on the terms of our relationship."

"Which were?" I pressed.

Her eyes narrowed. "He wanted to get married. I'm too young for that."

I howled.

"Bridget, you're nearly thirty-two years old. It's time to settle down," Mom said.

"You can say that again," Lisa muttered, joining in the conversation.

Lisa was my second oldest sister. Ever since we arrived, she'd been watching Ebony. For her to finally speak meant she must have formulated an opinion.

"Ebony, where are you from? You don't have a California accent."

"Charlotte, North Carolina," she replied.

"Wow, you're a long way from home. How did you end up here?"

The moment Ebony dreaded had arrived. I decided to give her some space, confident she could handle my sisters. I kissed her hand and continued to stand next to my father while she followed them to sit in the patio chairs. I stood in silence, listening to the flow of questions and answers between them. Lisa was obviously filling in for our older sister, Andrea, and would give her and Caroline a detailed report in private once they returned.

"Hand me a plate, will you?" Dad removed the hot dogs from the grill. "She's a looker, son."

I turned my attention back to Ebony. "Yeah, she is." I grinned with pride.

"Have you slept with her yet?"

My attention broke. I faced my dad as he casually took a long sip of his beer. He remained calm, cool, and collected. You'd think he just asked me to pass him the barbeque sauce.

"Uh ... no, not yet." I buried my hands deep in my pockets.

My dad and I talked about everything. From my first wet dream, to the first time I had sex. It was a rare occasion for him to ask a question that made me nervous.

This was one of them.

"What are you waiting for?" He paused to study me. His expression was serious. "Everything still working? You're not sick, are you?"

"Yes, Dad, everything works just fine and no, I'm healthy."

He continued to watch me. "Ah, I get it. You're serious; don't want to mess things up, eh?"

I looked back at Ebony. She seemed to have settled in. "I don't know, Dad, she might be the one."

His eyebrows rose in question. "Does she feel the same way?"

"I don't know. We haven't really talked about that. We're still in the beginning stages. We've kissed, but I don't want to rush it."

He nodded. "What about her family? You know your mother and I couldn't care less if Ebony were purple, as long as she's a good woman and you're happy. But if her parents are from the other side of the world —"

"They live in the U.S."

"You know what I mean. Things are different in the South. They may not be as liberal as we are. That's all I'm saying, son."

"We've talked about it … some. But we're here, not there. We're both consenting adults capable of making our own decisions."

"Whoa, boy, hold on. I'm not trying to tell you what to do." He put a hand on my shoulder. "After what happened with the last woman you dated, can you blame me? I'm just looking out for your best interest. Be sure your thinking with your head and not your *Johnson*." He paused when I laughed. "I'm serious. You should know from experience a man's heart is a fragile thing.

We try to hide behind the macho façade, pretending we don't get whipped. But deep down, when we find our own personal *Eve*, we're done. And if your *Eve* breaks your heart, well, it's hard to recover." He took a long pull on his beer before flipping the meat.

My own *Eve*. I'd never thought about a woman that way. It wasn't hard to understand where he was coming from. I studied the curve of Ebony's lips and the small crinkle in the corner of her eyes when she laughed. The relaxed pose of her body as she talked to my sisters. My heart warmed.

"What about you, Dad. Has your heart been broken by an *Eve*?"

His eyes followed my mother. "No. My *Eve*, my paradise, is right here."

CHAPTER 14

Ebony

B rian's sisters were an interesting group of women.

Bridget, by far, was my favorite. Not only did she favor Brian, she had a magnetic personality. Petite in stature, her hair wasn't blond, and her eyes were nearly gray, a direct contrast to Brian's deep blue. She'd stayed by my side the entire time, rolling her eyes at some of the questions her three older siblings threw at me.

Andrea, the oldest and most conservative of the sisters, had two teenage children. For the most part, she observed me in silence, commenting when necessary, allowing Lisa to ask the questions.

Lisa, by far the most talkative next to Bridget, asked me everything she could think of. It was obvious by the smile that popped in the corners of her mouth when she approved of my response. If I won her approval, the others would surely follow suit.

And then there was the sweet, and very pregnant, Caroline. My heart went out to her. With two weeks to go until her due date, she looked as if she were about to burst. She smiled and shook my hand, but her focus was getting her baby to come sooner than later. 'Damn the party, I need to have this baby tonight,' she'd said.

The only people I hadn't had a one-on-one discussion with were her parents.

I leaned against the back porch column and sipped my soda, enjoying the view of the landscaped backyard. Mrs. Young and her daughters migrated into the kitchen to put the final touches on the meal. I offered to help, but they told me, as a guest, I needed to relax. Personally, I thought they were taking the time to talk about me in private. The idea was unnerving, but it was bound to happen.

"That wasn't so bad, right?" Brian's deep voice startled me. He stood behind me and slipped his hands around my waist. "*Mm* ... you smell good," he whispered. His lips found a spot below my ear that made my body quiver. He'd never done that before. I desperately wanted him to do it again.

"Hey." I angled my head around and shared a quick kiss. "What are you doing?" We locked our fingers together. The heat of his body seduced me. I couldn't contain the nervous laughter and looked around to see who could be watching.

"They're all inside, and the kids are too busy playing to notice. Besides, I'm kissing my girlfriend," he murmured and — *oh yeah* — he kissed the spot again. "Was that an official proclamation or something done for my father's benefit?"

I honestly didn't know where the remark came from. Somehow, it felt … right. Brian introduced me to a side he rarely shared with other women. He wasn't the type of man to bring just anyone home. Once I got over being nervous, it felt like I belonged here. Maybe even to him.

"Do you want me to take it back?" I teased, looking over my shoulder.

"Hell no, I want you to be my girl."

"Yeah, I figured you did."

His chuckle went deep, vibrating in his body as I leaned against him.

"Why don't we do something to make it official?"

His whisper filled my ear making every nerve in my body go on standby. My heart beat a mile a minute at his invitation.

"What do you have in mind?"

"Hmm, I could think of plenty of things we could do to —"

"Ebony, could you come here for a moment?" Mrs. Young's voice floated out the open sliding-glass doors as his sisters filed out of the kitchen.

Bridget glanced at me and snickered.

Brian laid his head on my shoulder and groaned.

I forced myself from his arms and immediately regretted the loss of his body's heat. "Your mom hasn't talked to me yet." A chill went through me even though it was eighty-four degrees outside. "I'll be back."

I could feel his eyes on me as I walked away.

"Ah, there you are. I said I didn't need your help, but my daughters decided to take a break. Would you mind making the salad?"

I smiled. "Sure, Mrs. Young."

We both knew they were giving her the space she needed to get to know the new woman in her only son's life.

"Please, call me Laura. Mrs. Young makes me feel old."

Whatever her age, she wore it well. Brian got his blond hair from her. Her shoulder-length locks held faint streaks of gray, while her smile mimicked her son's. Her eyes were blue-gray, like Bridget's, and her figure was impressive for a woman who'd given birth to five children.

"I hope my daughters didn't scare you off." Her eyes twinkled with laughter.

"No, ma'am, they didn't. I have an older sister, so I know what it's like to bring home someone and have them interrogated by her. Though I'm sure from time to time my brother can be worse."

Laura pulled a bagged salad from the refrigerator. "Is he older or younger?"

"He's my twin."

"Really? How did your mother handle it?"

"With nerve pills by the time we were in high school. Trevon was a handful."

She chuckled. "Do me a favor and cut up some onion, tomato, and cucumber. Pre-made salad is convenient, but it's always lacking."

"Sure." I reached for the knife resting on the counter top.

"Forgive me for asking, but did you really pick my son up in a bar?"

I laughed. "No, ma'am. I was at the bar when he picked me up."

"That's what I thought. He doesn't usually do stuff like that. Well, not as far as I know …" She glanced away, apparently embarrassed by what she'd said.

"I know what you mean." I smiled. "To be honest, he picked me out of a crowd watching the band play. He came up to me, and I politely brushed him off."

Mrs. Young laughed.

"A few days later, Brian showed up at my house, hired by my roommate to cut our lawn and well … here we are. I can say one thing, he's very persistent."

"Oh yes," she agreed. "As a kid he used to flash those blue eyes at me all the time to get cookies from the jar before dinner. He's got eyes just like his father."

"He knows how to use them," I agreed. Brian did indeed have the same swag as his father who was strikingly handsome.

I glanced up and saw her smile.

"You are the first woman Brian's brought around here in a long time, Ebony. He likes you. I hope you feel the same way about him. I'd hate for my son's heart to be broken again."

I paused, mid-slice of an onion, and frowned.

"Oh, dear, I've said too much." Laura turned her focus to a pot on the stove.

Brian's heart had been broken? He'd never mentioned it to me when talking about previous relationships.

"I like Brian. I love his confidence and his desire to reach his goals, and he supports mine. That's why I'm with him. I don't know where our relationship is going to go, but I'm willing to stick around and find out."

We studied each other before she nodded.

"I can understand why he likes you. You speak your

mind. That's a good thing. He doesn't need a woman who'll back down. Keep that up, and you'll be fine." She smiled briefly and turned back to the stove.

That was unexpected.

Brian stood in the doorway of the kitchen, having appeared out of nowhere. "Mom, can I borrow Ebony?"

His timing was impeccable. He must have been watching from the patio door, waiting for me to finish.

"Go ahead, I'll clean this up. Thank you for your help, Ebony."

"We're going for a tour of the house," he told her.

"Don't be long. Dinner should be ready in twenty minutes."

"That's long enough," he muttered. He grabbed my hand and practically dragged me out of the kitchen, through the living room, and up the stairs.

I laughed at his enthusiasm. "Where are we going?"

"You'll see." He acted like a kid about to unwrap a present the day before Christmas. And I was the present.

Oh boy.

The excursion stopped at a door he pushed open.

"This is my old bedroom," he said, holding the door open for me to walk past him. It was a typical boy's room. Sports equipment from his high school days sat in the corner. Posters of his favorite band still adorned the walls. I walked to a dresser lined with trophies and awards. Next to them were framed pictures of Brian as a baby up until his college graduation. Evidence of Mrs. Young's use of the room sat in a corner. A sewing table, fabric, and various magazines filled the space.

I picked up the nearest framed photo. "You were adorable." A six-year-old Brian grinned into the camera. His two front teeth were missing, and thick blond curls hung wildly around his face.

He stood leaning against the doorjamb. "Apparently my mom felt the same way. I'd just fallen over the handle bars of my bike and knocked out my two front teeth. Fortunately, they were baby teeth. It took nearly a year before the new ones grew back."

I set down the frame and picked up another. A low clicking noise drew my attention. Brian leaned against the closed bedroom door, his eyes intent on me.

My heart kicked up a notch. "What are you doing?"

He didn't say a word when he walked over and removed the frame from my grasp. He pulled my arms around his neck and slid his hands around my waist. His lips came for mine, taking exactly what he wanted. His kisses before had been soft with a hint of heat, but not now. Now he took possession of my mouth without holding back. There was no question, only demand.

I gave in to him, accepting his tongue eagerly as I offered him mine. A sigh of pleasure escaped me when he pushed me against the dresser, his mouth leaving mine and traveling from my chin to my throat. His hands roamed the length of my body, down to my butt, and squeezed.

"Brian..."

"Shh..." he murmured, coming back to my mouth.

I arched as his hands journeyed back and found the hem of my shirt. He pushed the fabric up and slipped rough fingers over bare skin. My breath heaved in and out as I struggled to breathe. My hips pushed against his firm body and rubbed against the desire evident in his pants. I could feel every firm inch of him. I tried to pull my hands free of his shoulders so I could run them over his body, but to no avail. He kept my arms trapped.

"No, I don't have enough control. All I want is a sample." His voice was thick with need as his mouth went back for mine.

"Oh, God," I moaned when his attention turned to the side of my throat. I struggled to keep my voice down when he began grinding against me.

I was on the verge of coming, right then and there. Just as I was about to cry out, Brian covered my mouth with his, swallowing my gasp while torturing me even more with his body.

As intriguing and exciting as sleeping with Brian was, I was suddenly aware we stood in his old bedroom.

In his parents' house.

With his entire family outside.

Oh. My. God.

Worry flashed over me. Yes, we were grown and what we did and where we did it was our business. But here?

Visions of his mother walking up the stairs looking for us scared me. His family was wonderful and seemed willing to support our relationship. I didn't want to screw it up by becoming the *ho* who did her son in his old bedroom during the family barbeque.

"Brian." It was nearly impossible to speak while his tongue traced an erotic trail down my throat.

His mouth came back to mine, but this time, his kiss was slow, and the glide of his fingers light as he pulled my shirt back down.

My knees were weak, my brain scrambled, and my breath ragged. I forced my eyes open and found him gazing down at me. His eyes were heavy, filled with lust.

"I need to be alone with you," he said, dipping his

head down to kiss me again. "I want you in my bed, tonight. We'll stay for dinner and fireworks." He kissed me long and deep. "But after that ..."

Brian had been true to his word; he'd gotten to know me before showing me this passionate side of him. I had no doubt being with him would be worth the wait. He knew exactly how to make my body hunger for more. It was hard to think straight.

No matter how much I wanted to be with him, I felt guilty, as if somehow I'd let him down.

Brian brought me into his private world. But what did I have to give him in return besides my body? I felt like I'd cheated him out of something he deserved. My best friends hadn't known about him until the last minute. My family didn't know I was seeing him. And we'd been involved for a month.

I was a coward. I was in his family home about to eat his parents' food. He'd brought me as deep into his life as anyone could go. Yet in my world, Brian continued to be an outsider.

I doubted my family would accept him nearly as much as his accepted me. And despite what Brian believed, being in California did not make being an interracial couple any easier.

Once we slept together, what would happen next? What would be the expectation? Would he want more? Would I?

One thing was for sure, once we crossed the line, the rules were definitely going to change. But I wanted them to.

Because I wanted Brian.

CHAPTER 15

Ebony

"We'll be alone tonight," Brian said as he unlocked the front door to his house.

"I guess Javan is still out with Yasmine." I tried to hide the nervousness in my voice.

"He's got several women he deals with. I don't keep up with him."

The door closed behind us. I followed him through the foyer to the living room. He looked around the room apparently making sure everything was in order. "Would you like something to drink?"

"No thanks. I ate too much at your parents' house. I'll be full until next week." I set my purse down on the sofa and studied the room.

It surprised me that a house shared by two men was so clean. I didn't know what to expect, especially after seeing the way he usually kept his truck.

Brian walked over to a shelf containing the largest CD collection I'd ever seen. He ran his hand over the black wooden cabinet before looking up at me in satisfaction.

"Wow. How many CDs do you have?"

"At last count, 262." He laughed. "I've been collecting since I was in middle school. All of this represents every genre of music I play and artist I admire. My iPhone has pretty much every one of these discs and more."

"Amazing." I joined him at the cabinet and studied the titles.

He angled his head and watched me. I sensed his gaze and immediately thought of the kiss we'd shared at his parents' house. He was showing remarkable restraint for a man who'd been close to ripping off my clothes. "See anything you like?"

I glanced over at him and saw the mischievous twinkle. His question was an obvious double entendre.

"Yes." I selected a disk and held it up for his approval.

"Sade, old school, cool."

"Do you have a CD player in your room?"

His answer was a devilish grin and an extended hand. We walked down a hallway past the kitchen and a door I assumed led to his roommate's bedroom. Brian's room was just as neat as the living room. A full-sized bed with blood-red sheets was in the center below a set of windows. A desk with a laptop sat on one side, while a guitar and several smaller instruments were in the corner.

Brian closed the door and walked to the CD player on the nightstand. The sexy, sultry music was an instant aphrodisiac.

He sat at the edge of his bed, sinful desire in his cerulean eyes. "Come here."

I walked over to him and stood between his legs. He ran his eyes over my body, starting with my legs and stopping at my mouth. My legs went weak as his hands slid from the back of my knees, over my hips, and gripped my waist. He guided me down so that I straddled his lap, putting his mouth in line with my throat.

"You have no idea how bad I want you," he murmured as his lips grazed the side of my throat.

He had no idea how bad I wanted him. I slipped my fingers into the nape of his curly hair and held him as our lips met and mated. Neither of us wasted time. He greedily gripped the edge of my shirt, slipped it over my head, and lowered his mouth to the top of my breast, his tongue gliding over me. He pulled the cups of my bra down, and his hot mouth latched onto a hardened nipple. I arched and my head fell back. The bra hit the floor.

I moaned his name when he cupped my breasts, kneading them gently as his mouth found mine again. All sense of coherent thought left me. I rocked my hips against him, feeling his hardened flesh pushing against his jeans and between my thighs. I wanted him out, naked, and inside of me. Now.

I slipped my fingers between us and quickly unfastened the buttons of his shirt. Of all days to decide to wear one of these. Why couldn't he have on a pullover like always? A quick tug would have had his chest available to me in seconds. Now I had to work for it.

Buttons free, I forced the material over his shoulders and down to his wrists. He released me to help remove the shirt. In our haste, his wrists got tangled up. I bit my lip as I looked down at him. His eyes were the most intense shade of blue I'd ever seen. His mouth parted expectantly. His lips were swollen and pink from the way I'd sucked them. I wanted to own him. Every … last … inch.

A deep chuckle came from his throat. "What are you doing?" He tried to free his wrist.

"Don't worry, I promise you'll like it." I smiled wickedly as I fisted the makeshift handcuffs, trapping his hands on the bed.

I nibbled, lapped, and sucked my way to his throat while Brian groaned.

He smelled so good, so male. Barbeque and beer mixed with his musky cologne that held a hint of sweetness. His scent had driven me crazy all night. I took my time to savor every detail of his bronzed flesh, tasting every inch I could reach. But it wasn't enough. I lifted my head from his chest and teased him with my tongue, evading his mouth as he tried to capture mine.

He panted beneath me, his chest heaved in and out, but his eyes, those crystal blue orbs stayed on me. I was driving him crazy, and my time to be in control was running out. I was sure the moment his wrist were free, he would take me down and return the favor.

Perfect, because that was exactly what I wanted.

I slid off his lap, down to the floor, and placed myself between his parted thighs. I went for his belt buckle and worked quickly to free him from his jeans. Brian's body shifted. A quick peek showed him struggling to undo the twisted knot of his shirt.

Pants undone, I slipped my hand in, seized my prize, and stroked.

"Shit …" he bit out, his body bucked.

I let out a naughty laugh.

Free at last, Brian gripped my wrist. "Can't have too much of that just yet."

He held firm while leaning down, capturing and forcing his way into my mouth. He pulled my hands around his neck, lifted me from the floor, and dropped me down onto the bed. The sudden change of position and the bounce on the mattress forced out a seductive laugh. I felt so alive, so sexy and —

Oh. My. God. He was gorgeous.

Brian stood at the edge of the bed and finished the job I started. With a solid thump, his jeans hit the floor. My gaze traveled over the newly exposed flesh. Damn …

His body was more than I'd expected. His torso and legs were long and a well-toned set of muscles led down from his chest to his groin. Nearly every part of him was tan. His legs, his thighs … even his …

I'd never suspected him of using a tanning bed, but somehow his entire body was exactly the same shade. I had imagined a part of him being lighter than the rest because of his time spent working in the summer sun.

I moved to sit up but stopped when he shook his head.

"I want you to stay there. Don't move." He licked his lips and walked backward toward his dresser. He bumped into it and turned to dig into a drawer. He returned, holding a box of condoms and tossed it lightly onto the bed.

He studied me momentarily before dropping down to his knees, making himself at home between my legs. Leaning on my elbows, I sat up and looked down the length of my body. Brian smiled wickedly, leaned forward, and kissed my stomach. Slow, methodical kisses traveled to my navel. He dipped his tongue in and made me giggle.

The sight and sensation of him between my thighs made me ache to be free of the rest of my clothes. Brian stopped me when I went to grab the zipper of my shorts. He gripped my wrists and held them firm against the bed. He dipped his head lower on my body, kissing the exposed skin of my thighs, and glided his tongue down to my knees. He lifted my leg to his shoulder and continued to tease with fingertips and mouth. I reached for him, but he was just out of range.

He stopped long enough to remove my shoes and socks before repeating the delicious agony on my other leg. Both now rested on his shoulders.

"Brian," I begged. My legs were like rubber and vibrated with want, need, and desire so much I could not regain control.

"I want you ready for me. The moment I get you naked, I'm going to get inside you. But not until you're ready."

"I'm ready, I'm ready …" I wiggled my hips and tried my best to push up against him.

He was good. No matter how much I tried to sit up or lean forward, he remained just out of reach. I was about to go mad.

He lifted an eyebrow and removed his hands. The only contact came from my legs resting on his shoulders.

Seconds seemed like minutes. Minutes seemed like hours.

"God, Brian, please …"

Finally, he reached for the clasp of my shorts and

pulled them down. But damn it, my panties were still on.

"Leave them," he said huskily, dropping my shorts on the floor. His mouth went to my knees. His hands slid mercilessly up the inside of my thighs and parted them.

I watched as his lips followed. I could no longer see his eyes, only the top of his head, but man, could I feel. His breath was ragged, his mouth hot. At last, he came within my reach. I slipped my fingers in his hair and held on tight while he worked his way up my body.

And then his fingers, his large, firm fingers found me and stroked. He teased with his thumb. I arched off the bed and dug my fingers into the tangle of his hair.

I wanted his mouth there instead. But no, he sat up and watched me as he played my body like his guitar.

Our eyes connected, and I fought to breathe. My mouth gaped open, inhaling his scent. The moment he slipped a finger under the lace of my panties, I flew into ecstasy. My body tense, I cried out his name.

He wasted no time, quickly removed the final barrier between us, and covered himself. The weight of his body on mine when he slipped inside was beyond anything I imagined. He filled me, every inch, and moved slowly, as if searching for the perfect rhythm.

"Yes ... yes ... yes ..."

"Is this what you want?" His voice was deep in my ear, his breath labored as he moved inside me.

Unable to speak again, I answered him by tightening my legs on the backs of his thighs and pushed my hips up to meet him. He groaned in response to the added friction of our bodies as they danced in unison. My fingers were still in his hair, so I directed his lips back to mine and invaded his mouth with my tongue just as he invaded me.

Time no longer mattered. Our differences didn't matter. The only thing that mattered was that we were two bodies moving with the same desire.

Brian pulled back, braced on his elbows, and looked deep into my eyes. His mouth open, his face contorted with pleasure, his biceps taunt and straining from his obvious control. I had no idea how long we stayed that way. I just knew that it felt so good. He slowed our rhythm and lowered his mouth to me. And when we kissed, it was slow and hot. It was question and demands all wrapped into one. I moaned and let him take everything I had to give.

He released my lips and dropped his head onto my shoulder. With one hand, he balanced his weight, obviously not wanting to crush me, but I didn't care. He slipped his hand past my hip and to my thigh, lifting it high on his waist. The change in angle was mind-blowing. And this time, when he moved, it wasn't slow.

"I want you to come," he said, his voice hoarse.

He released my leg and reached for my bottom, lifting me off the bed and pounded into me.

Tears of ecstasy leaked from the corners of my eyes as I held on for the ride.

I tried my best to meet him stroke for stroke until my body tensed, clamping down on the point where we were connected, and let go. All breathing stopped, all thinking ceased. I could feel him deep inside of me and hear his breath catch as he followed my release and let loose something that sounded like a growl as he collapsed on top of me.

My heart raced. The ability to breathe came back.

The ability to see beyond the flashing white lights behind my eyes remained impossible.

Weakened, my arms and legs fell free from his body like rubber. I hadn't felt this good in more than just months. I hadn't felt this good ... ever.

There was more going on here. I could feel it in the way we'd made love. I could see it in his eyes when he'd watched me.

Oh, shit.

CHAPTER 16

Brian

I expected it to be like this.

The lack of feeling in my legs, feet, and inability to think straight, oh yeah.

The only thing I could feel was the heat radiating from her body. Every part of her was slick with sweat and inviting.

Ebony felt so damn good.

Having her for the first time was way better than I imagined it could be.

Too weak to move, my weight settled on her body. My first thought was she couldn't breathe. She'd been holding me with her arms and legs, but they fell away the moment I collapsed.

"Are you all right?" My thick voice sounded foreign in my own ears.

"Oh, yes." Her reply came out a sexy snake-like

drawl.

My face rested between her neck and shoulder. The scent of charcoal from the picnic was in her hair, the smell of sex on her sweat-dampened skin. I breathed deep to memorize the moment.

"I'll move in a minute, just ... give me a minute."

Ebony didn't speak, but I could tell by the motion of her head that she nodded.

My heart thundered like a bass drum, and hers raced in unison against my chest. Funny. Lying on her like this meant our hearts were practically side-by-side, nearly one.

As my heartbeat slowed, the blood in my body flowed to the needed places once again. Movement of any kind became doable. I lifted my head and looked around. We'd managed to travel the expanse of my bed.

I pushed up on my elbows and paused, too weak to move anymore, I peered down at her.

Her hair splayed across the mattress; her lips were full and pouty and calling my name. I didn't have the energy to give them what they needed. She appeared relaxed, her eyes closed while a slight smile played on those sexy lips. After all, she'd been a very willing participant. She'd given as much as she'd taken.

Her eyes opened just a little. The heavily lidded chocolate wells made my heart kick back into sudden overdrive. I wondered if she was as worn out as I was. Either way, I'd be ready for another round in, oh ... twenty minutes. Ten if she kept looking at me that way.

I leaned down, caressed her mouth with mine, and pulled out, immediately regretting the loss of heat from her body. I flopped down on the available space on the bed and removed the condom. That bit of effort cost me all the energy I'd recovered. I closed my eyes and drifted in the silent afterglow of sex.

Over the years, I'd been with plenty of women. One night stands, quickies, just because, and any other situation I could think of. I'd done things and had them done to me in ways that would have made the average man jealous. None of them compared to this. Sex with Ebony hadn't been just sex ... it had been making love.

I reached up and scratched my head at the thought.

When I met Ebony, sleeping with her was my initial goal, because hell, it had been impossible to ignore a body like hers. That night I was horny and in need of a release. If she'd responded to the free drink, she would have been like any other woman: a quick lay with no strings attached. But she didn't.

The way she'd looked me up and down and questioned my intentions threw me way off my ordinary game and into uncharted territory. Up for a challenge, I'd grabbed hold and refused to let go. The more I got to know her, the more I fantasized and lusted ... until now.

And somehow in between all of this I did the unthinkable and introduced her to my life. My music. My family. Since when did I start introducing women I had only known for a month to my family? Family was sacred. I never brought an unknown element into the center of my life. A rotten influence could disturb the entire balance of what gave me peace in the world.

My slice of perfection. My slice of paradise.

My *Eve*.

I chuckled. My father described his relationship with my mother that way. And yeah, I confided in him that I thought I'd found *the one*. But I had no true idea what that *one* was until now.

Never in my life had I ever been this satisfied after sex and yet still craved more. And the more wasn't just about sex. I wanted her smile, her company. I wanted her to be just as important in my life as my guitar.

Anything Ebony wanted from me, she could have. My time. My money. My heart.

Radiating heat in my chest had me rubbing that very spot. Love happened for me once, and it had taken months to cultivate, not weeks. And look how that ended. Did I really want that kind of risk right now?

Ebony wanted monogamy. Done, because I wasn't sharing. She wanted good sex, hell yeah, so did I. And it was beyond good.

Her declaration of boyfriend/girlfriend sounded like a high-school romance compared to what I felt. But what did it mean? Our first true conversation had been about *friends-with-benefits*. Is that what we were doing? I'm sure she wouldn't have shared the label with my father. Maybe it was just her way of telling me she wanted to have sex.

In the beginning, when she'd made it clear she didn't want to sleep with me, my response had been to ignore my desire and focus on developing a relationship because she intrigued me. That didn't remove the sexual tension; I just kept from making advances. And now after sex, I realized I still needed more from her.

Her mind, her body, her time. Every part she was willing to share.

I turned my head slightly and glimpsed her relaxed form. All that caramel skin, soft and delicious. Mine.

"*Mmm* ..."

Ebony's moan made the blood in my body drain from one head to another.

She shifted in bed and faced me. "Hi." She smiled.

"Hi, yourself." I couldn't keep a cocky grin off my face. Oh yeah, I'd given her more than she'd expected.

We studied each other in silence. It didn't feel awkward at all.

Ebony reached out and brushed a finger along my jaw, then rested her hand on my chest. Her gaze went down to my skin.

She smiled slightly. "You've got freckles on your chest." She traced them lightly.

I looked down. Her fingers were so soft. "Yeah, in a few places."

"I like them." She bit her lip and sat up on her elbow, seemingly entranced by my skin.

Enjoying her curiosity, I folded my arms behind my head, leaving every inch of my body at her disposal. She could have access to anything she wanted.

Her eyes traveled to the tattoos on my biceps. I gave a half grin. The markings on my skin always seemed to fascinate the women I'd been with. Somehow, they wanted to equate them with power or something else stupid.

She studied them intently. "What do they mean?"

Usually I made up some ridiculous story to entertain. But not this time. That was a first.

"I surf a lot. When I was in college, I made my way to Hawaii for a weekend with some friends. It was an awesome time to go. The waves were rough and wild, perfect for what we were doing. Anyway, there was one killer break none of us seemed to get hold of. After hours of trying, I finally did it. To celebrate, I decided to get a tattoo.

"There was this really old man who worked in the

tattoo parlor. When I showed him what I wanted, he frowned and said it was not the one for me. At first I was pissed, but then he explained. He said, 'Marking your body is a sacred thing. A tattoo represents what is dear to you. Don't waste time doing something you will regret when you get older.' He then removed his shirt and showed me some of the most amazing artwork I'd ever seen. His arms, chest, back ... all of his markings told the story of his life. I made the decision right then and there my tattoos would mean something."

I smiled as Ebony retrieved the pillow from the floor, folded it, and rested her head on her arms to listen to my tale.

"I was just twenty-one then, still wet behind the ears — no pun intended — and didn't have much of a story to tell. So he asked me what meant the most to me in my life. I told him, and he designed this." I pulled my arm from behind my head and flexed my biceps. "This is a shark and represents adaptability and strength. The dolphin," I moved my arm and pointed, "represents joy and friendship. Here is wind, which is protection and fertility. And my favorite," I adjusted my arm again, "is the turtle. This is for family and life."

I watched her eyes travel over the black figures. "They are beautiful, Brian." She glanced at my other arm and her eyebrows furrowed. "But why do you have two of them?"

"This one," I indicated my right arm "is for my family. My parents, sisters, cousins, and everyone I hold dear." I held up my other arm. "But this set, the one closest to my heart, represents my future family."

Ebony laughed lightly. "Family to come, huh? You like to plan in advance, don't you?"

"You've got to have a plan in order to get what you want out of life. You're doing a good job with the plan you have."

"Yeah, and it's a lot of work. I've enjoyed every opportunity, too. But I can't wait for this year to be over. I want school behind me, so I can focus on my job. I've got so much information waiting to get put to use, but I can't do it yet." She turned to lie on her back.

I narrowed my eyebrows and watched her sigh. "What's wrong? I thought you got to do a lot. I mean, you do more than shovel crap all day, right?"

She chuckled. "Yeah, I assist the head veterinarians when they do routine physicals on the animals."

"That sounds good."

"Yeah, *sounds* is the operative word. When I assist, my job is to stand there with a chart in my hand, taking notes about animal weight or medication. Nothing hands-on just yet." She rolled her eyes. "Okay, that's not completely true. I do some hands-on, but it's only with the little animals. I want to work with the big ones — lions, elephants, panda bears — for crying out loud."

"Stuck with the baby orangutan, huh?"

"I wouldn't say stuck. I love taking care of her. She's fragile and small. Her mother was sick and dying. It forced the vets to do a cesarean on her in order to save the infant. She was born too soon, but Nala is a fighter. She's just a month old and has packed on a few pounds as well as started to develop like other infants of her species."

Her eyes lit up as she spoke. For the first time I noticed the way the tip of her nose wiggled when she got excited. That was endearing.

"But now I wonder if ..." The twinkle in her eye

dimmed.

"What?"

She sighed heavily before turning back to face me. "I've worked my ass off for the opportunity for the full-time position next year, but sometimes I wonder if something is going to happen to change things. I mean, I get along with everyone. I always get to work on time and stay late even when not on the clock. I volunteer for the shitty assignments —" She smiled a little when I laughed. "Ha, ha, I don't mean literally."

"Yes, you do, admit it. There's no shame in shoveling shit. We all have to some time."

"Seems like I do a lot of it when I'm with you." Ebony nudged my chest. "Seriously, I saw something last month that's got me worried. My mentor, Doctor Jacobs, has been aiding me since I started volunteering, taking me under his wing. He's always been willing to answer any questions I've had. He's even shared information I never would have known to ask. Recently, he loaned me a stack of books along with detailed notes from his senior year in college. They're for the same classes I'll be taking this fall. He wants me to get the job."

I felt my eyebrows knit together, suddenly territorial. "He hasn't tried to make a move on you, has he?"

"What? No, no. Okay, once, but nothing happened." She waved it off.

"So what's the problem?"

"Well, I walked into a supply closet for some toilet paper and found him in there with his pants down around his ankles and the new intern on her knees."

Blood shot straight to my groin and my attention went immediately to her mouth. I wondered what her mouth would feel like—

"I slammed the door and hurried out of there."

I shrugged, forcing my attention away from her mouth and checked the time. Twenty minutes would be over soon. As much as I wanted to listen to what she had to say, I wanted to be inside her again.

"They were coworkers. Sex in the work place is nothing new."

One of her eyebrows cocked. "He's in his fifties, and the girl is just nineteen."

"Oh."

"Exactly. The zoo has a strict no-fraternization policy, but so does every job. It still happens. If no one reports it, then it's not a problem. It wasn't my first time walking in on a couple who decided to take private time on the clock. Honestly I couldn't care less. The age difference is a little creepy, but she's legal so it's not a crime." She paused and took a deep breath. "The problem is he pulled me to the side an hour later and told me he's worried about his job and has two kids in college to support."

"Hold up, he was getting waxed by a girl the same age as his kids?" I grimaced. "That's gross."

Ebony shuddered beside me. "Tell me about it. It gets worse; the girl was his daughter's best friend. He got her the job as a volunteer over the summer."

I whistled. "Damn."

"So he pulls me to the side and begs me not to tell anyone and promises to make me a shoo-in for the full-time position next year if I keep my mouth shut. He can do it, he's on the board in charge of who gets hired and fired."

Wow. Who knew there could be that much drama at

the zoo? "What did you say?"

"I would have told him to screw himself, but it had already been done," she muttered.

I howled.

"I told him I wasn't interested. I worked hard to get where I am and didn't need his help to make it. What he did is his business and not to get me involved."

I nodded. "I would have done the same thing."

She looked at me, chewing on her lip. "The only problem is now I'm worried he's going to try and hold it against me and mess up my chances. Since then, he's been keeping a closer eye on everything I do, as if he's waiting for me to screw up so he can have something to hold against me in case I change my mind. Work was stressful enough with the competition between the five interns for two positions."

I reached for her bottom lip and pulled it from between perfect teeth. "Stop. If anyone's going to chew on your lip, it'll be me." She shook her head and grinned. "Don't sweat it. You're good at what you do, and he knows it. If he didn't believe you were capable of doing the job, he wouldn't be interested in your education. There's no real need for him to try and find something to hold against you. You'll be able to get the job without his help. It sounds as if he's trying to find something to hold over your head, just in case you change your mind. Don't worry about it." Unable to resist the plump pink flesh still glistening from her tongue, I leaned into kiss her lip.

"*Hmm.*" Her eyes opened slowly. "You are so supportive. That's one of the reasons why I like being with you."

Instead of answering, I kissed her again. Man, could

she kiss. Before meeting her, I preferred kissing other places than just mouths. Lips had always seemed like a formality. The real action came when I focused on other parts of the body. With Ebony, kissing was pure pleasure, an opportunity to explore and plunder.

I pulled back and ran my finger along her flawless skin. "None of the guys you've dated have supported your career?"

"No. The last guy decided he wanted a family immediately, which meant I would have to quit seven years of college, become his wife, and start popping out babies." She scoffed. "That wasn't about to happen."

"You don't want a family?"

"Of course, I do, when the time is right. *That time* isn't right now. Once I finish school, it's going to take a few years to establish myself in my field. The strain of a relationship mixed with a new career isn't the right way to start a family. So children are not in the works for me, not right now."

"So what about us? What exactly are we doing?" I lay back on the bed while Ebony sat up. She looked down at me, her perfect breasts jiggled from her movements.

"I'm not sure. What do you want?"

Narrowing my eyebrows, I reached up, pushed stray hairs away from her face, and tucked them behind her ear.

"I want you, but not just like this. I want this to be more than just sex. I promise there will be no one but you. I'll be here for you whenever you need me, for support, conversation. Sex." I jogged my eyebrows.

Ebony laughed. "You're not looking for anything else right now?" Her gaze shot over to my tattoo.

"In time, but for now, this is what I want. Can you

handle it?"

She made a show of deep thought. "Yes, I can, because I want the same." She leaned down and kissed me.

Oh yeah, she definitely wanted the same thing. Ebony wasted no time straddling me. I gripped her hips as she settled down. I would have rather she just climbed aboard, but there was no protection in place. Her hands rested on my chest as she stared down.

"I could get used to this."

"Me, too." I slid my fingers over her beautiful bare skin. "So what are you waiting for?"

Her smile was sexy as hell as she leaned down and brought her mouth to mine. Time for round two.

CHAPTER 17

Ebony

Leaving Brian's bed behind had been hard. Over the last few weeks, we'd talked on the phone and gone out on several dates. I'd spent the night at his place and he at mine. But it wasn't enough.

Brian made me laugh and challenged my mind. Since being with him, my outlook on life had changed. Between white women giving me the evil eye and black men glaring at Brian, it opened my eyes to the ignorance in the world.

I had never been one to disapprove of other's relationship choices. Yet, I never would have imagined choosing differently for myself. Despite the difference in skin color, our relationship was just like any other. We had our likes and dislikes, things neither of us could relate to, and disagreements. None of those things changed the deeper feelings I had developed for him.

My biggest problem was not being able to stop thinking about him while at work. The memory of the way his hands felt on my body and the way he watched me when we made love were hard to put aside. I often found myself daydreaming instead of focusing on my job.

"Ebony, check the weight of the baboon, it seems off," Dr. Jacobs said, annoyance flashing over his face. He continued to examine the chart. "The calculation has to be exact before administering the antibiotic."

"I'm sorry. I'll take care of it right away." I hurried back to the holding pen where the baboon in question rested until the sedative administered before his physical wore off.

I felt my former mentor's eyes on me. A miscalculation wasn't good. I had assisted Dr. Jacobs many times during exams because he trusted my eye for detail. After refusing to accept his offer and promise to keep his affair secret, he'd watched my every move. I couldn't give him reason to push me out of the program.

I focused on my job and pushed thoughts of Brian aside. Moments like this were one of the reasons why I had never rushed into emotional attachments.

Eventually, it was my turn to take care of Nala. For the past two months, she had received around-the-clock care of being bathed, diapered, and bottle-fed. The hours spent doing those tasks reminded me why having kids would not be in my immediate future. I enjoyed caring for her as part of my job. But would I have it in me to do my job and then come home to care for my own child? And what about during the day? I paid attention when my sister spoke of the cost of daycare service for my niece. The thought gave me chills.

Then it dawned on me. I hadn't worried about pregnancy in months. Patrick and I didn't have sex all the time. Our hectic schedules kept us too busy to spend a lot of time in bed.

My relationship with Brian was very different. We took every available chance to see each other. The way we made love, not using any birth control would never be an option. I made a mental note to visit my doctor and review my birth control options.

I had Brian on the brain again when my cell phone rang. Thank God I was at home. A check of the caller ID revealed my sister's name on the screen.

"Lashana, how are you?"

"I'm good, baby girl. We haven't heard from you in a while. What's going on? You haven't been bitten by a lion, have you?"

I laughed. Lashana had been one of my biggest supporters when I decided to become a vet, even though she didn't like wild animals.

"No, I haven't worked with the big cats yet."

She groaned. "I'll never understand your fascination with those things. As far as I'm concerned, black people and lions don't mix. You all should both go back to Africa, so he can chase you up a tree … it's the natural order of things."

I shook my head at her ludicrous comment. "And where will you be? Carrying a bucket on top your head?"

"Hell no. I'm fine right here at home in the air conditioning, drinking a glass of wine. I said y'all because you're crazy."

That was my sister. We'd grown closer as we aged.

For the longest time I thought no other woman would be as forthcoming with her thoughts. Until I met Yasmine. She was my sister to the tenth degree.

"Why haven't you called Momma? She's been dying to call you for the past few weeks. I've been keeping her preoccupied to give you some breathing room."

"Thanks." She'd been running interference since my move to California. Seven years had passed, and my mother still had a hard time accepting my choice.

"We expected you to call on the Fourth of July. That was how long ago?" she asked pointedly.

"I was preoccupied at the time." Thoughts of lying in Brian's arms that night made me smile.

"Translation, you were doing the horizontal mambo with Patrick. Didn't you guys break up?"

"We did, months ago. He's getting married, by the way."

"Damn. Okay," she drawled. "If it wasn't him then it was someone else. Come on. Let it out. It's my job as big sister to make sure you've got your head on straight."

"I do have my head on straight."

"Oh, you're snippy. Interesting. Don't hold back, girl, spill the beans."

I closed my eyes and rubbed the bridge of my nose. It doesn't matter what she or anyone else in my family thought. Yeah right. "His name is Brian. He plays in a band."

"Okay ..."

"He owns a lawn maintenance business and plans to get hired working for a recording studio soon." I cursed silently.

There was no reason for me to try and convince her of anything. Talking up Brian's attributes would never make a difference to my family. He could be a million-aire, and they'd still have something to say about his race. But then again...

"Let me get this straight. He's in a band. He cuts grass for a living, and his dream job is to work in a studio? How old is this guy?" She laughed through the phone. "He sounds straight out of high school. Not to mention, you're studying to be a doctor, well not a human doctor, but still. You need someone who's more on your level. A real professional."

Her comments set my teeth on edge. Brian's career choice made no difference to me. He worked hard and was good with everything he did. He had goals and was on his way to meeting them. That's what mattered to me.

My family seemed to believe my ideal man would have a well-paying job. And be black.

"And what black man does that?" she continued. "Wouldn't he be out trying to be a rapper?"

"He's white, Shana."

I could practically hear the crickets from back home chirping through the phone.

"Did you say I'm right? Something must be wrong with the connection because it sounded like you said he was white."

"Brian is white." I steeled myself for her retort.

"Oh. Hell. No. What are you doing messing with a white guy, Ebony? Are you crazy?" she hissed.

"No, I'm not crazy. I'm just ... Brian's a really nice guy. I decided to give him a chance."

"Give him a chance? You slept with him, didn't you?"

"That's none of your business, Shana. The way

you're acting right now is why I didn't bother telling you in the first place." I fought to keep my voice down. Why waste time getting upset?

"Excuse me ... you have noticed racism still exists, right? What good is being with a white man going to do for you? I could understand if he had a good job and made a lot of money, but damn, he sounds as broke as you. And, oh, God, what if you got knocked up?"

I wanted to scream. "He's not going to knock me up. I'm being safe."

The line went quiet. "I'm calling Trevon."

"What does he have to do with this?"

Lashana didn't answer, only clicked over and left me on a dead line.

I'd long since gotten off the bed and paced back and forth across my room. I was too close to blowing a blood vessel.

"Hello? Ebony, is everything okay?" Trevon's deep voice broke the silence.

I hadn't heard my twin's voice in months. We emailed each other all the time, but catching each other on the phone proved difficult due to the time zone differences and our work schedules. I worked during the day, and he worked at night.

"No, everything is *not* okay," Lashana's aggravated voice broke in.

"Yes, it is, Tre, I don't know why she called you. It's not going to make me change my mind," I said.

"So nobody's hurt or dying, right?" he asked.

"No," I said.

"Our sister's has lost her damn mind," Lashana said.

I exhaled loudly. "I have not lost mind. I'm a grown woman, and I can date anyone I damn well please."

"Whoa, whoa, will somebody please tell me what the hell is going on with the two of you?"

"Your twin is dating a white man," Lashana interjected.

"We've been seeing each other for a while, but it's not that serious." Yet.

"Really? But you've slept with him," she retorted.

"You slept with Tony on your second date!" I threw back at her. "Don't try to call me a *ho*."

"Ladies." Trevon chuckled. "Calm down. Man, this reminds me of home. I always refereed. First of all, nobody's a *ho*, though, Shana, Eb's got you there."

"Oh, grow up," she said sourly.

"I have, quite nicely. Now, let me get this straight, Eb, you've gone white?"

I pinched the bridge of my nose, attempting to kill the headache threatening to emerge. "Yes. He's a good man, better than some knuckleheads I've been with since moving here. He took me to meet his family over the holiday at his parents' house —"

"Oh, God," Lashana mumbled.

"They have no problem with our relationship," I added quickly. "Especially his sisters. Sorry I can't say the same of my own."

"I find that hard to believe," she said.

"Are you serious about this guy? Does he treat you right?" Trevon had remained silent during our verbal sparring.

I knew then Trevon was on my side. He always understood me. Even as children, he always had my back.

"Yes, I wouldn't be with him if he didn't. To be honest, I have no idea where this could go. Marriage isn't what either of us is looking for. I like spending time with him because he's not domineering and doesn't expect me to live up to his expectations. He can put up with my mouth—"

"He must be the silent type," Lashana muttered.

"No, he's the likes-the-way-I- talk-and-gives-it-right-back-to-me type." I chuckled. "He's persistent, that's for sure. He kept after me even when I told him no. And he's a hard worker, not a slacker at all. He doesn't use his love of music as an excuse not to work in the meantime. He's realistic about what he wants and is supportive of my dreams. That's what I love most about him."

"Love?" Lashana sighed. "Look, Eb, I bet the guy is a good catch for someone, just not you. You don't have to settle for the first man who smiles at you and says nice things."

"He's the first man who's appreciated what I'm doing with my life and hasn't tried to change me, which is exactly what Patrick wanted to do. He supported me as long as he got what he wanted. When he wanted more, he demanded I waste my education and stay home to bear his children. I had to draw the line."

"I didn't know. Why didn't you tell me?" Lashana sounded hurt.

"I told you what you needed to know. Brian's not like him at all."

"Sounds as though you've got your mind made up," Trevon said.

"Yeah, I guess I do."

"Have you thought about what Mom and Dad are going to say when they find out?" Lashana tried again.

"Yes, and honestly, I'm scared. But this is my life, not

yours or theirs. Shana, when you found Tony, you didn't let what Mom or Dad said stop you."

"It's not the same. At least he's black."

Trying to convince her any further was a waste of time. She'd come around ... eventually.

"Well, sis, I can't say I'm surprised. Didn't I tell you it would happen when you moved to L.A.?" Trevon asked.

"What do you mean?"

"That you'd find your Mr. Ed." He began laughing.

I groaned. "Not that stupid joke again."

"What is knucklehead talking about?" Lashana asked.

"White horse, white man, she's a vet ... Mr. Ed ..." Trevon reminded her.

"Oh, please." Lashana lost the battle to keep from laughing.

I joined in. "Tre, you're dead wrong."

We laughed before silence descended on the line again.

"Look, guys, I don't expect you to understand why I'm dating Brian, and I'm not asking for your approval. This is who I'm with right now, and it works for me. Just do me a favor. Don't tell Mom or Dad."

"What?" Lashana said.

"I'm serious, Shana. I'll deal with telling them in my own time. Right now I want to see where this goes. Until then ..."

"Your secret's safe with me, Eb. Just make sure you're happy. If this guy does one thing to hurt you, I'm on the next flight out of Atlanta to kick his ass."

"Shana?"

There was a moment of unintelligible mumbling on the line.

"Fine, but this doesn't need to go on forever. Don't wait until you decide to marry the guy before telling them."

"Thanks. Marriage is nowhere in my future. For now, I'm satisfied with not being alone."

CHAPTER 18

Brian

"Today was one of the longest days in my life, baby. I thought I'd be too tired to make it over here."

"I'm glad you did," Ebony said, her smile audible in her voice.

We sat in the living room in her house. Remnants of our dinner — a nearly empty pizza box and soda cans — littered the coffee table. I sat on the floor in between her legs while she massaged the tension of the day out of my shoulders. This was heaven.

"Oh yeah, right there." I angled my head, giving her complete access to my aching muscle.

"Right here?" She kissed my ear lobe.

A lazy wave of desire shot to my groin. I groaned. "Baby, don't tease me. I might be tired but —"

"Sorry, can't control Mother Nature." Her laugh was

sexy.

I had the feeling she was enjoying this way too much. "Exactly, so don't add to the torture."

Her fingers stilled. "Are you saying not being able to get some is going to keep you away?"

I pulled away from her hands and twisted around to face her. "Never. Bring those lips down here."

She obliged, giving me a kiss that made me wish we could do more. "Good answer."

I turned back around and sighed as she resumed the massage.

"Hopefully Peter can come back to work tomorrow. I wouldn't have taken on these new clients if I didn't have them working for me. One thing is for sure, Dylan earned his keep. We busted our asses to get all four jobs done in ten hours."

"Wow, they weren't all private customers, were they?"

"No. My new clients are an apartment complex and a small strip mall. I'm beat. It'll probably take the weekend to recover."

Despite being tired, I needed to be with her, even if our clothes stayed on. Even though a hot shower left my body weeping for sleep, spending time with her was worth the twenty-minute drive. Besides, I could always crash in her bed tonight.

"Thanks." I pushed my aching bones up off the floor, stretched, and sat at the opposite end of the couch. I patted my knee; it was my turn to reciprocate. "What's new with you?"

A funny look passed over her face as she rested her feet in my lap. "Work is okay, I guess. I talked to my sister the other day."

I fought the urge to let my curiosity be obvious. We had barely talked about her family since our first couple of dates. She'd made it known they probably would not approve of our relationship. To counteract that negativity, I made sure she met mine. My mother adored her. Every time we talked, one of her first questions was about Ebony. Were we still seeing each other? Was I happy? To each of those questions. my answer was a resounding yes.

"How's your family?" My focus stayed on her foot.

"Okay, I guess. The conversation dealt more about me than her."

I risked a glance and saw her staring down at her fingers. Uh oh.

"I told her about us." Her gaze met mine.

"And?"

"And … she thought I had gone crazy. She called Trevon, and well, it was a very interesting phone call."

Nervousness grew in the pit of my stomach. I'd been down this road before, and the consequences had not been good. A fact I had yet to share.

I held my breath while she continued.

"Trevon said he predicted I'd end up dating a white man."

I furrowed my eyebrows. "Are you serious? How did that happen?"

Ebony's lips turned up. Her eyes brightened slightly as she giggled. "The night before my family drove me to L.A., I was in my room stuffing every article of clothing in my suitcase. Well, he walked in as my bag popped open and my underwear fell onto the floor. I'm a tomboy, remember?"

I nodded, giving her eyes, and her foot, my full attention.

"The year before, Shana talked me into wearing thongs, something I hated. Well, to my surprise — and embarrassment — thongs of a variety of colors fell onto the floor. Tre picked up one, a white one, and made a crazy joke. Now that I think about it, I'd rather not repeat it." Her face screwed up as if she'd said too much.

"Oh no, you don't. You brought it up, and now you've got to share."

"No, never mind, it's stupid."

"You said he predicted our relationship. I want to know how that happened."

Ebony covered her face and groaned. "You're not going to let this go, are you?"

"Nope." I put on the most evil grin, which made her crack a smile.

"Okay, fine, you asked for it." She paused and took a deep breath. "Do you know who Mr. Ed is?"

I thought about it. "You mean the talking horse? My parents watched reruns of the show on *Nick at Night* years ago."

She bit her lip. "Yeah, that's the one. He said since I wore thongs, I would get a boyfriend named Mr. Ed because I was studying to become a veterinarian. And since Mr. Ed was white ..." Her voice trailed off as she chewed her lip.

"Since the horse was white and I'm white, that makes me Mr. Ed?"

She nodded.

I laughed so hard I could barely breathe.

She snorted. "Are you okay?"

I held up a finger and nodded as I regained my breath. "When can I meet him? I like him already."

Ebony looked relieved. "Not anytime soon since he lives in Atlanta. Unless you hurt me, then he'll fly out here and kick your ass."

That statement hit a little too close to home and quickly sobered me up.

"Oh, man, did I say something wrong?" Ebony's eyebrows creased as the smile left her lips.

I realized my thoughts must have been obvious on my face.

"No, you didn't. Something you said reminded me of a bad dating experience, that's all." I tried to wave it away, but the expression of concern and curiosity on her face made me reconsider.

"About a year ago, I dated a woman, and things were going pretty good. We'd been seeing each other for more than six months. Well, one evening we were standing at her door kissing. The next thing I knew, someone grabbed me and started punching. I fought back, thinking we were being mugged until I heard her screaming for the men attacking me to stop. It turns out, two of her brothers decided I wasn't the right man for their little sister."

Her eyes widened. "Was she black?"

I nodded. "Apparently she hadn't told her family about us. Somehow they got wind, and her brothers decided to take matters into their own hands. Luckily they didn't break anything, and I didn't press charges. I just wanted the chance to meet her family and talk. She didn't return my calls for a few days. Then one day, she shows up at my door with a small box of things I'd given her and told me she couldn't see me anymore. I spent the next two weeks trying to convince her to give us another try. I begged her to let me speak to her family. She insisted they wouldn't listen. Then one day, she changed her cell number, and I knew it was over."

Ebony sat in silence. Her voice was soft when she spoke again. "Did you love her?"

That was a tough question. How did I tell the woman I was falling in love with I had loved someone else, not several years ago, but just last year?

"I can't lie and say I didn't have feelings for her. What I feel for you is nothing like that. You're so much more of a woman there is nothing to compare. I believe things happen for a reason. Dealing with her and her family was just a practice run before meeting you. I'm glad things ended, or else I wouldn't be here with you."

Ebony had a wary look in her eyes as she studied me.

"It sounds corny, but I'm serious, baby. I'm glad we're together. You don't know how much it means to me that you shared our relationship with your family. What did your parents have to say?"

"I haven't talked to them yet."

Before I could ask her why not, my cell phone rang. I checked the caller ID. The number wasn't one I recognized, so I chose to ignore it. It was nearly nine p.m. and no reason for any potential clients to be calling. But money was money. I apologized for the interruption and hit redial.

"Hello?" an unfamiliar male voice answered.

"I missed your call."

"Ah, yes. Is this Brian Young?"

My business cards didn't give my full name. Great, a bill collector managed to get my private number. I didn't have many outstanding bills, but it didn't mean I felt like negotiating a deal on what I did owe.

Too late.

"Yeah," I didn't hide the resignation in my voice.

"Mr. Young, we've never met, but I got your name from my great grandfather, Harry Lieberwitz ..."

"The name is not familiar."

The man chuckled. "According to him, you played in a band at a dance he recently attended. He said he was about to get lucky when you came and stole his girl."

Immediately the image of good old Harry at the retirement home with his hands on Ebony's derriere came to mind.

"You mean Harry, the man whose hands were all over my date," I corrected. A quick glance showed Ebony watching me in confusion. I shrugged.

"That would be him. My name is Abe Lieberwitz. I'm with B and D Records."

Curiosity replaced irritation. B and D Records, a well-known label, represented several of the hottest musical acts in Southern California.

"I'm putting together a promotional tour right now. Have you heard of ..." He rattled off a few of the artists.

"Yeah, I'm a fan of their music." I wiped my sweaty palms on my pants and tried to stay cool and avert Ebony's questioning stare.

"Good, you're familiar with our sound. I'm in a bind. In a month, we're going on tour for twelve weeks. We'll be hitting major cities in Cali, of course. We're also going up north and hitting a few spots in the North-west. I got my band together, but my bass player broke his leg last week. He's out, and I need someone ASAP."

This couldn't be happening, could it?

"Long story short, I've auditioned a few guys but they don't mesh with the band. My grandfather mentioned you, so I got your number from Mrs. Devero at the home. I did some checking around, and you come highly recommended. I'd like for you to come audition for me."

Disbelief took over and made my hands numb. The expression on my face must have been dumbstruck because Ebony gripped my knee and mouthed *what*?

"Let me get this straight. You want me to audition for a spot on a twelve-week concert tour with your record label?"

I stared wide-eyed at Ebony, whose hands shot to her mouth.

"Yes. Will that be a problem?"

"Hell no ... I mean, no, not at all. Tell me when and where."

"Good, give me your email address and I'll send you the information. It will include sheet music for the tour. Be prepared to play at least two of the songs. The members will decide which ones."

I stared at the phone when the call ended. Holy shit. The chance of a lifetime materialized out of nowhere. Unbelievable.

"Brian?" Ebony's questioning eyes watched me.

I swallowed hard and relayed the entire conversation.

"Baby, I'm so proud of you!" She scooted across the couch, into my arms, and planted a congratulatory smack on my lips.

"Do you know what this could mean? I've been trying to get into those closed auditions for years. It's because of you."

"Me? I didn't do anything."

I chuckled and reached for her hand. "Yes, you did. Harry, from the home, is his grandfather. He remem-

bered me because of you. You're my good-luck charm."
I kissed her hand and watched her blush.

Enough time had gone by so I checked my email on
my Smartphone. As promised, the email waited with
attachments for the sheet music, instrumental tracks,
and directions to the audition location. Then I looked
at the time.

"Damn," I muttered.

"What?"

"The audition's tomorrow night," I scrolled through
the downloaded information and found three files of
music. "I've got to learn all three of these songs by tomorrow evening." I looked up at her. "I have to cancel
our date for tomorrow."

A hint of disappointment flickered in her eyes.
"That's okay, Brian. I'm not mad. This is about you." She
ran a slender finger over my cheek.

If I wasn't already falling in love, this would have
been the moment my heart decided Ebony was the one.

"Yeah, well, it also means I need to get started now.
I've got twenty-four hours to learn these parts."

"You can do it." She smiled. "I've got faith in you because my baby's got mad skills."

"Thanks, but those skills have to be worked on all
the time." I looked around the living room at the pile of
trash. "I'll help you clean up, and then I've got to run."
My chest stung from regret.

"No. Go do what you need to do. I'll handle this, but,
Brian." She held my head between her angel-soft hands.
"Get some rest. Don't push yourself too hard or else
you'll be no good. Promise?"

I nodded, swimming in the pools of her eyes. Staying
the night would have been the perfect end to my day.

"Go, baby." She leaned in to kiss me. My mouth opened for hers, and I took the time to savor every drop of her essence for motivation.

She walked me to the door.

"I'll call you tomorrow, okay?"

Ebony nodded. "I don't go in to work on Wednesday. Let me know when you're done, and I'll come spend the night, if it's okay."

"I'll be looking forward to it." I kissed her quickly, headed for my truck, and resisted the urge to run. Excitement pumped through my veins.

An opportunity had presented itself, and I was not about to let it go. Even though it fell in my lap, I still had to work for it.

I put the truck in reverse and backed out of the driveway, but paused and saw Ebony standing in the doorway of her house, her auburn hair illuminated by the porch light. She waved.

My goal would be to make her proud.

A sudden wave of energy ignited inside me, and all hints of tired and aching bones disappeared. I was a man on a mission.

That job was going to be mine.

CHAPTER 19

Ebony

T ime flew by. Brian's audition had been three weeks ago. Since then we'd hardly seen each other.

It didn't surprise me when he announced he'd earned the spot in the band. I was so proud of him and wasted no time calling Lashana to brag. She had been shocked into speechlessness after what she said about his profession.

But as time went on, he had less time for me. Practices at various times during the night and day made it hard for us to find time to connect. Costume fittings, show rehearsals with the artist, sound and stage crew … the list went on and on.

Even though I knew from the start the opportunity would separate us for three months, the closer we got to his date of departure, the more anxious I felt.

I, the woman who'd been queen of having my head in a book for seven years and barely thinking about men, did not want to let him go.

Of course, we wouldn't be breaking up. The night he came back from the audition bearing the news, our relationship was the first thing we discussed. Neither of us had done the long-distance thing, but we were determined to make it work. I sated the both of us by saying my final year in school would be starting around the time he left. With him gone, I could focus on starting the year off right. I would be hitting my stride by the time he came home.

He seemed to believe me. I pretended I would be okay.

Unfortunately, the last week became one spiraling disaster after another.

First, my part-time job at the exotic animal hospital lost one of its partners. As a result, the remaining partner decided he no longer needed a full staff. Since my job was temporary to earn college credits and pad my résumé, I was the first to go.

And there went my additional income for the past two years.

With fall approaching, the amount of seasonal zoo volunteers decreased. The majority were high school and college kids. With public school and college about to be back in session, those available spaces were filled with fresh interns who needed to be trained. At first it seemed like a Godsend. More hours would cover the lost income and cut back on the amount of time spent between two jobs and school.

Until my college adviser informed me that I needed more hours of experience working at an animal hospital. In order to have the amount needed to graduate in the spring, I had to find another job doing the same thing... immediately.

Worst of all, my book allowance through my scholarship was short due to budget cuts. I could afford all of my textbooks and supplies, except for one. It would take at least two weeks of paychecks from the zoo for me to afford it.

Thank God I'd been able to pay off my small car note.

I was on break at work, staring at my bank statement, bills, and note pad. No matter how many times I blinked, there was no way to fill the amount of empty spaces in my ledger. It was time to make an executive decision. Ask my parents for a loan or pawn the title of my car to have enough money to buy my book and pad my account for a couple of weeks. Decisions, decisions, decisions.

There was another option. Brian received a signing bonus as a part of his contract with the record label. He planned on putting the majority of it into savings and paying off a few of his debts. He'd asked me if I needed help with anything, and I'd told him no. Man had things changed in a few weeks. If I asked him for help, he'd do it willingly. But I didn't want to. I was not his wife and refused to become financially dependent. Period.

For the past seven years, I'd made it on my own. There were times when things had gotten rough, but this wasn't as bad as some of the others. This was just a setback. I would manage.

The chime on my cell phone alerted me of a text message. Brian sent a video of him walking around the practice room, introducing some guys in the band. The video ended with him beaming into the camera, promising to call as soon as he could. Seeing his enthusiasm and listening to his voice made me smile. In no mood to send a video reply, I settled for sending a text instead.

Ask him for help, idiot.

Maybe ... but for right now, I would manage.

"Ms. Campbell, can I speak to you for a moment?"

Dr. Jacobs stood in the doorway of the breakroom, his expression stern.

Great, just what I needed, more stress.

I kept my sigh inaudible and gathered my things. "Yes, just a moment." I stuffed my belongings into my locker and then followed behind him.

We walked down the long corridor beyond the restrooms, past the infamous supply closet, and stopped outside in the open air. He apparently didn't want anyone hearing what he had to say.

"You will be starting fall classes soon, correct?"

Straight to the point, no small talk.

"Yes, next week."

He nodded, adjusted his glasses on his slender nose. Dr. Jacobs was a decent man, though he lacked a lot in the looks department. He had an over-the-belt belly that reminded me of my dad and a receding hairline. In his day, he must have been a hell of a catch, at least to Mrs. Jacobs. What I didn't understand was what a nineteen-year-old college freshman saw in him. What kind of favor did she earn by getting down on her knees for her best friend's dad?

I rubbed my eyes and forced the memory away.

"I take it you've finished reading the text books I loaned you," he continued, pushing his glasses up on his nose.

"Um, well ..."

"You've had sufficient time to study them, nearly three months."

It was more like two-and-a-half, but I was not about to correct him.

"I need them back. I can't afford for you to be caught with them when school is in session. Someone might think I helped you cheat."

"Help me cheat? I've never cheated —"

"Shh!" He waved his stubby hands at me and glanced around to make sure no one was within earshot of my brief outburst.

I ground my teeth and lowered my voice. "Dr. Jacobs, you've known me for the last four years. You know I would never cheat. I never viewed your loaning me those books as a way to breeze through my classes."

"Yes, well, others may not see it that way. I need you to return them tomorrow. The notes too, all of them. I trust you won't forget." Finished, he walked back into the building. I could have sworn there was a satisfied gleam in his eye and pep in his step.

Why the hell couldn't he understand none of his games were necessary? I couldn't care less who Dr. Jacobs screwed. Two months had gone by, and I hadn't said a word. If holding his infidelity over his head was my goal, it would have been done months ago.

Fine. He could have his damn books back. And every last note card. They were outdated by twenty years anyway. What good could they do me? Outdated chemistry charts and facts would not compete with the modern day methods of animal husbandry.

But deep down, it felt like I was the one getting screwed. And it wasn't in a good way.

***

Sprawled out on my bed, I massaged my temples while nursing a headache. I was too broke to afford a Coke and a smile. My laptop sat beside me, and the job ads were open on the screen. There were plenty of jobs that would provide the amount of money needed to stay afloat. The only problem is none of them were animal hospitals. Working at a gas station would not earn me the hours needed to secure the full-time zoo position.

Seven years suddenly felt like a total waste. I had enough money to manage my expenses for at least two months without having a second job. After that …

I didn't want to think that far ahead for fear my brain matter would melt down to mere sludge.

Two months. That meant if I didn't find another job soon, by the time Brian came back, I would be getting ready to quit school. Wouldn't that be a wonderful welcome home present?

Brian would get off the tour bus, ready to welcome me in his arms. He would still be handsome but his clothes would smell like beer, smoke, and God knows what else happened on the bus.

Wait a minute; he'd better not get off the bus smelling like another woman …

If there was one thing I learned during our time together, it was this: Brian was a man of his word. If he promised monogamy, he'd do it. If he wanted more or someone else, he wouldn't waste either of our time. He'd come right out and say it.

Did I think he'd cheat on me while he was away? He was a man, and all men have needs. Somehow, deep in my heart, I didn't think he would. What else could I do but trust? If I wasted time suspecting or questioning him, the only thing I'd do was push him down that path. If he did stray, then somehow the truth would come out. It always did.

Damn, one week until he left for three months. At least he wouldn't be around to watch me go into scramble mode. It would not be pretty. What he didn't know wouldn't affect his ability to play. The last thing I wanted to be was a distraction in any way.

I supported his decision to go on the road, knowing how much it would boost his career. Now, I needed to focus on mine.

My headache subsided enough to sit up and turn on the light in my darkened room. It was nearly dusk, and Brian hadn't texted me yet. Another sign of a long day for him. Maybe if I focused on pleasing him for the next week, it would take away some of my own stress and help me see things from a different prospective. Then I may be able to navigate my way through this financial mess.

I forced myself off the bed and walked to the closet. Brian would be leaving Sunday morning. His band planned a big farewell party at the club where they performed Saturday night. Brian was ecstatic when he showed me one of the flyers. The turnout promised to be bigger than any of their regular shows. They had a large following. The band had already found a replacement bass player, someone Brian had recommended. On his last night at the club, he would play a few songs for old time's sake before officially handing over his spot on stage to the new guy.

After that, the rest of the night belonged to us.

My original plan had been to buy a slinky dress that would keep his eyes on me all night long. His eyes never wandered when we were together, but still.

That was before I lost my part-time job. Now ...

I pushed through the clothes hangers until I reached the last one hiding in the back. What do you know? The infamous dress I swore never to wear again.

The little black number that started it all.

Wearing it again would be ... perfect.

CHAPTER 20

Brian

Time had run out.

I glanced at my watch. Ebony would be ready for me to pick her up in a few hours. A quick shower, shave, bite to eat, and I'd be on my way. Oh yeah, make sure the room was straight since this was where we'd spend the night.

I really wanted to get a hotel room, but she insisted it would be a waste of money. Her logic made sense. My intention was to leave with a memory of a night neither of us would forget. But it didn't matter where we were. Just being together would be enough.

My clothes landed in a heap on top of my laundry basket. I grabbed my outfit for the evening and lay it on the bed. Black slacks, a black dress shirt, complimented by a blue-and-black tie. I would even wear my black dress shoes for the occasion.

A glint of silver tinsel resting on my nightstand grabbed my attention. Ebony's gift. She was going to love it. I debated all day about surprising her when picking her up, but decided tonight, when we were alone, would be the perfect time.

While in the shower, I reviewed the list of things handled in preparation for my departure.

Dylan and Peter had been working for me for months. They knew my customers, but didn't know the amount of work it took to run the business. I decided to entrust Peter with the finer details and the computer software used to track the finances. After two weeks, they were prepared. Since neither of them owned a vehicle capable of carrying the tools required for the job, I left my truck — and the equipment in it — in their care. Even though it cost money, I added them to my automobile and business insurance for the next few months. I had confidence in their ability to take care of the business. But hey, shit happened.

Upon signing with the label for the duration of the tour, I received a check. I'd never seen that many zeros on a piece of paper with my name on it. Ever. After paying on some bills, like my student loan, I paid my half of the rent and utilities for the duration of my time away. My one splurge was buying the guitar I really wanted, a sweet Fender Rodger Water's Precision Electric Bass Guitar. The original price had been a breathtaking twelve hundred dollars, but I found it on sale for eight hundred, brand spanking new.

The rest went into my savings account where I'd been squirreling away money, bit-by-bit. As much as it took a load off of my pocket having Javan for a roommate, it was time to get my own place. I had a future to plan.

A dog ... a wife ... kids.

I wanted Ebony to be my wife. If we could make it through the next couple of months apart, we could make it when I got back. Before I asked her to marry me, I needed something to offer her. Getting my own place would be one of the first things I researched upon my return.

But, first things first.

I stared into the bathroom mirror and adjusted my tie. Damn, I looked good. I added a few shots of the cologne Ebony loved.

A knock on the doorjamb startled me. I peered over my shoulder and saw Javan's hulking frame.

"Looking good, man. It's about time you picked up my sense of style. It's a shame it took hooking up with a sista' to do it," he ribbed.

"Hey, I know how to dress. I just don't need to strut around like a peacock."

"Oh, you've got jokes."

I grinned and turned out the light.

Javan moved out of the way and followed me down the hall. "You all packed?"

"Yeah, I'm good."

"You leave on Sunday, right?"

"Yep." I palmed my keys and stopped in the kitchen for a bottle of water.

Javan shook his head.

"What?" I gulped the ice cold liquid.

"All those women ... man, it'll be *ho* central. I'm jealous."

I lifted an eyebrow and laughed. "I'm working, J. Besides, I don't have time for anyone else. I've found the woman I want."

"Ebony?" He chuckled. "You sure about that? You know what they say, when the cat's away, the mice will play and all that shit."

"Nah, I'm not worried. She's waiting for me, and I'm saving it all for her." I disposed of the empty bottle.

Javan eyed me for a moment. "A woman like her, wait? Yeah, right. I'll tell you what; I'll keep an eye on her while you're gone. Believe me ... she'll be well taken care of."

Every muscle in my body went on alert. I turned slowly and faced him. "What did you just say?"

"I said, don't worry. I'll keep an eye out, you know, in case Ebony needs anything. Damn, man, what did you think I meant?"

I studied Javan's eyes for any reason why I shouldn't trust him. Yeah, he'd made hints of wanting to get with Ebony, but he'd backed off when he learned we were a couple. We'd even double dated with him and Yasmine several times. Ebony didn't let on that he still bothered her.

I couldn't find a hint of deception. It was probably my possessiveness, making a simple comment into something more. "Guess I misunderstood you."

"You got that right. I'll be gone tonight so you love birds can swing from the rafters if you need to." He grinned.

That solidified it. I needed my own place, even if it was an apartment.

"Thanks." I glanced at my watch. "Gotta go." I shook his hand and left.

My foot was a lead weight on the way to Ebony's place.

By the time I rang her doorbell, the anticipation of seeing her again had driven me crazy. The front porch light came on, door opened, and my love stood illuminated by the light.

My heart stopped beating, and my body went into full attention. How was it possible after I'd seen, touched, kissed, and lusted over every glorious part of her naked body that it felt like I was seeing her for the first time?

Her auburn hair sat high off her shoulders and hung in springy spirals, which framed her lovely face. She wore the same black strapless number she'd worn the night we met, leaving my eyes free range to travel across her delicious throat, to the necklace that was a constant decoration, and over ample cleavage.

I loved the way the black liquid fabric hugged every inch of her body. It felt like I had x-ray vision and could see through the silky material. I would never be able to forget the image of her chocolate nipples, and her taste forever imprinted on my tongue.

I allowed my eyes to wander farther down, past the midpoint of her thigh where the dress ended. Black strings wrapped around sexy calf muscles and down to her barely-there heels.

"Tonight, I only want you wearing the necklace and nothing else." I let my eyes roam over her body again. "Well, you can keep on the heels."

Her naughty laugh made me grip the doorframe to keep from carrying her up to her bedroom and making it happen now.

***

At the club, we were in the center of VIP. The guys

toasted my success and promised tonight's performance would be memorable. Ebony stood in front of the crowd and danced for me as I played. It was like déjà vu except this time the sexy woman on the dance floor was going home with me.

Finally, we were back at my place. True to his word, Javan had left the house to us.

In my room, I turned on music to set the mood. Not like either of us needed it. Tonight, I was letting her take the lead. She was the director of the beautiful music our bodies would make. I was the instrument waiting to be taken into her arms and played.

"It appears you have everything packed," she commented, studying the bags resting in the corner.

"I'm ready. Though, honestly, the most important thing is my guitar; it's the money maker."

She faced me, her leg set at an angle making her luscious hip pop. "I would have thought your hands were the money maker."

I chuckled. "Put the two together..."

She pursued her lips. "True. I can think of other places where your hands are much appreciated."

"Really?" I tilted my head and watched her.

An inviting smile shaped her lips as she walked slowly toward my large suitcase and slid the zipper open. "Would you like me to show you?"

"I can figure it out."

Her seductive laugh shot straight to my groin.

She pulled the lid open and peered inside. "Looks like you're missing something."

Before I could ask her what it was, she made a move that left me speechless.

With slow mesmerizing movements, Ebony lifted

the hem of her dress, revealing a sexy pair of underwear. Red lace sat between her shapely thighs with edges as thin as a shoestring. Then, her fingers slid smoothly over the material, gripped the edges, and pulled them down. I followed their journey, memorizing every seductive movement. When it reached her ankles, she steadied herself on the edge of the suitcase and kicked them over her heels. The thong disappeared in a compartment of my bag. Once it was zipped, she shimmied her hips, smoothing the dress back in place.

"That's so you don't forget about me."

"Oh, baby, there's no way I'm going to forget about you."

She smiled and walked toward me, her hips swaying to the rhythm of the music. I loved watching her walk.

When she reached me, she put her hand on my chest and nudged me until I started walking backward. We stopped when my back hit the door.

She bit her lip and began unfastening my belt.

Oh yeah. Time to play.

I unfastened my tie and the buttons of my shirt. After the third button, I pulled the thing over my head. The shirt and the tie landed somewhere on the floor. Her mission accomplished, Ebony sunk down on the floor, taking my pants and briefs with her. Oh yeah.

She started at my navel and worked her way down, running her nails along my thighs. I ran my hand over her hair and removed the pins. The curls fell lazily around her face, not that I could see it because she was busy working my anatomy like a pro.

"Damn, you're good," I gritted my teeth and lay my head back against the wall.

My breath caught and my body quivered. I fought to

focus on something to keep from losing it too soon, yet enjoy the pleasure she gave me. Multiplication tables, the theme song to *Sesame Street* ... grandma wearing a bathing suit.

Soft caresses with her hands and mouth alternated with the strokes of a master. She was good at this. If it weren't for the support of the door behind me, I would have been down on my knees.

The list of things I would miss grew exponentially. Every last one of them had to do with Ebony. All of them weren't about sex, but this was somewhere near the top.

All too soon, she rose to her feet, her lips trailing my abs with her hands in the lead. The moment she reached my neck, I placed my hands in her soft hair and kissed the hell out of her.

Her moan went down my throat and into me.

"Turn around," I commanded.

She did, and I reached behind her and slid my lips over the side of her neck. I nipped and teased her while pulling the silky skintight fabric of her dress down, freeing her breasts. I unhooked the strapless bra and dropped it on the floor. Her breasts free, I palmed the voluptuous weights in my hands, running fingers over firm nipples. She arched, pushing them against my fingers.

She moaned her pleasure when my fingers left the first stop of the night and ended at the hem of her dress. Sliding it up, I revealed her perfectly round ass already free of its constraints. I gripped her hips, pulled her against me, and teased.

"Oh yes ..." she moaned.

I loved the sexy sound of that word as it rolled off

her tongue.

"Do you like the way this feels?" I whispered in her ear.

"Yes ..." she purred, her body moving in time with mine, forming a rhythm of our own.

She angled her head for a kiss, our tongues mating ... tasting ... taunting.

I slipped my hand to the place I called home. Ebony shuddered in my hand, ripe and ready.

Without pulling away, I walked her toward the bed. When we reached it, she bent forward and assumed the position.

And then I saw it.

A blue winged butterfly was etched into her hip.

I ran my finger over the tattoo lightly. We hadn't been together in one, long, agonizing week. The new mark had nearly healed.

"I got it last week. Do you like it?"

Did I like it? Was she kidding? It was as seductive as hell. I leaned over and ran my lips over it.

"It's perfect," I murmured and continued the journey over to her spine and up her back. We'd discuss the beauty of it later. Right now, I was on a mission.

Her hips swayed, her body called my name. I answered without hesitation and gave her what we both wanted. In one fluid push, we were one. Her body rocked against me while I gripped her hips and slid deep inside over and over again.

Forget her? That was impossible. I'd never forget the woman who not only rocked my world, but was also my world, my rock, my inspiration, my heart.

My one and only *Eve.*

Tonight, I was determined that she not only hear

how much I loved her, but she would also feel it, too.

All. Night. Long.

I didn't need to sleep; I could do that on the bus.

It didn't take long for her body to spasm as she cried out my name. Damn, I was going to miss that. I needed to hear it again, so I pulled out, turned her around, and lay her down. I continued to give her what she wanted, and take what I needed. I memorized every moan, every gasp, and every sound our bodies made as we slapped against each other, storing it for the long, lonely nights ahead.

When she came again, her body pulled me along for the erotic ride. When it was over, I panted, riding the euphoric wave.

Yeah, no way in hell I'd ever be with another woman.

Ebony collapsed back on the bed. Exhausted, I positioned my body beside her. We faced each other. She had no idea how desirable she was after sex. The way her eyelids hung low from gratification, her parted lips as she panted, her once well-put together hairdo mangled beyond recognition.

"Hey, you still have the dress on," I reached over to grasp the fabric bunched above her hips and below her breast. "Your necklace and heels were the only things you were supposed to be wearing."

A laugh of satisfaction came from her sexy lips. "You should have pulled it over my head." She nodded at me. "You still have on pants, socks, and shoes."

Resting on my back and still unable to sit up, I kicked my feet. The weight of the fabric and shoes were hard to miss. "Oh?" I wagged my eyebrows, which caused her to laugh again. I pulled together enough strength to toe off my shoes, kick off the pants, and dispose of the condom.

"Oh shit."

"What?"

There was no condom. I'd just made love and emptied every ounce of me inside of her without protection.

"I screwed up ..."

Ebony looked down at my empty hands. When she looked back, her eyes were wide with horror.

"Baby, I'm sorry, I—"

She held her hand up and silenced me. Not good. I slapped my forehead. This could not be happening. I was about to leave town in a few hours. I wanted to give her a night to remember, not leave her pregnant.

"I'm sorry, Ebony. I wasn't thinking ..."

"Me neither." She sat up on the bed and gripped the fabric pooled around her hips.

I sat up to join her.

"It's not your fault, I usually check to make sure we're safe but ... damn it, Brian, I wanted you."

"Baby," I reached for her hand, "I wasn't trying to get you pregnant."

She nodded, but didn't speak, her eyes focused on the other side of the room.

I studied her face, worry taking over. I stroked the back of her hand with my thumb. "Ebony, baby, talk to me."

"I'm not on birth control."

My eyes widened. "What?"

Her eyes closed. "It makes me sick. I haven't been on anything for the past year. I was supposed to see my doctor to discuss my options, but I've been so busy with school, work, and looking for another job …" She faced me, eyes wet with tears. "We've always been careful, Brian. I'm sorry. I wasn't trying to trap you or —"

I wiped her tears. "I know."

Damn. All it took was one time to get her pregnant. Never once did I ask if she was on birth control. I did my part in protecting us both by making sure we always had condoms. Tonight, I'd lost all control and look at what happened.

"How long will it take before you know for sure?"

Ebony ran a hand over her face and sniffed. "There's a test, but I have to wait to see if I miss my period. That won't be for another two weeks."

"Okay. Tell me what you need, and I'll pay for it. Just —"

Before I could finish, she got up from the bed, pushed the fabric over her hips, and kicked it into a corner of my room. She dug into the dresser and pulled out my old baseball jersey she slept in when she stayed over. Without another word, Ebony walked out of the bedroom in the direction of the bathroom. I heard the door shut firmly behind her.

Reality slapped me upside the head. I was an ass.

Neither of us needed her pregnant, not now. I wanted her to be the mother of my children, but the timing was off.

I was well on the path of making the money needed to support a family. But this wasn't about what I wanted. Ebony hadn't graduated college, let alone established herself in her field. Damn, I could have just screwed her life up … literally.

A myriad of possibilities ran through my mind. Was this mistake going to cost Ebony her career? Would

Ebony end up hating me for the rest of her life? What if she decided she didn't want anything else to do with me and had an abortion? Or worse, what if she had an abortion and never told me she was pregnant?

Scenario after scenario ran through my mind, none of them had a happy ending.

What had I done?

CHAPTER 21

Ebony

I leaned over the sink and splashed ice-cold water on my face.

Just when it seemed like things couldn't get any worse ... loss of a mentor, a job, my bank account low.

And now the chance I could, at this very moment, have a new life growing within my womb. The image of the miraculous explosion of DNA splitting and duplicating as soon as sperm met egg, from a show on the Discovery Channel, forced me to sit on the closed lid of the toilet.

A baby.

But not just any baby, Brian's baby. The man I loved and wanted to have his children ... one day. Was it possible fate decided to speed up the timetable against my will?

Okay, the chances of me not getting pregnant were

equal with the chances of me getting pregnant, fifty-fifty.

My mind went blank. I stood and splashed more water on my face. I could only imagine what Brian felt. He was ready for a baby just as much as I was. His career was about to launch off the pad in hours, while mine raced toward the finish line.

Having a baby right now could sabotage both of our careers.

Yet, as crazy as it sounded ... a small part of me wanted to have some part of him left behind for the next few months. Getting pregnant would be a way of making sure he came back to me.

Oh, great, not only was I insecure, I was turning into one of those women who trapped their boyfriend into staying with them.

How would Brian feel after spending months on the road, with women coming up to him wearing next to nothing and size-two waistlines? He'd come home to discover his already voluptuous girlfriend had taken on the profile of a barge.

Brian wanted to have a family. Maybe he would be happy. But on the other hand, if he viewed this mistake as a forced reason to hang around ...

What good would speculation do? I could be completely wrong.

I flushed the toilet and washed my hands to carry on the pretense of leaving to use the bathroom. I closed the door behind me silently.

Brian was sprawled out on the bed, naked. One of his hands rested on his chest, his fingers drumming silently. His other arm was draped across his face, his mouth was drawn tight in what I assumed was disappointment. "You hate me right now, don't you?"

His question startled me.

"No, I don't."

"Ebony, baby, don't lie. Just tell me the truth. I'll understand." He removed his arm from his face, his electric gaze zeroed in on me. He was serious.

I settled on the bed, leaned down, and kissed him lightly. "No, Brian, I'm not mad, this is on both of us. Besides, the chances are fifty-fifty, right?"

Though with my family, it was more than that. My chances were more than slim.

Since not being sexually active, my focus was not on maintaining protection. I didn't take the pill because of blood-clotting issues in my family. Hormone shots caused weight gain and uncontrollable nausea. I stopped taking birth control all together once I broke up with Patrick. I should have known better.

The history of women in my family's ability to conceive like the Virgin Mary flooded my already half-frozen brain.

My mother told me once that every time my father looked at her, she got pregnant. Plus, twins ran on her side of the family. My sister wasn't any better. She'd been on birth control religiously since the age of sixteen before she and her husband decided they wanted kids. Once she stopped taking the pill, she thought it would take a year before she would conceive. Imagine her delight when she found out she was pregnant four months later.

Four months.

With a family like mine, what were my chances? I decided to keep that information to myself. The last thing Brian needed was an unnecessary distraction because of guilt.

And, oh, boy, Brian's side of the family seemed pretty potent as well. After all, Mr. Young helped add five lives to the world's population. What if Brian inherited his father's potent gene, as he'd inherited his intense blue eyes?

Brian studied me without speaking.

I pulled back the sheets and crawled into bed. After a minute, he joined me.

"Ebony, there's something I need to tell you." He waited until he had my full attention. "I had already planned to say this, but now the timing just feels ... wrong. But it's still true." He watched me with imploring eyes.

Uneasiness settled in the pit of my stomach. "Tell me what?"

He reached for my hand and kissed it tenderly. "To tell you how much I love you."

I felt my eyes widen, not because of his words, but because of the sincerity in his voice and eyes. The eyes never lie.

"We've been together for less than three months. This last month has been crazy. We haven't been together as much, and there is still much more for us to learn about each other." He looked down at our linked fingers. "Baby, you don't know how much your support has encouraged me. If it weren't for you, this opportunity wouldn't exist. Having you by my side and not be angry or discouraging has made me aspire to be more, to do more for you. I want to make you happy."

"Brian, I'm happy, because I'm in love with you, too." I smiled, blinking back the tears gathering in the corners of my eyes.

He returned my smile and wiped the tears. "Good, because when I come back, I'm going to do everything in my power to keep you happy. The first thing is looking into getting my own place. I need a place of my own, so when I ask you to marry me —"

I gasped and covered my mouth.

" … that part of our life will already be established." His grin went a mile wide. "Yes, Ebony, I want to marry you. We'll take the time to really get to know each other first, but believe me … I'm going to buy you the biggest ring I can find."

I laughed. The fear disappeared. The issues plaguing my life were no longer important. The only thing that mattered was hearing him say he wanted to marry me.

Not just because I could be pregnant, the *P* word hadn't been mentioned, just that he wanted me.

His hand went to my flat belly as though he'd read my thoughts. "If we just made a baby, it came from the love I feel for you, it's not an accident. If not, then when we start our family, there will never be an *oops*, just pure, unadulterated love." He angled his head, his smile charming. "Can you handle it?"

"Oh, yeah." I beamed.

"One more thing." He released my hand and dug into the nightstand. He removed a box of condoms and left them available for easy access. "Not trying to play baby roulette."

I giggled and nodded in agreement.

He dug in again and pulled out another box. A beautiful shade of purple paper and glimmering silver tinsel sat in his hand. I felt my mouth drop open. Since my hands were in my lap, Brian placed the wrapped box in my palm.

"Open it."

It wasn't a ring; the box was the wrong shape. I wanted to shake it to see if I could guess what hid inside. It was a struggle not to rip apart the beautiful packaging; the anticipation drove me crazy.

What I found left me speechless.

"Do you like it?" Brian's brow creased as if my approval of his gift were a life-or-death issue.

In my hand was a 14-karat-gold charm bracelet with three charms: a guitar, a heart and … I studied the third charm. "A giraffe?" I laughed my surprise.

"I told the sales woman you took care of an orangutan for a living, and she looked at me like I was crazy. It was either this or a cat or dog. I wanted it to represent your dream job. This was the closest thing they had."

"It's beautiful. I love it. Thank you."

Brian let out a sigh as his shoulders relaxed. He slipped the gold chain from my fingers and looped it around my wrist. "This is a promise. I chose these charms because they represent our hearts, our desires, and our future. As we grow together and accomplish more, I will give you another charm to celebrate." His eyebrows furrowed. "Adding a baby bottle was not the first charm I planned to get you. I was thinking of graduation and marriage."

I pushed him back on the bed, moved the covers, and climbed on top of him, settling in the only place I wanted to be.

"Whether we have a baby now or later, I love you, Brian." I leaned down and kissed him deeply.

His fingers ran over my hip. I cringed and sat up. "Ow, it's sore."

He looked down at his hand and realized he'd

gripped my tattooed hip. "Sorry." He pushed the shirt I wore aside and studied it from the angle where he lay. "It's beautiful by the way. What made you get a butterfly? Why not a heart or a rose?"

I sat up and stared down at his marked biceps and traced them. "You told me your tattoos were symbols that mattered. I decided my tattoo would do the same." I reached for both of his hands and pulled them to my chest.

I marveled at the subtle differences in the pigment of our skin. My caramel to his cream; the two complimented each other like a perfect blend of coffee. I could imagine what our baby would look like. Our child would be light skinned, with skin as bronze as his, only naturally. The hair would probably be brown with golden streaks and eyes as blue as his. Beautiful.

"Butterflies don't start out as butterflies; they're caterpillars, ordinary insects you rarely pay attention to. Then one day, they disappear into a cocoon and emerge changed, different. They're no longer ordinary; they are magnificent, beautiful winged creatures." I pulled his hand to my heart.

"Since meeting you, I've come out of my cocoon. I was alone with a one-tracked mind, but you've changed me. You've challenged my mind and made me see life, love, and relationships in a way I never thought would work for me. We went from friends, to lovers, to … being in love. You've supported me and taken interest in ways no other men have. These differences," I held up our linked fingers and kissed his hand, "mean nothing. The heart is what's important. So, I chose the butterfly. And it's blue because of your eyes. They're the first thing I noticed about you."

"I may be pushing the man-code here, but that has got to be the most beautiful and sincere thing anyone has ever said to me." He chuckled. "Come here."

I lowered my body to his chest, and this time when our mouths met it was like magic. Every inch of my body tingled, warming me from my head to my toes. Brian deepened the kiss as he slid his roving hands up under the jersey and pulled it over my head. Naked again, he rolled me over onto my back. He pulled back and stared into my eyes. For the first time, I truly felt loved. This was home. This was perfection. This was the one thing I would never be able to be without again in my life. Not just love, but the love of this man.

Brian was my soulmate.

He pulled one of my hands from behind his head, linked our fingers, and pulled it between our chests.

"You are mine, and I am yours. No matter how far apart we are, my heart, my body belongs to you. There will never be another woman for me. Do you trust me?"

That was such an odd combination of words that for a moment I couldn't answer.

"I need to know, Ebony, do you trust me to be away from you and know I'm not sleeping around?"

"Yes ... I trust you."

His eyes closed as he sighed in what must have been relief. When he opened his eyes again, he focused on me with a soul-searching gaze.

"I trust you, too, with my heart. I need you to understand, I've never given my heart to another woman, not like this. Please, please, wait for me. Everything I've promised you will happen as soon as I come home. Don't doubt that."

"I'm not going anywhere. After tonight, no one else

will touch me except for you. My body and my heart are for no one else but you."

There was nothing else to say. I pulled his mouth back to mine and sealed the deal. Brian didn't waste time. With our hands linked, our mouths mated. He parted my thighs with his and eased between my legs. His kiss traveled down my throat to my breasts while his free hand ran the length of my body.

"I want to be inside you and stay until I have to leave," he whispered as he worked his way back up to my chin.

I moaned, wanting the same. He made a move to enter me, but stopped abruptly and reached for the condom box.

"Baby roulette," we said in unison. One day, in our old age, we would look back at this night and laugh.

A deep groan emanated from his throat as his head dropped down on my chest.

"Damn, it's empty," he said in frustration.

"Look in my purse, I always have some." I pointed to my side of the bed where it sat on the floor.

Brian released our fingers and shifted for the bag. Not willing to search, he dumped the contents onto the floor. I seconded his impatience.

"Yes!" He sat up, covered himself, and slid right into home.

Our lovemaking was slow and beautiful and everything I ever wanted.

Tonight would sustain me until Brian came home.

CHAPTER 22

Ebony

This cannot be happening.

The contents of my oversized purse littered the cashier's counter. "I put it in my bag…"

An annoyed grunt came from the man standing in line behind me.

Irritation made my cheeks hot. I stuffed my things into my purse. "I'll come back." I grabbed my backpack from the floor and moved out of the way.

So much for buying my book today. School had been in session for less than a week, and I had already fallen behind. My final year of college shouldn't start like this. I stomped out of the campus bookstore while muttering under my breath.

I could only hope my professor would be lenient since this was the first assignment. Who was I kidding? He'd already made it clear that if the assignment wasn't on his desk by the deadline, I would be screwed. I needed that book. It was my fault I didn't have it on time. I'd spent the last few weeks focusing on finding another job, managing my finances, and spending as much time as possible with Brian before he left.

I climbed in my car and slammed the door shut. Where in the hell was my school ID? Paying full price for the book was not my idea of money management. As it was, I barely had enough money to get the book at the discounted price. In hindsight, maybe I shouldn't have spent money on that tattoo. At the time, I'd been able to afford it. How was I supposed to know my job situation would change?

I emptied my purse on the passenger seat and continued to search, as if it would make a difference. A scan of the seats, floor, and other surfaces yielded no results. The only other option would be paying for another card and waiting until my next paycheck to buy the book. By then it would be too late to turn in my assignment.

If I had accepted Brian's help in the beginning, I would not be in this situation. And now I was paying for it.

I resigned myself to ask my roommates to borrow money. I could afford to pay for another ID with the money I had now, but it wouldn't do any good. Student services closed thirty minutes ago. By the time they opened again, I'd be at work. Wasn't that just great?

I lay my head back against the headrest and massaged my temples.

Today sucked.

I tried to stop stressing about the outcome of my grade for this paper and wished I could talk to Brian.

Hearing his soothing voice would not make my ID card appear, but it would calm my nerves enough to mull over the matter with a clear head.

He had been gone for less than thirty-six hours, and I missed him like crazy. We'd spoken last night before I went to bed. Our goal was to talk to each other every day, at least before he went on stage. His new schedule revolved around practice, show time, and travel. And after-parties.

Women threw panties at him when he performed at the club. I remembered watching him and listening to women behind me talk about what they could physically do for him. As vain as it sounded, I enjoyed watching their mouths gape open when Brian came off stage, pulled me into his arms, and kissed me.

I trusted Brian, but the right set of circumstances could lead to a slip up. Like a drunken after-party.

I promised myself not to dwell on it any more. All I could do was trust him. Focusing on the *what ifs* would only bring it to fruition.

I reached for my phone as it vibrated. It showed a missed call and voice message. I'd forgotten to take it off vibrate when class ended. I turned up the ringer and checked the message. Brian had called. My heart leapt in my chest at the sound of his voice. Praying he'd still be available, I hit redial.

"Hey, baby." His unbelievably smooth voice coated my irritation.

I closed my eyes and zeroed in on his timbre. "Brian, are you busy?"

"Kind of. We're waiting for the stagehands to rearrange the stage so we can do warm ups and sound checks before full-show rehearsal. I've got a few minutes. How was class?"

I laughed ruefully. "Class was fine. Homework is another story. I'm screwed because I don't have an important book."

"I thought you got everything weeks ago."

"Well, I did except for one book that cost so much it was out of my budget. I put it off until I had the money. Now my student ID is missing. I need it to get a student discount."

"Wait, you needed money and didn't tell me?" An exasperated sigh came through the line. "Ebony, I told you I would help you with anything you need. You know I would have bought it for you."

"I know, it's just ... you've got your own bills to worry about. Besides, I've been handling this sort of problem for years on my own."

"But you're not on your own anymore; you've got me. I want to see you succeed. But it won't happen if you don't have everything you need. Don't mess with your education because you're too proud to ask."

"Brian—"

"Let me take care of you, baby. With the way they're paying me, I can help you with anything you need."

"But —"

"There are no *buts*. Look, I can't be there with you right now, at least let me do this, okay? Text me your account number, and I'll deposit the money into your bank in the morning."

I breathed a sigh of relief. "Thanks, Brian. I'll pay you back."

"There's nothing to pay back. Now, your ID, when did you see it last?" I could hear the cackles of men around him.

"It's usually in my purse. I've checked everywhere." I thought back to the last few days' activities and groaned in realization. "Your house, in your bedroom. Remember when you were looking for a condom?"

Brian chuckled. "Oh, yeah. I dumped your bag on the floor."

"We overslept and were running late to get to the bus. I grabbed everything I saw, but didn't think to look under the bed." I couldn't help but laugh. "Wow."

The background noises in the phone lowered as I heard Brian excuse himself. His voice was low, husky when he spoke again. "I can't stop thinking about that night."

My body tingled in all the right places. "Me neither." I'd woken up in need of a cold shower just this morning from dreaming about it.

"Have you ever had phone sex?"

"Are you serious?" I giggled.

"Very. Some of the guys say they've done it with their girlfriends. Or a better idea ... we could Facetime."

Brian continued to share creative ways for us to be together via technology. Some of them sounded like fun, but I drew the line at naked text messages. Facetime was one thing, but having a naked picture of me stored on his phone, where someone might find it ... Uh-uh, not this girl. My luck I'd be up for a promotion one day, and my *girls* would go viral. Still, just the thought that he wanted to see me cheered me up, but all too soon, the conversation winded down.

"Baby, I've got to go. I'll tell Javan to let you in. You should be able to get it tonight."

"Thank you." I paused, studying the bracelet on my arm. The guitar glinted in the sun. "I love you."

"I love you, too. I'll text you later."

We disconnected. Hearing him say he loved me would hold me over until the next time we talked.

Brian was right. I could have avoided a lot of my anxiety over the last few weeks. Accepting his help would have given me time to focus on finding another job and not stress about all the other details. I would chalk it up as a lesson learned.

Armed with a plan and the possible location of my ID card, I felt better, knowing I would rectify the situation by nightfall.

***

Several hours went by before Brian's text came through; Javan was home. I checked the time and saw it was nearly eight p.m. A quick check of the house had shown that my roommates weren't home yet. I called both of their cell phones and got no response. That wasn't unusual; they both worked late.

The idea of going to Brian's house unescorted made me uneasy.

I contemplated my options: wait until one of them showed up, or wait until tomorrow and meet Yasmine over there once she got off work. Another option would be to ask Yasmine to go look for it. Neither scenario worked because it would be after the bookstore's hours of operation. I needed the book tomorrow. Besides, the more I thought about it, I wanted to do it myself. I wanted to get his baseball jersey. It smelled like him and sleeping in it would be like having him near.

A quick in and out, ten minutes tops. With any luck, my ID would be peeking out from under Brian's bed.

The entire house was dark when I arrived. The porch

light didn't come on until I rang the bell for the third time.

The door opened, and I immediately felt on edge.

Javan didn't speak. His dark eyes made no effort to hide his thoughts. The man projected sexual heat. It was clear to see why Yasmine liked him.

He and Brian were the same height, but that's where the similarities ended. Once upon a time, before meeting Brian, a man like Javan would have gotten my attention.

Javan's milk-chocolate skin stretched over a body that boasted of hours spent in a gymnasium. His shoulder length dreads rested against the nape of his neck, held by a thick band. From the looks of it, the man spent more time at a hairdresser than I did. Whatever he did, Yasmine sure liked it.

Ignoring my discomfort, I focused on the white set of silk pajamas. The button-up top hung open, exposing his defined muscular chest.

I imagined Brian wearing them in a shade of blue that matched his eyes. Then again, he didn't wear anything to bed except for the skin he was born in, especially when I spent the night.

"Hi." I forced my voice to sound normal and made myself meet his probing gaze. "Sorry it's late. You look like you were expecting someone else."

Yasmine and Javan were in an open relationship. The chances of her showing up tonight were fifty-fifty. Regardless, I didn't care to be here when one of his play dates arrived.

Javan's eyes shifted to my car. "I wasn't expecting anyone except you." His eyes traveled over me again.

I felt self-conscious. My shorts weren't too tight,

and my tee hung loose over my hips. What was he looking at?

"Oh, um ..." I ignored the implication of his words. "I won't take long then." I waited for him to step aside.

He moved slightly; there would be no way to avoid walking past without brushing against him.

I held my breath. His cologne reeked of dark spices and irritated my nose. Fortunately, my man had better taste.

In Brian's room, I went straight for the side of the bed where the contents of my purse had rested. My ID wasn't visible from where I stood, which meant it would probably be under the bed. Getting on my hands and knees shouldn't have made me uncomfortable, but Javan's hulking frame hovered in the doorway and made it impossible to lose the nervous feeling. Why had he followed me?

I contemplated the best way to get on the floor without putting my butt or back in the path of his roving eyes. Unfortunately, the desk was in the way, leaving no other option.

"You need help?"

My heart kicked up a notch. Javan's shadow moved over the light from the ceiling when he moved from the doorway to the side of the bed where I kneeled.

I closed my eyes, pushed my hand under the bed, through the dust on the hardwood floor, and prayed my fingers would find what I searched for.

Finally, success. I clung to the flimsy piece of plastic, as if my life depended on it. "No." I moved to get up as quickly as possible. To my chagrin, Javan stood right behind me, his huge outstretched palm waiting to help me.

The way he positioned himself made it impossible to get up without his help. I gripped his hand, pulled myself up quickly, and backed away from him. I wiped my sweaty hands on my shorts. He now blocked my path.

Every nerve in my body stood on edge. Was I over-reacting? After all, he was Brian's roommate and my best friend's lover. I could not control what he did with his eyes. All things stated, I should be able to trust him.

My internal alarm said otherwise.

Javan continued to block my path, caging me between the bed, dresser, and wall. The plastic card nearly slipped from my fingers as my hands began to shake.

"There's something I've never been able to understand about you." He crossed his arms and looked around Brian's room.

"What?" I forced my voice to stay steady.

His dark eyes trailed over to the bed. "What do you see in him? You are a very desirable sister. Why are you fucking a white guy?"

My eyes felt like they would bulge out of my head. Did I just hear him right? He was supposed to be Brian's friend. Why question me about my racial preferences? The look in his eye quickly dispelled the remark that wanted to leave my mouth.

"What's the problem? Couldn't find a brother to satisfy you?"

"That's none of your business, Javan. Excuse me." I moved to get past him, but he stayed rooted to that spot. For a moment, I contemplated climbing over the bed and scampering out into the hall. I had the feeling being in any position on the bed would be a bad idea, though.

He watched me before he stepped aside, once again, forcing me to brush against him.

"Maybe you weren't with the right one. I know Yasmine talks about how I handle her." His laughter was smug.

"What goes on between the two of you is none of my business." I focused on walking calmly down the hallway instead of breaking into a mad run.

I had escaped the bedroom and almost made it to the front door, but somehow, Javan managed to slip from behind me and block my exit to freedom.

"True, or it could be something going on between the three of us." The expression on my face must have caused him to reconsider his ridiculous offer. "Okay, it can be just us then." He took a step toward me.

I bit back a gasp at the wild look that blazed in his eyes.

Everything about his body language said he was determined to get what he wanted.

I knew then no matter what I said or did, this was only going to end one way. I looked around the room and tried to spy another path to the door. Maybe if I moved fast enough, I could reach the front door, then my car, and get away from here.

But there was no place to go except the way I'd come. If I made it to Brian's room, I could lock the door and call for help. But, oh, God, there wasn't a phone in his room, and my cell was in my car.

Why did I leave my phone in the car?

Reasoning was my only option. "Javan," I struggled to force my voice out of a dry mouth. "I'm not interested, okay? I don't want to do anything to hurt

Yasmine. She's really into you, and I value our friendship. I'm sure you feel the same way about Brian."

Javan's dark laughter sent ice-cold fear to my heart. "What goes on between us has nothing to do with either of them. Brian pretends to be all innocent." His laugh was chilling. "Don't believe the act. He used to fuck with more than one girl at a time. Then you came along and changed him." He closed the distance between us in two long strides.

I moved as far away from him as I could and backed into the living room until I bumped into the CD collection.

"What is so special about you?" His voice lowered to a murmur as he ran a hand through the loose strands of my hair.

My body quivered, and I gasped in fear, no longer able to keep it in. What was I doing here? Why was this happening to me?

"You must be good in bed. I can hear the sounds you make. Bet I can make you yell more and come harder." He leaned toward me and breathed deeply. "You smell good."

I whimpered, hating the fact I wore the perfume Brian loved, and backed into the shelf behind me. The card I'd come to retrieve slipped from my fingers and hit the floor. Brian's prized CD collection shifted as the weight of my body pushed against it, knocking it into the wall. Discs crashed down around my feet.

Unable to look away from his eyes, I reached blindly behind me, searching the shelves for something of significant weight to protect myself. I only came away with a lightweight plastic CD cover.

Javan sneered as his large fingers left my hair and

traced down my collarbone to the front of my shirt. Tears sprang into my eyes. It seemed the more I tried to get away, the more eerie excitement grew in his eyes. I had to get away from him ... I needed to find a way out.

"Javan..."

He grabbed one of my breasts, his humongous body towered over me. There was nowhere for me to run with the shelf at my back.

"Please stop ..." My voice was barely audible to my own ears. I closed my eyes to the sadistic sneer on his face and yelled in pain as he gripped my nipple through my shirt. I smacked at his hands, but his grip only hardened.

"Oh, come on, that's not how you sound when you're with him."

"Please ... don't do this," I begged again. My voice was thick with terror. I had never felt so helpless in my life. No matter what I did, he was too big for me to stop him.

There was only one thing I could do; only one weapon of defense in my female arsenal.

Javan leaned in to kiss me as I struggled.

I aimed my knee for all he held dear, pushed him off, and ran. I was inches away from reaching the door. Once outside, I would scream bloody murder to draw attention from the neighbors, jump in my car, and get away.

I peered over my shoulder. Pain and anger mangled Javan's face, and he seemed to have recovered from the damage I'd inflicted.

I turned back and reached for the doorknob, frantically twisting it with sweaty fingers, fighting to get a grip.

But then I slipped on the rug at the door and hit my

head.

CHAPTER 23

Ebony

No matter how hard I tried, it was impossible to get rid of the smell.

Dark spices.

Neither the fragrance of my cucumber-and-melon body wash nor the tropical-scented soap could get rid of the stench.

My skin flamed red, my inner thighs raw. I ached everywhere: my breasts ... my back ... the very heart of me.

I squeezed my eyes shut to block out the memory.

It was impossible.

How could this have happened? What did I do wrong? How had I let him rape me? No amount of fighting back prevented what Javan had been determined to do.

A wave of revulsion hit. Dry heaves forced me to

double over in pain. There was no foreseeable end to this nightmare.

I sunk to the tub's floor, crossed my arms tightly across my chest, and watched the soapy water swirl around the drain. My body shook as heavy tears mixed with the lukewarm water, rained down my hair and face.

Nothing short of bleach could get rid of Javan's pungent scent.

I should have waited for Yasmine or Kaitlyn.

I should have paid for the damn book.

The repercussions of my procrastination and stubbornness were coming back to bite me. If I'd accepted Brian's offer in the beginning, then none of this would have happened.

I wouldn't have a failing grade in class.

I wouldn't be a victim of Javan's deceit.

In the end, it was my fault. I'd asked for this.

I deserved every bad thing going on in my life.

The water ran cold, making my already aching limbs hurt worse. How long had I been in the shower? Had my roommates gotten home yet?

I dragged my bruised body out of the tub and to the bathroom mirror. Faint traces of black-and-blue marks emerged under my light brown skin. Javan had been merciless in his assault, taking whatever he wanted. He'd been sure not to leave marks where they'd be visible to the world. For that, I should be thankful.

I was thankful for still having my life.

One hip ached worse than the other. I rubbed it gently with the towel before twisting around to get a look. Oh, God, no ... my tattoo. Javan's humongous hand marred my dedication to Brian and our relationship. The skin around the bright blue butterfly was swollen and red.

A fresh wave of tears ran down my face. How much more crying could I do? It had been hard to drive home with bleary eyes.

My heart felt like it would break into a million pieces.

And oh, God, Brian ...

Only hours after promising Brian I'd be faithful, my words were no longer valid. And to think I worried about him sleeping with another woman. Now, another man ... his friend, had taken me, used me and ...

Oh, God, what had I done?

I wanted to call Brian and tell him what happened and how much I needed him. My hand rested on the bathroom counter, my fingers inches away from grasping my phone.

Javan's leering voice flooded my mind, growling, sending chills down my spine. "Tell Brian." He'd smirked as he pulled his pants up. "Go ahead. He's not going to believe you. You cheated on him. At least that's what I'll say. Why would he believe you? You're just another black slut who walked away from him to be with a brother."

I wanted to jump on him and beat him and gouge his eyes out for what he'd done to me, for what he'd said about me ... about Brian. But what could I do? He'd already demonstrated that he could overpower me.

I could call the police and have Javan arrested. But then what?

Brian was on tour. Word would get back to him; he would break his contract and come home. His reputation would be ruined, his chances at establishing his career gone because of my mistake.

And what about our relationship? Hadn't he just asked, no, begged me, to wait for him? He wanted to marry me and start a family.

My hands immediately flew to my stomach. I could be pregnant now. Oh, no, what if I was and lost our baby due to this violent act?

My knees grew weak and forced me to lean over the counter's edge. Now, I would be nothing but damaged goods.

If Brian ever got wind of what happened and believed Javan's story over mine, our relationship would be over. He'd known Javan for years; we'd only been involved for months. Brian said we needed more time to get to know each other.

If this ever came out, my unexpected chance at love would be over, gone forever. And where would that leave me? Broken hearted and alone.

Losing Brian would be far more devastating than Javan raping me. I could put this act of violence behind me and pretend it never happened.

But there would be no way to pretend our relationship never existed.

I wiped tears from my eyes and stared at my battered body. These bruises would be long gone by the time Brian came home. The blemishes would disappear, but deep down, I would never be the same.

I pulled on a pair of sweatpants and a long T-shirt.

Sudden pounding on the bathroom door made my heart jump. I gripped the counter. I'd locked the door. Could Javan have followed me home? Had Yasmine given him a key?

"Ebony, girl, you're hogging all the hot water! Hurry

up!" Yasmine's exasperated voice filtered through the door.

Yasmine. Should I tell her? She needed to know about her man. But would she believe me?

We became best friends when we met in college. We confided in each other and connected in a way that bonded us as sisters.

She'd had her own share of relationship trials over the years, her life altered by people she'd thought were her friends. They not only used her, they went behind her back and ruined her outlook on dating. It was why she refused to be seriously involved again.

I could not risk becoming another one of the women who'd hurt her.

When I'd threatened Javan after he defiled me, he mocked, "*Your girl's in love with me. If you tell Yasmine about us, you'll become another ho who used to be her friend.*"

Javan had it all figured out. Who was I fooling? No one around me would believe, not even Kaitlyn. Besides, she never had been good at keeping a secret.

There was no one to confide in without them getting hurt, too.

Brian. Yasmine. Kaitlyn.

My mistake had started weeks ago. The repercussions of my decision had snowballed beyond belief.

I would be the only one to pay the cost for this mistake. This was my secret, my burden to bear alone.

Dressed, I gathered up my bathing supplies, balled up my torn clothes, and wrapped them in my towel out of sight of prying eyes.

Yasmine leaned against the wall, tapping her toe impatiently when I opened the door. "It's about time. I bet the hot water's gone," she grumbled. "I've had one hell of a day. All I want to do is shower, crash in bed, and pretend this day never happened."

I walked by, gripping my towel, unable to make eye contact. "Sorry," I muttered. My foot crossed the threshold of my room when she stopped me.

"Look at me, being all insensitive. Are you okay?" Her voice softened.

I ran a hand over my bloodshot eyes. "I had a long day, too. Headache."

Yasmine tilted her head and studied me. In the years we'd known each other, she'd learned to read me well. "That's not all." She walked over and put a hand on my aching shoulder. I flinched. "What's really bothering you?"

For a split second, my lips parted. I nearly blurted out everything.

Oh, no, I could not go there, not now, not ever.

"You miss Brian, don't you?" She shook her head and pulled me into her arms. I leaned in and absorbed strength from that small contact. "It's okay. I'm sure lover boy is sitting around pining over you, too." Yasmine chuckled. "I feel the same way when I haven't seen Javan in a few days. The crazy part is it's been a long time since I felt that way about anyone." She kissed my forehead and rubbed my back. "Three months will be over before you know it."

She let go and headed for the bathroom. I stood rooted in place and leaned against the doorjamb before closing my door.

In my room, I swallowed aspirin, and climbed in bed to wrap up in the security of my sheets.

***

I awoke with a start. My heart raced, my head and body ached. It took a moment for the nightmare to dissipate and realize I was alone in my bed. But the moment I closed my eyes, images of my nightmare bombarded me, sending me back to that hallway.

And then I heard it, the ringing of my cell phone. I reached for it and saw Brian's cheerful smile on the screen. My finger grazed the talk button. My need to hear his voice overwhelmed me, but if I answered now, I would spill everything and our relationship would be over.

I closed my eyes and prayed for strength as the phone continued to ring. When it stopped, I waited until it notified me of a voicemail. I held the phone and listened to his message.

"Hey, baby, it's me. Tonight was awesome! I wish you could have been here. I have so much to tell you, and you won't believe everyone I've met. I can't wait to talk to you. I didn't mean to wake you because I know you've got a busy day ahead. Did you get your badge? I called Javan, but he didn't answer. Don't worry; I know you'll do well in class. Just hang in there, okay? I'll send the money in the morning. Until then, I plan to dream about you. Good night, Ebony. I love you."

Tears flooded from my eyes and the lump in my throat made it hard to swallow. I wished more than anything in this world I could have been with him tonight.

I wished I'd paid for another ID.

I wished I'd just bought the damn book in the first place.

I wished he would've had a roll of condoms and not emptied my bag on the floor.

Oh. My. God. I sat up so fast my head began to swim. Condoms.

Javan hadn't used one. He'd been reckless and didn't pull out and ...

I leaned over the edge of my bed and searched frantically for the trashcan. To my surprise, there was still something left to vomit.

Gonorrhea. Hepatitis. Herpes. Chlamydia. AIDS.

The chances of me conceiving had just doubled.

As soon as my stomach settled, I went online and researched my options. My search led to an over-the-counter morning-after pill to decrease the chances of pregnancy. The thought of taking the pill was unnerving. Even though it couldn't compare, in my mind, deciding to take the pill to reduce the chance I could have gotten pregnant from the rape was the equivalent to having an abortion.

But what if I already carried Brian's baby?

What if I didn't and was now pregnant with Javan's?

I couldn't live with the possibility of having another man's child.

My head spun. I needed to make a decision now. I had forty-eight hours from the time of unprotected sex to take the pill in order for it to be effective.

Brian and I had been together less than forty-eight hours ago. It had been nearly two hours since the rape.

If I was pregnant, a paternity test during the pregnancy would determine if Brian was the father. In order to have his consent, he would have to know about the rape. That could not happen.

Taking the pill meant not only killing the sperm Javan left behind; it meant killing the possible life Brian and I might have created. Either way I'd be killing a part of myself.

If I avoided testing and kept the truth to myself, Brian would go for months being happy, thinking the baby was his and planning to be the father I knew he could be ... until the baby was born. A child born looking like Javan without any hints of being the light-skinned, blue-eyed bi-racial beauty I saw in my dream would reveal my secret. No matter what I said, Brian would believe I cheated on him. It would be too late to tell the truth.

There was only one decision I could live with, without disrupting the lives around me.

I got dressed and headed for the nearest all-night pharmacy.

CHAPTER 24

Yasmine

Three months later ...

"Ms. Phillips, you have a call on line three."

I forced irritation out of my voice. "Thomas, how many times have I told you, call me Yasmine?"

The young, pimpled faced kid, who worked the front desk, blushed. He looked like he'd pass out on the floor if I smiled at him. Talk about a teenage crush.

"I'm-m-m-sorry, I just can't —"

What he couldn't do was get the words out without stammering half to death. Where had my father found this guy?

"It's okay, just send the call through."

Thomas shut his mouth, nodded, and walked into the doorframe. He looked at me again, his face even redder from embarrassment.

I allowed a half-smile, not wanting to throw too much at him for fear of having to transfer the call myself.

He responded with a dorky grin and headed back to the front desk.

The Phillips' Family Inn had been in business since I attended high school. I'd held the title of Assistant Manager of this location since graduating college. My parents sweated blood and tears to open the establishment.

After years of planning, my great-grandmother's death left my mother enough money and the perfect property to build their dream.

Twelve years later, there were two locations with the possibility of a third. Talk about following your dreams.

My dream did not include running a hotel for the rest of my life.

Fashion was my thing. I spent every free moment researching and using my family and friends as test dummies. As far as they were concerned, I became the go-to person when needing to dress for the occasion. My best friend, Ebony, was one of my better case studies. The day we'd met, she wore a pair of jeans and an everyday T-shirt that hid her beauty. It took a few months to break her shell.

My goal was to start a business as a fashion consultant. I had the skill, the talent, and the motivation. All I needed was time and a location to work out of.

I chewed on my lip and pulled out my calendar. Time ... time ... time ...

A date circled in blaring red ink made me pause. Javan and I had an anniversary coming up. We'd been dating for eight months. How had that happened?

Long-term relationships and I did not get along. Too many chances of happiness had turned to heartache. The last man who'd broken my heart had hammered a nail into the coffin. Looking for love no longer interested me.

I wasn't gay; I loved men. I loved their attitudes, their style, their swagger ... hell, I loved sex. A man could have me all day in any way. But my heart was forbidden. No man would ever reach there again.

Yet, somehow, Javan had slipped through a loophole and planted himself there. For eight months. Most of my friends-with-benefits relationships barely lasted three months.

Maybe watching Ebony and Brian's relationship grow had rubbed off on us. Especially since he'd left Ebony behind to pursue his career. Since he'd been gone, Javan started spending more time with me. He became interested in my mind as much as my body.

The phone rang and snapped me out of my thoughts.

"This is Yasmine Phillips, manager of the Phillips' Family Inn."

"Yasmine, its Brian, how are you?"

"Brian? How have you been? How's the tour?"

He laughed. "Man, it's been one of the best experiences of my life. I've learned a lot and met so many people. It's an experience I'll never forget. But honestly, I'm ready to come home. That's why I'm calling. We'll be back in a week, and I want to do something special for Ebony. It's been three months since we've been together and ... well ..." Nervous laughter came through the phone. "We need some time alone, you know? Could you hook me up with something special for me and my girl?"

"Say no more. I've got the perfect room for you guys. It has a balcony overlooking the rose garden."

Brian exhaled in what had to be relief. "Thanks." He wasted no time giving me the details of what he wanted. Ebony would be very pleased.

"I like your style, Brian. Maybe you can give Javan some pointers. Our anniversary is coming up soon —" His unexpected outburst made me pause. "What are you laughing at?"

He cleared his throat. "Did you say anniversary?"

"Don't be a smart ass, Brian."

He chuckled. "Sorry, you were saying?"

I rolled my eyes. "It's next week. Maybe we can meet up for dinner or something. I'll fill Ebony in on the details later. Do you think you guys can unwrap yourselves long enough to join the festivities?"

"Sure. Let us know, and we'll be there."

"Cool. Now if that's all ..."

"Actually," Brian paused. "Yasmine, can I ask you something?" The tone of his voice changed.

"What's on your mind?" I doodled on a note pad.

"You've been friends with Ebony for a while ..." He paused again.

I tapped the pen on my desk. Patience was not one of my strong suits. "What do you want to know? If it's something private because of the sister code ..." I shrugged even though he couldn't see it.

"I understand. Have you noticed anything different about Ebony? I mean, is she okay?"

I sat the pen down. Of course, she'd changed. She was in full school and work mode. I admired her dedication. Once she set her mind on something, she went all in.

"She's good, just stressing about school as always. It's her last year, and the pressure is intense. Besides, with you gone, who else is she going to play with besides the monkey?"

That made him laugh. "Yeah, I guess you're right. I've been so busy I thought I missed something important."

"Don't worry about her. I've been busy myself, but I'll check on her."

"Thanks, Yasmine," he said and ended the call.

Now that I thought about it, Brian was right. Ebony had changed. Her hard work and dedication to her job were nothing new. But once he'd left, she started working harder than usual. She ate, slept, worked, and talked to him when she could. But when it came to Kaitlin and me ...

I could understand why she avoided us. After all, we were spending time with our boyfriends while she waited by the phone. And the three months without sex thing ... damn. I'd be a freaking lunatic by now. Ebony needed an intervention, a girl's night out. The mission: get her back to the way he left her. It was way past time for her newly acquired frumpy look to go.

Time to plan. I called Kaitlyn, and she agreed with my idea.

Only one thing left to do. Call Javan and cancel our plans for the evening.

Jazz music played through the line while I was on hold. Calling him at work irritated me. I wished he would keep his cell phone on.

"Thank you for calling Franklin and Associates. How may I direct your call?"

I ground my teeth. I hated the receptionist. She

never hesitated to play games when she transferred my call. She also had no qualms letting me know her eyes were on my man.

"Sandra, I've been waiting for more than five minutes. Is Javan available?"

"Oh, Ms. Phillips, I'm sorry. Hold the line for a moment, I'll check."

I wanted to reach through the phone and slap her.

Another minute passed. "Hello?" Javan had the sexiest voice.

"Hi, baby, it's me."

"Ah, Yasmine ..." The moment he realized it was me — because the bitch would never tell him — his voice dropped an octave.

I found it hard not to fidget in my seat. "Were you busy?"

"No, my last patient left a while ago. I'm wrapping up paperwork now."

"One of these days, I'm going to cuss her ass out," I said hotly. "She left me on hold for five minutes."

Javan's husky laugh tickled my ear through the phone. "Should I warn her now or wait to pull you off?"

"Don't tempt me." I could visualize his receptionist's skinny ass running around the office.

"*Hmm*, the idea of you fighting over me turns me on. Why don't you swing by in say ... thirty minutes? We can have lunch in my office. You'll end up eating in your car, but I'm sure you'll leave a very satisfied woman."

Having *lunch* with Javan was always creative. A time check left me disappointed. "Unfortunately, our computers had crashed for the second time this week. I've got an emergency call in for a computer tech now. I'm stuck."

"We all have to work." I could hear the rustle of paper through the line. "Then tonight, my place. Both of us naked with you on top?"

The visual image of his body drove me crazy. Tight muscles under smooth-chocolate skin. The man could have been the spokesperson for the Hershey's corporation. There always seemed to be a sexual current flowing around him. It pulled me in like a magnet.

"That's why I'm calling. I've got to cancel. Brian's coming back in a few days, and my girl needs help. Ebony's been in her own little world since he's been gone. Who knew she'd be stuck on him?" I laughed.

The rustling noise stopped. "What's wrong with her?"

"She's been MIA for three months, stuck in her room not wanting to talk. I think she's a little jealous."

"Of what?"

"Of our relationship. Plus, Kaity's got Luke. Think about it, she was with Brian a few months, and then he left."

"Yeah, I'm sure that's it. Look, I've got to go." All sense of flirting left his voice.

"Okay, me too. The computer geek is here." I studied the man who'd suddenly appeared in my doorway. "Love you."

"Yeah, later."

I hung up the phone. Why didn't Thomas notify me the computer technician had arrived?

Always eager to appreciate a good-looking man, I studied him.

He wore dark-rimmed glasses, black pants, and the standard white shirt and black tie worn by geeks across America. He had cocoa-colored skin with shoulders hinting at a nice build beneath his shirt. He wore his hair in a low cut, typical black-male fashion. A trimmed goatee surrounded generous lips. Although he didn't hold a candle to Javan's thick frame, he was attractive ... in a geeky sort of way.

"Sorry to disturb you, Mrs. Phillips, my name is Zachariah Givens. I'm here to service your computers." He pointed over his shoulder down the short hallway leading to the front desk. "I rang the bell twice, but no one was out front."

I exhaled in exasperation. "Thomas must be on break." I made note to address him about leaving the front desk unmanned without informing me. We were a small hotel chain, but we ran our establishment as if we were one of the big kids. "And it's Ms. Phillips. Come in."

I rose from my chair and smoothed the tight fabric over my hips. My skirt stopped at the mid-point of my thigh, my legs were naked without pantyhose, and I wore sensible, yet stylish heels. Most men would have watched the movements. He didn't. Guess I'd offended him with my comment.

"Look, I didn't mean anything by calling you a geek. You reminded me of —"

"No problem." His voice was flat and impersonal. "I hear it at least five times a day. It comes with the job."

O ... kay. So he was a geek with no sense of humor. Fine. But his voice had a hoarseness that was as sexy as hell.

I moved out of the way so he could sit at my desk.

"What type of problem are you having?" He adjusted the chair to fit his height.

I frowned. I wasn't that short.

It took five minutes to run down the problems we'd been experiencing.

"So can you fix it?" I asked.

"I'll have to run a diagnostic on the system and check each terminal before I can tell what's going on. It's possible you've got a virus, or," he studied the computer set up, "your system is outdated and can no longer handle the workload."

That was not the news I wanted. My father wouldn't be pleased either.

He glanced at his watch. "It's going to be a while; you might want to grab lunch. Leave me your number, and I'll call when I've got my diagnosis."

What the hell? Was he kicking me out of my own office?

My jaw clenched, I breathed deeply and exhaled slowly. I didn't know this man, and he didn't know me. Did he assume he could just waltz in here and take over my office?

No way in hell was that about to happen. I paid him, which meant he worked for me.

I crossed my arms and glared. He stared back with hazel eyes that shouted intelligence beneath those black frames. They were gorgeous.

"It's not time for my break," I said firmly. "I'll wait." With that said, I sat in a chair in the corner of my office and crossed my legs. My skirt hiked up a few inches exposing my thigh.

He broke our challenging stare and glanced at my legs. About damn time he noticed.

"Suit yourself." He turned back to the screen and began keying in code, tuning me out as if I didn't exist.

Well, damn.

CHAPTER 25

Ebony

"**D**octor Lofton, are you sure?"

"Ebony, go home. There's nothing you can do. Nala is being taken care of." The head vet led me out of the clinic and pointed in the direction of my locker.

"Please call me if—"

"If anything changes, I'll call you. Go home and get some rest. You need it."

The clinic door closed firmly in my face. As much as I wanted to keep a watchful eye on the orangutan, what Dr. Lofton had said rang true. I was exhausted. Spending the weekend in the overnight room on a cot and taking showers in the staff bathroom had not been the best place to rest.

Then again, I barely got rest at home.

I cleaned out my locker and headed for my car.

The last three months were taking their toll. Nightmares plagued me. Coffee and five-hour energy drinks kept me on my feet. Neither was good for my health. I even managed to lose a few pounds.

My grades were slipping, and the three-point-nine GPA I'd maintained for the past seven years dropped a point.

To my dismay, I found myself thinking about the offer Dr. Jacobs made months ago when everything was right in my little world. I'm sure at this point the terms would have changed. Although I hadn't threatened him in any way, I still could, and therefore secure the position of Veterinarian Technician in the spring.

As sick as the thought of stooping to his level made me feel, the idea of losing everything I'd worked for over the last seven years made me sicker.

The last couple of months changed my entire outlook on life and left me a hermit in my own home. Keeping the secret of my rape wore me down.

With Brian gone and me avoiding my friends, caring for Nala had become my lifeline, the one thing grounding me in a life that had turned into one big fat lie. It seemed as if I lied to everyone around me.

"Busy, but okay," had become my typical response when Kaitlyn asked.

Although I had never outright lied to Yasmine, it was a lie by omission when she talked about her relationship with Javan, and I remained silent.

I lied to Brian by using work and school as an excuse for feeling down.

As much as it hurt lying to him, he was the one thing keeping me from giving up and moving back to North Carolina.

The bright spot in my life was the fact he would return home in a few days. No more waiting to hold him, smell him, or feel him lying next to me. Knowing Brian loved me was not enough. Nothing replaced seeing it in his eyes and feeling it in his touch.

I needed him desperately.

But the need brought fear. Fear that he'd somehow find out about the rape. Fear Javan's threats would come true. Fear Brian would leave me.

I could not dwell on those thoughts.

When I arrived home, my roommates' cars were in the driveway. That was odd. Normally, Yasmine arrived home after I did and Kaitlyn came last. As an assistant costume designer for a T.V. show, Kaitlyn worked long days, traveling for costume fittings or purchasing new pieces.

If they were both here, something had to be wrong.

I closed the door behind me. "Kaity, Yaz? Where are you?"

"In the kitchen," Kaitlyn said.

I dropped my book-bag down in the living room. The aroma of Mexican food greeted me from the kitchen.

"Surprise!" they yelled in unison.

"What's going on?"

Yasmine stood at the counter, a bottle of tequila in one hand and a daiquiri mix in the other. Ice sat in the blender.

Kaitlyn sat at the table, spooning portions of take-out food onto plates. "Girls' Night of course, what else?" she said in her Texas twang.

"Don't even think about saying no. We took off work early for this. No excuses. I don't care if you've got a project due tomorrow and you haven't done a thing to get started. Which is highly unlikely." Yasmine paused, started the blender, and then tasted her concoction. "Damn, that's good." She filled three empty glasses before continuing. "Tonight is about us women and everything feminine."

"Right, Yaz is gonna do manis and pedis. I've picked out these cute little outfits for us." Kaitlyn waved a hand up and down her body, indicating what she had on. "Don't laugh, they're supposed to be crazy lookin'."

For the first time, I paid attention to their attire. Tank tops, booty shorts, and flip-flops. Hawaiian leis were on their necks and ridiculously large sombreros were on their heads. Yasmine wore a pair of extra-large sunglasses around her neck.

"Before you say a thang," Kaitlyn continued, "I know you're wonderin' where your fabulous outfit is. Check your bed. Go on. Go change. We'll be waitin' on ya." She made a shooing motion with her hands.

"But —"

"This daiquiri is not going to stay frozen forever. Hurry up, girl," Yasmine added.

I shook my head and allowed a small smile to grace my lips. Hanging with the girls doing silly stuff at home had been a monthly tradition since college. I couldn't remember the last time we'd done it. Despite my efforts to evade their questions for the past three months, I missed this. Maybe, just this once, it would be okay to let my guard down and pretend everything was normal. No matter what all went on in my life, I still had my friends. And soon I would have Brian again.

The sting of excitement brewed in my chest. I ran upstairs to change into my crazy get-up.

They laughed upon my arrival into the kitchen; it immediately felt like old times. We ate, drank, danced, and cleaned up the kitchen while listening to music. For the life of me, I couldn't remember the last time we'd had this much fun.

The next phase of the evening turned to watching movies. Over the years, we'd collected a vast amount of romantic comedies. Since we could never agree on what to watch, we'd devised a system in which we picked a number. The highest number and corresponding DVD would be the winner. Tonight's selection was *Fools Rush In.*

None of us really watched the movie, since we'd seen it more than fifty times. Instead, we sipped on our third round of daiquiris while taking turns getting our nails done. Before long, men became the subject of the evening.

"Luke's a pretty good guy. He is so tall I have to stand on a box to kiss him," Kaitlyn said.

"What happened to Justin?" I asked.

Both women looked at me. "Uh, we broke up two months ago. Girl, you've been in a whole 'nother world," Kaitlyn said. "But I understand. It won't be long before Brian's back."

"I can't wait." I felt the dreamy smile spread across my face. They laughed.

The drinks were definitely working their magic. For the first time in months, I acted like my old self.

"Speaking of which," Yasmine said, "I'm planning an anniversary party for me and Javan."

"What?" Kaitlyn asked in surprise.

My mouth went dry. Anniversary? They were still together? I was sure my expression echoed Kaitlyn's statement.

"How long have you guys been goin' out?" she asked.

"Next week will be eight months." Yasmine peered down in her glass, as her voice lowered. "I think it's turning into something serious."

I was unable to keep my mouth closed. Bile began boiling in my stomach.

"As crazy as it sounds, I'm in love with him," Yasmine continued. "I said it would never happen again, but it has."

Kaitlyn looked on in awe. "Wow, I thought he was just supposed to be a straight hit-and-get-it guy."

Yasmine burst out laughing. "Kaity, that sounds so crazy coming from you."

"What? I've been around you guys long enough to get hip." She added a finger snap to punctuate her statement.

The conversation became background noise to my thoughts.

This wasn't right. Yasmine wasn't supposed to love him. Her standard operating procedure was sleep with a guy for a few months, dump him, and move on. Why was she still with him? I banked on, no, counted on, her leaving him. If that happened, he would be out of my life as much as possible. So what if Javan was Brian's roommate? I could avoid going to his house and dealing with him. I could avoid being in the place where my life changed for the worst. After all, Brian said he intended to move when he got back.

If they were together, I couldn't avoid seeing him at my home.

"Marriage may be in the works,." Yasmine said, snapping me back to the conversation.

Kaitlyn squealed and leaned over the sofa to give her a congratulatory hug.

Maintaining as much composure as possible, I excused myself, moved quickly down the hall, and emptied the contents of the evening's festivities into the toilet.

CHAPTER 26

Ebony

Visiting my gynecologist had never been one of my favorite things to do. Sitting on the cold piece of paper wearing nothing but a glorified paper towel did not make me comfortable or keep me warm, even while wearing socks.

The walls in the room felt like they were closing in on me. I never had more than one physical a year. The reasons that led me here again made me nervous.

A knock on the door announced the doctor's arrival.

"Ms. Campbell, it's good to see you." She smiled warmly and shook my hand before turning her attention to the file she held. "It seems you were here in August and tested for STDs. All of your lab work came back negative." Her eyebrows scrunched. "And now you want to be tested again? I applaud your willingness to monitor your health, but this is odd. You've been my patient for the past five years; you've never needed more than the normal screenings." She flipped through my file again.

I sat quietly, fiddling with my fingertips.

"You're also requesting a pregnancy test." Her eyebrows rose in question, studying me intently. "As your doctor, I have to ask, is everything okay?"

Good question, one I wanted to avoid. After the rape, when I got screened, my first thought was to visit a free clinic where testing would be anonymous. No unnecessary questions, no evidence of what happened left behind in my permanent file. If the results were negative, it would be as if nothing had ever happened.

But reasoning prevailed. Seeing my doctor made sense. She knew my medical history and would know immediately if something were wrong.

"Dr. Chambers, I'm fine, thanks for asking. There was an ... accident a few months back ..."

"Accident as in broken condom?"

The memory of the last night with Brian made me smile. "Lack of would be more like it."

On both occasions. My smile faded at the thought of Javan.

"*Hmm*. What about your partner? Has he been tested?"

"Brian? We'd talked about it before we slept together; he's clean. He's a good man. Plus, I've always been selective." My words were passionate.

Dr. Chambers didn't fail to notice. She made notes on my file. "You're not on birth control. All you use are condoms?" She glanced up at me.

I nodded. "I was supposed to come in to talk about using birth control, but my schedule has been hectic."

"We can cover that when we're done with the physical." She added another note. "Any missed periods? Difference in bleeding?"

I hesitated. "A little. My last two periods haven't come exactly on time and have been lighter than usual." That alone made me paranoid beyond belief.

"We'll do the pregnancy test in a few minutes. Let's check your vitals." She put my file on the counter, picked up her stethoscope.

Eyes, heart, lungs, reflexes, and breasts exam followed; Dr. Chambers took her profession seriously.

"Okay, put your feet in the stirrups."

I complied.

"Any recent sexual activity?"

"No."

I stared at the ceiling and listened as Dr. Chambers washed her hands and put on sterile gloves. She sat on the small stool at the end of the examination table. The crank of the forceps made me jump. How could even an exam make me feel violated?

I gritted my teeth, trying not to cry as the exam continued. It lasted only a minute but felt like hours.

She removed the forceps. The snap of the gloves made me jump again. Water splashed in the small sink while the smell of soap and hand sanitizer filled the air.

I removed my feet from the stirrups, glad this part of the exam had ended. I wiped away a stray tear.

"Ebony." She paused. "Are you okay? Is there something you want to share?"

My eyes went wide. My first reaction: deny, deny, deny. Embarrassment followed.

"I ... no, I ..."

She patted my knee. "It's okay." She retrieved tissue

for watering eyes that betrayed my secret. "Was it your boyfriend?" Her voice remained gentle as she sat back down on the stool.

"No, please, don't …" I begged when she reached for my file again. She put it down. "No, Brian would never …"

She waited for a beat. "Do you know the man who raped you?"

I hung my head, unable to meet her concerned gaze, wondering how she'd known. "Yes."

"Have you filed a police report?"

"No!" Dr. Chambers watched, but didn't seem surprised. "No," I said again, in a calmer voice. "I can't file a report. It was my fault."

"Rape is never your fault, Ebony. If you were having sex with someone, even if it's your boyfriend, and you change your mind, it would still not be your fault."

"I shouldn't have been there …" Every ounce of guilt that I'd packed away came barreling down on me. Tears that disappeared months ago flooded back and ran down my face.

"Still not your fault," she repeated, her voice stern. "Have you told anyone what happened?"

I shook my head and dried my eyes. "You're the only one who knows. Not even my boyfriend … I couldn't tell him."

She waited before speaking again. "Do you plan on telling him?"

"I can't … it's complicated."

Her eyebrows furrowed. "Have you had sex with him since the rape?" Genuine concern blazed in her eyes. It felt good having someone to talk to, even if I wasn't sharing everything.

"No. He's been out of town for the last couple of months, working. This happened after he left." I looked down; the tissue in my hands was nearly shredded. "He'll be back soon. I don't know if I can handle sleeping with him."

Dr. Chambers nodded. "Don't do anything you're not comfortable with. To be honest, Ebony, you need to tell him. If you keep it to yourself, he'll never know there's a problem. Keeping it inside won't help you recover mentally or physically." She patted my knee again, then gave me privacy while I was getting dressed. A few minutes later a nurse came in to collect samples for my tests.

I knew deep in my heart what my doctor said was true. It would be impossible to be with Brian again without sex being involved. After being apart for three months, he'd made it clear how much he wanted me.

My period wouldn't be due for a few more weeks, and there were no other valid excuses to buy myself time. Not knowing what would happen between us made me wary.

Dr. Chambers handed me several pamphlets when she returned. "Look over these."

I read the titles. They were about recovering from rape. I opened my mouth to protest, but she held up a hand.

"How you handle this is your business. What you've told me was doctor/patient confidentiality. Your life doesn't seem to be in danger, and you're not a threat to yourself or anyone else. I don't know how you're coping with this, but I strongly suggest you seek counseling. You can't hold it in forever, Ebony. If seeing a counselor makes you uncomfortable, confide in someone close to you. You need to seek help or else it could affect your health. As it is, your blood pressure is elevated. The pregnancy test results are negative. Stress is probably what's affecting your period. You need to remove as much stress from your life as possible. Your emotional health is just as important as your physical health."

Counseling.

I stuffed the pamphlets in my purse. I would review them in the privacy of my bedroom.

It felt good telling Dr. Chambers without her judging me. Talking to a professional could be a good thing, but seeing one would mean an obvious change in my routine. Brian's return would make it hard to explain absences without lying and saying nothing was wrong.

But something was wrong. He just didn't need to know about it.

Ever.

There were five days until his return.

Three days until the results of my STD test came back.

Please, God, let everything still be okay.

***

Brian waited on the other side of that door. The man I loved and desperately wanted to be with.

The man I'd hidden secrets from.

My heart raced as I shifted the overnight bag in my hand.

When Brian told me of his plans for the weekend, I'd nearly screamed for joy. The idea of seeing him again made my heart soar.

Until I thought about how much Brian looked forward to having sex. He'd made his intentions clear on the phone. My moment of euphoria took a nosedive, crashed and burned.

Our reunion should have been fraught with happiness, joy, and sex — mad, crazy, wild, happy-to-see-you-and-baby-did-I-miss-you sex. Instead, sex was the last thing I wanted to think about, yet the only thing I could think about.

My tests came back clean; no STDs. As grateful as I was for the information, it didn't mean I was ready for the intimacy Brian expected.

The doorknob twisted and a second later, he appeared. Tall, tanned, and wearing a five o'clock shadow. His hair had grown longer; the blond curls rested at the nape of his neck.

But his eyes, those deep wells of ocean blue, pulled me in hard and fast; I could hardly breathe.

"Ebony ..."

He took two steps and lifted me off the ground. My bag slipped from my fingers and dropped to the floor as he carried me into the room. The door closed heavily behind us. His kisses rained over my face, my mouth, and my neck.

"I've missed you, baby." His mouth met mine in a kiss that melted the ice that had formed in my veins since the night of my attack. "Are you crying?" His fingers wiped gently across my cheeks.

I could hear the concern in his voice and see it in his eyes.

"I don't know whether to laugh or cry," I stuttered.

Not true, I wanted to cry. A lot. I wanted to wrap my arms around him and confess every lie I'd told him. I wanted to hear him say everything would be okay, and he would never leave me. I wanted to tell him about my ordeal, so he could help me survive.

But I couldn't.

Brian smoothed hair from my face, chuckled, and kissed me again. He took my hand and led me to the edge of the bed. Every nerve in my body tensed. My heart raced and my hands shook. He wanted to make love. Could I handle it?

He sat on the edge of the bed, pulled me into his lap, and held me tight. His arms were strong and felt like home. His head rested on my shoulder. He wasn't rushing; this was pure, physical contact. This I could handle. This I needed.

I rested my cheek against his soft curls. His damp hair smelled of shampoo. His cologne, the sexy, male scent he wore, called to me. My Brian was home.

"I didn't know I would miss you so much," he whispered.

"Me neither."

He looked up into my eyes. His finger traced the side of my jaw.

All I saw was love. The man I'd yearned for, wanted, and needed was back in my life. My world had teetered back and forth for months as I tried to find some form of balance. Yet just looking into his eyes made it all right.

I no longer questioned or felt fear. Just love, pure love, want, and desire. How could I deny what he deserved?

"Make love to me." The words came effortlessly.

As if he'd been waiting for my queue, Brian gave me what I asked for. He kissed me deeply, passionately ... slowly.

Love and longing sent my heart racing. Heat my body hadn't felt since our last night together washed over me, solidifying my need to be with him.

Rough fingers that knew my body well unbuttoned my shirt. "I've missed these," he murmured, his fingers slid over the exposed swell of my breasts. Lips and mouth followed as he lowered the cups of my bra.

I closed my eyes and let my head fall back, reveling in the contact of hot mouth and fingertips. For the first time in months, I allowed myself to relax, for my body to be touched, stroked … loved.

After Javan's vicious attack … Oh, no, please, not now …

Images of that night began to emerge. Pain. Vulnerability. Helplessness.

The memory threatened to break my vow of silence. My heart now raced for a completely different reason.

"Baby, what's wrong?" He stopped kissing me. The lust in his eyes turned to concern as he massaged my back. "You're tense. Did I hurt you?"

I blinked and forced myself back to the present. I was here, in a hotel room with Brian. This wasn't three months ago; this was now.

I forced the thoughts of the past from my mind and centered on the man who watched me with love and genuine concern.

I could do this. I could exorcise the past and be the woman Brian had left behind. I wanted to be … I needed to be.

Instead of answering, I stood, pushed off my shirt, and unhooked my bra. Partially naked, I straddled him. Brian's gaze traveled down at my exposed skin. He wasted no time pulling his shirt over his head. His smooth sun-kissed skin begged for my attention. Heat flashed in his eyes when I pushed him back on the bed.

Inch by inch, I ravaged him with teeth and tongue.

"Ah ... that feels so good ... baby ... protection ... we need ..." he managed to say in between his sounds of pleasure.

I forced my mouth away from his flesh and stood to remove his pants. Even though I'd worked out the details of birth control with my doctor, I wasn't about to skip this step again. The pain of my decision months ago still lingered and would never go away. "Where?"

"My bag ... in the chair."

I followed the line of his arm, willing myself over to the bag and emptied its contents on the floor. Prize in hand, I tossed it over to him and shimmied out of jeans while he moved farther up the bed, his eyes intent on me.

"A lot of women try to get with band members, Ebony. None of them could get my attention because all I could think about was you." He slid the condom in place. "Come here, beautiful."

Naked, I crawled up the length of his body. My eyes were on his as I straddled him and guided him home.

There was pain. Pain from not having sex in three months. Pain from the healed flesh inside of me.

My body wasn't as ready as it needed to be to accept him, but I didn't care. I needed him. The feel of him, the firmness of him against me, inside of me, made me whole.

Brian had no idea of the whirlpool of emotions surging inside of me, yet he moved slowly, caressing my back, my hips, and thighs. He reached up to brush fallen hair out of my face. Then our eyes met, silently communicating what we wanted as our bodies moved in unison.

Pain slowly gave way to pleasure, as I focused on the here and now. On the softness of his touch, the urgent need of his kiss, and the wonderful feeling as he filled the very heart of me.

"Baby, let me ..." His grip on my hips tightened as he moved to roll me on my back.

"No, like this." I planted my hands beside his head, and leaned down to kiss him while holding him in place.

He wanted to take charge of our lovemaking; his urge to push deep inside me obvious on his face. But I wasn't ready for that. Even though we were making love, having him tower over me would bring back the memory of...

No, not again.

I needed the control. In the past, our lovemaking was about desire and need. Rough and hard, even when we started off slowly. Brian was an amazing lover. Even though he may have wanted more, he seemed to sense my need to take things slowly and didn't push to change positions.

I sat up, rested my hands on his smooth chest, and rocked harder, faster. The shift of my body, forcing him deeper, made us both cry out in pleasure.

"God, Ebony ... I love you." He gripped me tighter and pushed up to give me everything he had.

When I came, there were tears in my eyes. He followed right behind me, his eyes focused on me.

This is what had been missing. My physical healing had been over long ago. Maybe now my emotional healing could begin.

I melted onto his chest and nestled in the warmth of his body. His arms folded around me and held firm. We remained connected, neither one of us moved.

My lips grazed his throat. "I love you, too, Brian. I'm glad you're home." I wiped the silent flow of tears.

He kissed me. "I promise never to leave you like that again." His words were gentle despite the conviction in his voice.

"No, Brian. Don't promise me you won't leave again because it's not fair. If another opportunity like this comes up, you take it." I poked him in the chest with my fingernail.

"Ow." He rubbed the red spot.

I sat up to look him directly in the eye and wiped my face. "Promise me, Brian. Don't give up on something you've been working for since before we met. Don't give up your dream because of me."

Brian's eyes widened. "Ebony, I don't want —"

"I don't want you to jeopardize your career. You'd end up hating me in the end."

He pulled me back to his chest. "There's no way I'd hate you. How about a compromise? We'll talk it over first. I didn't do it this time, and the guilt nearly killed me. In the end, the decision will be mine." A finger ran down my cheek. "You're part of my life. What I do affects you, too. Just like your decisions affect me. If your job needs you to go away, believe me, baby, I will support you."

I swallowed hard. He had no idea how much his statement rang true. My secret would go with me to the grave; no way would I let my mistake ruin his life. Besides, I'd handled it this long.

"That's fair," I conceded, my throat dry.

He smiled and kissed me again.

I would never get enough of his kisses or listening to

the rhythm of his heart.

"Tell me about it, Brian." I shifted off him and snuggled in his arms. During his time away, he'd told me numerous stories about his experiences, both good and bad. Right now, hearing his voice soothed me.

My head bounced as his chest moved when he laughed. "Didn't you hear enough of those stories?"

"Yeah, but tell me again."

Brian lowered his head and looked at me skeptically. "If it will make you happy ..."

I was beyond happy. We were together again, and I was in his arms in a room that smelled like ... roses.

For the first time, I noticed my surroundings. Roses, dozens of them — red, pink, and yellow — lined the dresser, the nightstand, and the table. Even the bed had red and yellow rose petals scattered across the sheets.

We'd made love on a bed of roses.

The room was a pale shade of burgundy accented with antique furniture, a deep mahogany, and fit the room perfectly. The headboard of the king-sized bed nearly reached the ceiling.

On the nightstand, sat a metal bucket filled with ice and an unopened bottle of what appeared to be champagne. Next to it sat a box of my favorite chocolate.

Even though the sun still glowed outside, the shades were drawn, and candles burned brightly around the room. The lights led a pathway to the bathroom where more candles illuminated the giant bathtub.

My heart swelled. "Oh, Brian ..."

He stopped talking. "What's wrong? You're crying again." He knuckled away my tears.

"It's beautiful, the room. I didn't notice it before."

"Well, you were crying then, too. I know it's too

soon, but this is the honeymoon suite." Worry displayed in his eyes again. "Are you sure you're okay?"

I stared deep into his eyes. So many emotions ran through me. Happiness, fear, joy, and sadness. "Yes, I'm okay."

I prayed I would never have to lie to him again.

CHAPTER 27

Brian

W hy did Ebony's *"I'm okay"* sound like a lie?
From the moment Ebony had arrived,
she'd been crying. I suspected something
was wrong for months. But what?

Ebony never gave me the impression of being needy
or clingy. She was strong and independent with a good
head on her shoulders. Why the sudden change?

It still irritated me that she had refused my help before I left. Some of the women in my past would have
jumped at the opportunity. I didn't get it. Why would
she think my helping her would be an inconvenience?
Didn't she know how much I loved her? How much
I wanted to take care of her? I'd made my intentions
clear.

We'd been together for nearly five months. We'd just
scratched the surface of each other's lives. A typical

relationship would mean we would know more about each other than we did right now. But our relationship wasn't typical.

While I was away, a part of me worried she would one day refuse my calls. Nothing, not even how good the sex was, required her to wait for me.

I risked everything we'd built when I accepted the job. I never asked how she felt about leaving her behind. I assumed everything would work out, because it's what I wanted.

The opportunity of a lifetime.

But love, true love, only happened once.

Did my decision to leave cause the change?

What I felt was real, and she seemed to feel the same way. We'd talked every day I was gone. I'd faithfully deposited money in her account every week, even when she said she didn't need it.

I looked over at the love of my life as she slept. Ebony had no idea how beautiful she was. This was the image I took to bed with me every night while away. This is what I thought of when woman followed me around at the after-parties or hung around backstage offering sex in order to get closer to the artist we played for.

Two weeks into the tour, I stopped counting how many women sneaked into my bedroom with offers I ordinarily wouldn't have refused. Nobody could take Ebony's place. Losing her because of some stupid one-night stand would not be worth it.

Now that we were together again, why the hell was I paranoid?

For the last couple of months, I'd asked what bothered her. It always seemed to be work, school, or that damn orangutan. I wasn't buying it. If she'd had a problem with me leaving and told me, we could deal with it in the open. Holding it in only built pent-up anger.

Now that I was home, there was no way for her to avoid telling me how she really felt. I'd learned to read her body language during our first few dates. There would be no way for her to continue to hide from me.

I was ready and willing to work through any problem she threw at me. All she needed to do was tell me the truth. We had two days to spend in our own world, thanks to Yasmine. There would be plenty of time to catch up. When we returned home, I would know the truth.

Ebony shifted in the bed, deep in sleep. During the course of the evening, she'd fallen into a deep slumber as I'd never seen. For the longest time, she'd held me as if she was afraid I'd leave and never return.

I replaced my body with the pillow my head had been resting on and went to the bathroom. She looked peaceful when I returned. I pulled on a pair of jeans and walked down the hall to retrieve more ice to keep the champagne chilled.

When I returned, she hadn't moved an inch. Her naked body lay exposed for my viewing pleasure. I stepped back to appreciate every curvy inch. Her caramel skin was as soft and smooth as I'd remembered, though she'd seemed a little slimmer. The sexy fragrance she wore mixed with her own natural scent, called to my primal urge to claim her. Not just as my lover, but as my woman, my wife.

But Ebony was not mine to own. She gave herself willingly; I appreciated that more than I could ever explain.

I loved her mind and spirit the most. Ebony's desire to work hard to achieve her goals was a quality to admire. Her selfless support was a trait not easily found in goal-oriented women.

No woman from my past would ever compare. I honestly didn't think another one ever could.

Almond-shaped brown eyes peered up from the pillow she clung to. *"Mmm ... I didn't mean to sleep."* She yawned and rolled over on her back. Her chocolate-covered nipples had my mouth watering. Damn she was distracting.

"You look tired." I slipped out of my jeans and back into bed, bringing the sheet up to cover our bodies.

She maneuvered herself into my arms again. Her arm wrapped around my waist possessively.

Unable to resist, I ran my hand down her arm, across smooth, soft skin.

"It's been a busy week. School, work, and watching Nala. Nothing I can't handle."

I studied her eyes; she looked away.

Then it hit me. I was an ass. Three months had gone by since the last time we'd been together.

How could I have forgotten? Being on the road, moving from city to city, practicing, and playing day after day ... The only time I thought about that night had been to distract me from temptation knocking on my door.

"Ebony, what's on your mind?" I angled my head to watch her.

A flicker of fear passed in her eyes. "What do you mean?" She shifted slightly, pulling the sheet tighter across her chest.

I tried to remember the moment she'd taken off her clothes. My focus had been getting inside her; I didn't pay attention to her stomach. Had it been flat? Had it changed to a slightly rounder form?

She'd been on top when we'd made love; I didn't explore her body the way I wanted to. Ebony kept me lying on the bed unable to give her what I know she liked.

Was it possible I would hurt the baby?

"Are you pregnant?" I took a deep breath and waited for her reply.

Her eyes widened. "What?" She sat up.

I did the same. "Did you find out? If you're pregnant just tell me. We can work through it."

"I'm not pregnant, Brian. I've been having my period."

"Are you sure? I've heard my sisters say they still had a period at least a month before realizing—"

"I took a test last week." Her grip on the sheet loosened as the corners of her mouth tilted. "Wait a minute. You paid attention to your sisters' talk about being pregnant?" She laughed, a genuine sound that eased the moment of tension. "My brother practically ran away the moment Shana or I mentioned the words bra, tampons, pads, or periods."

"Hey, I was the only boy in a house with four older sisters. There was nowhere to go." I returned her smile. "Besides, I figured the information would come in handy one day."

Ebony continued to laugh as she slid out of bed.

"Where are you going?"

"To take a closer look at this enormous tub in the bathroom. I wonder if it can fit two?" She threw an alluring glance over her shoulder.

I watched her perfect body's seductive glide into the candle-lit bathroom. Wicked thoughts came to mind as she leaned over the tub and ran water.

Unable to resist an open invitation to try something new, I grabbed the ice bucket, champagne, glasses, the chocolate, and the box of condoms. I didn't plan to leave the tub until the water turned to ice or our bodies shriveled beyond recognition.

Tonight we would catch up on everything physical. After that, I'd find out what was really bothering her.

CHAPTER 28

Brian

My bedroom had never looked so inviting.

After three months of sleeping in the cramped quarters of the tour bus with six grown men and crashing in hotels, this was paradise. Well, not exactly, because my *Eve* wasn't here.

Ebony and I made the most of our weekend. The establishment run by Yasmine's family had been the perfect place to reconnect.

Once she'd stopped crying.

We spent most of our time in that room. Oddly enough, we were in the Honeymoon Suite, the perfect backdrop for my future intentions. We lived off room service, wearing nothing until our last evening. We'd walked hand-in-hand in the rose garden outside of our room. Ebony posed for some beautiful pictures I took with my cell phone. By the end of our stay, her smile and the glow in her eyes had returned.

But that was on the surface. I still hadn't discovered what problem dwelled beneath the smiles she forced for my benefit. When she didn't know I was looking, strained emotions took over her flawless face, as if she were in actual pain.

All of my attempts to ask had failed. Ebony knew exactly how to redirect my intentions with a flash of skin. After three months without her, it didn't take much to lose my desire of intelligent conversation.

Now it was time to jump back into the real world.

First things first, open up the window and let in some fresh air. The room smelled like a closed-up tomb. No doubt, the door had remained closed the entire time I was gone. Everything was just as I left it. Including the clothes hamper, which held what I'd worn the last time I was here. They needed washed just like the clothes in my suitcase.

Maybe my mom would be so happy to see me that she would do my laundry. I chuckled. Yeah right. My mother stopped washing my clothes when I was in college. She'd found a thong as she pulled clothes out of the drier. It wasn't mine, of course, but she'd decided quickly she had no interest in what I did outside of her house.

I emptied my clothes from my suitcase into the basket. I could wash clothes when I visited my mom. My family knew I'd returned and respected the fact I needed to spend time with Ebony first. Her red thong fell out of the bag and onto the floor. I smiled and stuffed it into its new home in my nightstand. She wasn't getting them back.

Which reminded me, the sheets needed washing. I

stuffed those in a bag too. I planned to have her over as soon as possible and didn't want her lying on sheets that had been on the bed for months.

Everything needed to be perfect. I intended to get to the bottom of things the next time we were together. By the end of our first night at the hotel, I'd realized expecting a straight answer about what was on her mind was foolish. Reconnection on a primal level was the one thing both of us needed. We held conversations over the phone for months. We were aware of what was going on in each other's lives. There was nothing else to catch up on except the basic human need of physical contact. Long, lustful, erotic-as-hell sinful contact. We'd got that one down in record time.

My stomach growled, reminding me of another basic need: food. I scavenged the fridge and came up with a bottle of beer. Javan always kept beer, but the pickings for something edible were slim. I was the one who kept the refrigerator full. He tended to eat out or pick something up on his way home. I glanced at my watch. Javan wouldn't be off work for another five hours. I made note to grab some wings and fries from the Hot Wing Café on the way back from my parents'. We'd catch up over dinner.

In the living room, I walked over to my CD collection in search of music to listen to in the truck.

Strange, the disks were out of order. I kept my CDs in alphabetical order by genre.

Ebony. She probably grabbed a few disks when she'd come for her ID. It was the only explanation that made sense. Javan never touched my music.

After thirty minutes of reorganization, two disks were missing. I decided to worry about it later.

My cell phone chimed, alerting me to an incoming message. Peter confirmed our scheduled meeting for this evening. After replying, I grabbed my clothesbasket and headed for my truck.

My cousins had done a good job of running the business. I felt like a proud papa. They'd rarely called to ask questions, and my customers continued to be satisfied. They didn't know I kept tabs.

I checked my business account weekly. Peter made sure deposits were made on time and in full amounts. They'd done such a good job I planned to let them run the business for a while longer.

After returning to L.A., B and D Records offered a paying studio job. Accepting the offer had been a no-brainer. The only problem was it hindered my ability to run my business effectively. I needed to clear my schedule as much as possible. I could be called in at any time during the day or night. My routines would revolve around whatever artist they assigned me to work with. I couldn't afford to be in the middle of cutting grass, hot and sweaty when I got the call. I had to be sure I had time to shower and change before reporting to the studio.

My cousins, on the other hand, could manage the business around their school schedule. I would let them keep the lawn tools and customer base. Thanks to their father, Dylan had inherited an old work truck. It was perfect for a teen with no wheels; plus they could use it to get from job to job.

If they accepted my offer, I would officially have two full-time employees.

***

A few hours later, I returned from my parents' house with a hamper of freshly washed clothes and nearly half of my father's apple pie. My mother swore Dad would be okay with sharing. Apparently, I was the only one who snagged pieces, which meant his waistline expanded while I was away. He hadn't made it home before I left to confirm, so I'd taken her word for it.

Visiting my mother yielded two things: a dinner invite for Ebony and me on Sunday and the knowledge my mother had spoken to Ebony nearly once a week while I was away.

Ebony never mentioned it. I wondered why?

Javan's car was in the driveway when I returned home.

He wasn't in the living room when I walked in carrying dinner and a fresh six-pack of beer. "Yo, Javan, where are you?" I set the meal down on the kitchen counter and roamed the house.

He wasn't in his bedroom either, which meant one thing.

I walked into the weight room, formally known as the garage and storage space. "Hey, man."

Javan was on the bench, lifting weights as I walked in. He sat up, shirtless, with sweat pouring down his forehead and chest, his breath ragged.

He nodded in my direction but didn't get up. "What's up?" He appeared to have benched 175 pounds.

I'd done my fair share of weightlifting, but intense workouts were never my favorite thing to do. When we were roommates in college, the testosterone of being eighteen flooded our bodies and drove us to compete regularly. Weights, running, sit ups, women. You name it ... we'd probably competed in it. We both experienced our fair share of losses and wins.

Eventually, I found other means to satisfy my need to show off. Joining the band and surfing became my outlets. My business took up the rest of my time. Unlike Javan, my father didn't send me checks every month to support me.

His father was a well-known psychologist in Atlanta, Georgia. Once Javan graduated, his father gave him a Dodge Charger and pulled strings for him to get a job at a local practice.

Javan was used to getting what he wanted. The words, *no* and *hard work* were obscene in his vocabulary. To this day I couldn't understand why we remained friends after college.

He wasn't a bad guy. Yeah, he could be selfish, arrogant, egotistical and, at times, a straight pain in the ass. But when I needed him, he'd been there.

"You haven't missed a day lifting weights."

Javan flexed. "Gotta give the ladies what they want." He eyed his biceps longer than necessary.

"Ladies? I heard you were down to one now." I walked over to spot him when he leaned back and gripped the barbell again.

"Yeah, well ... we've gotten ... kind of serious ... since you've ... been gone ..." He paused to catch his breath. "A lot has changed."

"You can say that again," I muttered.

He did another set of presses, sat up, grabbed a towel, and wiped his face. "So, did you guys hook back up?"

"Oh, yeah." I grinned at the memory. "I didn't know I would miss her so much."

He laughed. "Yeah, a good piece of ass is hard to forget."

"Ebony is not a piece of ass, but you're right; she's hard to forget. If everything keeps going this good, I'm going to marry her."

"Marry her? You're seriously thinking of marrying a black woman? Have you met her family yet?"

I hooked my thumbs in the front pockets of my jeans. "No. I plan to spend the next couple of months getting to know everything about her, including her family. In December, I'll take her home and meet them." At least that was my plan. Ebony didn't know a thing about it.

Javan snickered. "I'd love to be a fly on that wall."

"I'm not worried. If … when I marry her, it will be Ebony who's my wife, not her family. If they won't support us, mine will."

He grabbed a bottle of water, gulped, and watched me. "Have you wondered why she's still with you? I mean, could dating you be an experiment? You know what I'm saying? What if you got all wrapped up and found out she really wants to go back to black?" His chest puffed out. "What if she used you as a means to stay busy while waiting for her dream man? I'm sure her parents will have a lot to say about who she marries." He gathered his towel and strolled back into the house. When he reached the door, he paused. "You might want to see if she cheated while you were gone."

"What?" I stared at him.

"Think about it. You guys hadn't been together long. Then you leave her alone." He shrugged. "It wouldn't take much for a brother to," he sucked his teeth and smirked, "pick her up and take care of where you left off. Yasmine mentioned she'd been acting weird lately.

But don't pay me any attention, what do I know?" He laughed as he walked off.

I stood rooted to the floor and watched as he disappeared through the door.

My chest felt tight. Ebony cheating on me was the last thing I was worried about. She didn't waste time telling me if she didn't want something. She'd made that clear the night we'd met.

She hadn't shown any signs of wanting out of our relationship. Did I miss something? Could that be the reason why she'd changed? Was there someone else waiting in the wings for her to push me away?

Maybe spending time at the hotel had been too much. Maybe her intention had been to break up with me, face-to-face, but I messed up the plan by surprising her with a romantic weekend.

Damn. I didn't know what to think.

We needed to talk. We were in my bed the first time we made love. It was there we'd promised to be together when I returned. Maybe when I got her there again, in my arms and in my bed, she'd be ready to tell me what was really going on.

CHAPTER 29

Ebony

"Ebony, hello? Are you in there?"

The tap on my shoulder and waving hand in my face nearly caused me to jump out of my skin.

"Are you okay? You seem distracted." Laura, another zoo intern, stood staring at me.

I blinked rapidly while shaking my head and focused on the sleeping infant in my arms.

Nala hadn't gotten any better over the weekend. Instead, her condition had worsened. Watching her energetic spark burn out, depressed me. Her eyes were sallow and her weight continued to decrease. I'd spent the past three months wrapping my life around caring for her. It felt like her demise warned of the failure of my own future.

Nala had been born the week I meet Brian. As she

grew, so did our relationship. Her illness had started after Brian left, after my rape. Since his return, she continued to get worse.

Right after I'd looked him in the face and lied.

It seemed as though no matter what I did, the lie compounded. Any effort to rectify it would expose my secret.

"I'm okay, just tired," I said. "Brian came back in town, and we spent the weekend together." Which made no sense. It was Wednesday, not Monday. It didn't stop busybody Laura from getting a kick out of it, though.

"You're still worn out? Way to go, Ebony!" Her laughter filled the room as she pulled supplies out of a cabinet.

If it were only that simple.

The most rest I'd gotten in months came from sleeping in Brian's arms. But that had changed the moment I opened my mouth.

Continuing my claim of being *okay* didn't seem big at the time. But I never expected him to ask about pregnancy.

After our one-night *oops*, neither of us had spoken of the situation again. Brian's hectic road schedule kept his mind on music. I struggled to forget the rape and the chance of catching an STD. Keeping my secret was more important to me than mentioning the results of a pregnancy test.

The possibility of carrying Javan's child had scared me more than having Brian's baby. The guilt I'd had after taking the morning-after pill and knowing I could have killed the baby of the man I loved would never leave.

Brian assumed something was wrong and had tried to question me. Trying to keep his mind diverted had worn me out physically. Not that I was complaining. Being able to make love repeatedly chased away some of the demons that plagued me.

But I was still a liar. I'd stolen something from him and needed to give him an explanation.

How could I explain it? *Brian, to be sure you didn't get me pregnant, I took measures to kill our baby.*

That would be the biggest lie of all. Whether I was pregnant or not, intentionally killing our baby never would have happened. *"A child made from love,"* Brian had said when he placed his hand lovingly on my belly.

A wave of nausea hit me as I imagined saying, *I got raped. There's a chance I could have gotten pregnant. To be safe, I took a pill to get rid of anything growing inside me. Oops.*

The truth would be just as bad as the lie.

The implications of my decision made my head spin.

When it was time for my break, I handed the sleeping orangutan to another volunteer before heading for the breakroom. I found an empty table and spread out my notes for school.

I had a lot to catch up. Since the rape, my grades had slipped. Keeping my mind focused on my responsibilities had gotten harder. Three months of not sleeping in order to avoid nightmares had left me exhausted.

The one bright spot in my life — besides Brian's return — had been finding an animal clinic that allowed me to work and earn credits needed for graduation. Unfortunately, it wasn't a paying job. Brian's continued donations to my bank account were the only things making it easier to breathe. Damn, I hated taking his money. No matter how many times I'd told him not to put any more in the account, the more it seemed to show up in larger amounts. Honestly, I didn't know what I would have done without him.

I owed him so much, yet I'd held back from him.

My conscience was eating me alive.

Guilt plagued me when my cell phone rang.

"Hey, baby, are you busy?"

I closed my eyes and focused on Brian's voice. Despite my guilt, his voice continued to soothe me.

"Taking a break, what are you doing?" I closed the notebook and gave him my full attention.

"I'm leaving practice at the studio. I was on my way home and started thinking of you. The days have been flying by. Even though you're not far away, it seems as if it's just as hard to be with you."

"Yeah, I know. I should have a few days off later this week."

"I hope one of them is Sunday. My mom invited us for dinner."

"I'm off then. Visiting your parents would be fun."

"Good. By the way, why didn't you tell me you'd been talking to my mom?"

"Oops, busted." I laughed lightly.

"You can say that again. Why didn't you tell me?"

"I didn't want you to think of me as the clingy girlfriend. I called her one day to say hello. And I don't know, talking to your mom felt as though I was near you."

I hadn't told her what happened, but hearing the voice of wisdom from an older woman after my attack had reassured me. I could have talked to my mother, but she would have known something was up within five minutes of calling. Mrs. Young didn't know me, so there was nothing to fear.

Brian was quiet on the phone.

"I'm sorry if I crossed a line by not telling you."

"No, that's fine. It just surprised me she was the one who told me."

Lie by omission. Thank God I wasn't Pinocchio.

"Well, your mom enjoyed sharing childhood stories." I needed to get his mind off asking more questions. The demeanor coming through the phone felt as if he was going there again.

Brian groaned. "I don't like where this is headed."

I forced out a laugh. "My favorite was when your father jumped on the phone and told me you were a junior."

Another groan.

"You never told me your full name was Winfred Brian Young the Third." This time my laugh was real.

"Your response is the reason why I choose not to tell people." He tried to sound upset, but a chuckle slipped out.

"So you were never going to tell me? When was I going to find out my lover was really named Winfred? When we got to the altar?"

Brian's laugh faltered slightly. "I don't know. Maybe I planned on taking my secret to the grave."

I cringed. That was an odd thing for him to say. Did he know what secret I held?

"So, no calling you Winfred?" I kept my voice light.

"No. The only Winfred is my dad."

"*Hmm*, okay, so Winky is out, too?" I waited for his response.

His father, Winfred the Second, had me rolling on the floor in tears as he shared the story of Brian's childhood nickname. After years of having girl after girl, Mr. Young grew resigned to not having a son. Then one day, Brian slipped in. Mr. Young, ecstatic at no longer being the only penis in the house, nicknamed him Winky because his penis wasn't the same size as his. The nickname stuck until Brian got old enough to understand what it meant. He threatened to run away from home if they called him that again.

Seconds passed without a response. Maybe now had not been the time for jokes.

"Just for the record, you outgrew the Winky nickname a long, long time ago." I lowered my voice to sound sultry without drawing attention from my coworkers.

He chuckled. "Care to prove it tonight? You've damaged my ego. It could use some stroking."

I closed my eyes. The tense sound in his voice seemed to dissipate. I would love to spend time with him again. I needed to figure out how to answer whatever questions he had without digging a bigger hole for myself.

"What do you have in mind?"

"My place, tonight. Pack a bag and spend the night with me."

For once, I was glad we were on the phone. It would be impossible to hide the horror in my eyes. I could not go back to his house.

Javan would be there.

My heart raced, my lips went dry, and my entire body shook. I'd managed to avoid him for the past three months. Especially when he came to pick up Yasmine.

269

Brian's presence would never ease my fear.

I steeled my voice in an effort to sound as normal as possible. "I can't. I have a paper due Friday. If I come over tonight, it'll never get done." *Liar, liar, pants on fire.* Dammit.

"You had my hopes up. My ego will never recover."

"I'll make it up to you. Why don't you come over Friday night? I'll be worth the wait."

"You're always worth the wait." His voice lowered, taking on a thoughtful tone. "I guess I can suffer through a few more days." He paused. "We need to talk, Ebony. Please be free on Friday. Whatever it takes, I'll be there. Okay?"

My internal alarm went off. *We need to talk.* Those words never led to a happy ending.

"Is everything okay?" I blurted.

"Yeah. I realized something the other day, and it's my fault. We'll talk about it Friday."

"Okay, my place as soon as you're free."

"Your place." The line went quiet for a moment. "I love you, Ebony." His words seemed to leave a lot of something unspoken.

I swallowed hard. "I love you, too."

CHAPTER 30

Brian

I waited patiently in the living room of Ebony's house for her to come downstairs. As excited as I was to be with her again, I dreaded the conversation we needed to have. How did I approach it? What did I say?

I'd been musing over the thoughts for the past few days and still hadn't come up with an answer.

She looked as beautiful as always in a brown dress, which complimented her complexion and eyes. We kissed when she reached the bottom of the stairs. But in the truck, we rode in silence.

Ebony's gaze focused out the window, taking in the scenery as we drove.

It was Sunday evening, and we were driving to my parents' house for dinner. I was glad to be with her again. I'd canceled our plans for Friday night due to a last-minute late-night recording session. It pissed me off when we waited for nearly three hours for the artist to show up. We worked well into the wee hours of the morning before quitting. On Saturday, I slept most of the day.

Now it was Sunday, and we both were on edge.

Over the last few days, I'd pushed what Javan said aside. Why should I believe him? Ebony couldn't have made love to me the way she did if she wanted to be with another man. She couldn't fake what I'd seen in her eyes or her whispered words.

I couldn't ignore the changes, but I was sure it didn't involve another man. It couldn't.

The only valuable advice Javan gave me regarded dealing with her family. The last conversation we had about family dealt with her sharing her brother's and sister's opinions about us. We still hadn't talked about her parents. In the end, their influence would affect our future, good or bad.

Since we were on the way to visit my family, there was no time like the present to bring it up again.

I reached for her hand. It felt soft in mine.

"Can we talk?" I focused on her eyes as mine left the road.

The nervousness came back.

Although she smiled with her lips, it hadn't reached her eyes. She squeezed my hand. "What's on your mind?"

I turned back to the road. "Family. I'm glad you get along with mine. It means a lot to me."

"You were right, Brian. They are wonderful people."

"I wouldn't have it any other way. That's what I want to talk about. Have you talked to your parents yet?" I risked looking at her again. She seemed surprised.

"When we started dating, you were adamant about their opinions. You told me how your brother and sister felt. What about your parents?"

She turned her attention back to the road. "My parents ... they don't know."

I inhaled sharply, forcing myself to think before I spoke again. I glanced over at her profile. "You haven't told them?"

"No." Her attention stayed on the road.

"Why? If your siblings know, why keep your mom and dad in the dark? Are you ashamed of me?"

"No, Brian, why would I be ashamed of you?" This time she did look at me. "I'm not ready to hear their opinion, that's all. My parents aren't as understanding as yours."

I clamped my jaw shut to keep from shouting the thoughts in my mind. I didn't care whether they accepted me or not, I just wanted her to acknowledge our relationship to her family, the same way I'd told mine.

"Would your parents be opinionated about someone you're in love with?"

"I don't know. And honestly, I don't want to know. I like the way things are between us. It's you and me. I don't care what my family thinks. The only reason Tre and Shana know is because she talked it out of me."

I faced her when we reached a red light. "You mean you wouldn't have told them?" Something in the pit of my stomach dropped.

"I honestly don't know. What I do know is when she asked, I didn't hold back. I'm not ashamed of you or this relationship. I would rather not invite unnecessary issues into it." She faced me. "I'm sure you don't understand my reasoning. Do I plan to tell them? Yes, in my own time, when they'll be more understanding. Telling them I'm dating a white man when every time I talk to them they're telling me about an available black man ... it's not how I want to tell them about you. I don't want them to think I'm with you because of what they say. When they meet you, they need to have fresh eyes. I want them to accept you and appreciate how happy you've made me. I don't want them biased."

The light turned green, and I pushed on the gas. She had a valid argument.

"What if that day never comes? Do you think they'd stop pushing guys at you if you let them know you were in a relationship?"

"I don't know." A flicker of uncertainty passed over her face.

I pulled her hand to my mouth and kissed it. "Don't wait for our wedding day to tell them, okay?"

"I'd never do that. I want my father to walk me down the aisle and give me to you with his full approval."

"I do, too. But this is about us, not them. You're the one I want to marry."

She glanced over at me, a slight smile on her face. "You still want to marry me?"

"Always," I said with as much conviction as I could muster.

Our fingers intertwined. She hadn't answered all of my questions, but it would be enough for now. Everything from now on would be about actions. Ebony was with me because it's what she wanted. Dredging up anything else would be asking for trouble.

"I've never been more serious about a woman in my life." The words popped out of my mouth. "I want to make you happy."

Ebony unstrapped her seatbelt and leaned across the middle console.

"What are you doing—"

She planted a big kiss on my mouth and slid back to her side of the car. "You have no idea how happy you make me."

This time, I could see she meant what she said. It was in her eyes. The knot in my stomach unraveled.

"I'm glad there was no oncoming traffic." I licked the flavored lip-gloss she'd left behind.

"I checked first." Our fingers locked together again.

Our conversation had only scratched the surface, but it would be enough to keep our relationship moving toward our goal. For now.

***

Cars jammed my parents' driveway and the curb when we arrived.

"Whoa, what's going on here?" I looked over at Ebony. "Do you know?"

She appeared surprised too. "Not a clue."

We held hands as we walked to the door. Before I could ring the bell, Bridget pulled the door open and flung her arms around me.

"Baby brother!"

Ebony laughed as our fingers slipped apart from the force of the hug.

"Ow." Man, love hurt.

"He's here!" she yelled over her shoulder before turning back to face us. "Ebony, it's good to see you." Bridget hugged her as well. "Come on guys, everyone's out back."

Bridget's enthusiasm was infectious as she tugged

us through the house to the patio. When we entered, everyone cheered.

I glanced around the backyard before Bridgette pushed me to the receiving line. A WELCOME HOME banner hung on the newly built gazebo. My father had fired up the grill again, and the family had added folding tables to the yard. All the trimmings for a Young family barbeque were in place, along with coolers filled with ice and drinks.

Hug after hug came from family and friends as I walked down the line of waiting arms. Everyone seemed to be there: aunts, uncles, grandparents, nieces, nephews, and my sisters.

My mother and father waited at the end of the receiving line. I'd just finished hugging my mom and shaking my father's hand when a voice I hadn't heard in two years floated over his shoulder. "I knew you'd do it one day."

My cousin Brad emerged from the crowd.

"No shit!" I laughed.

"Brian!" My mother swatted my shoulder.

We grabbed each other in a bear hug. "What are you doing here?" I punched him in the shoulder as we stepped back and appraised each other.

Brad had gained weight since I'd seen him. We were thick as thieves as kids. He was two years older than I was and had dark hair and blue eyes, and yet girls often thought we were brothers. He'd gotten a good job offer and moved to Florida two years ago. The man was a graphic designer wiz.

"Aunt Laura told me you would be home this week. I came out to visit my mom. Imagine my surprise when I found out you'd been traveling doing concerts. That's awesome, man." It was my turn to take a punch.

"Thanks. It looks as though life's been good for you." I reached over and poked his midsection.

"It definitely has." His chest poked out in pride.

"We've got a lot of catching up to do."

"Tell me about it. Let me start by introducing you to my wife." Brad held out his hand and a dark-colored hand connected with his.

I followed the arm to a green-eyed beauty with long curly hair. Brad had married a black woman. It was hard to keep my mouth from dropping open. We always had similar taste in women.

"Brian, this is Tierra."

I shut my mouth and grinned. "It's nice to meet you." I gestured Ebony over. "Baby, this is my crazy cousin Brad and his wife, Tierra. Guys, this is my girlfriend, Ebony."

We stared at one other before sharing a laugh.

"It's nice to finally meet you." Tierra gave me a hug. "Brad has told me so many stories." She repeated the gesture to Ebony. "It's nice to meet you, too."

"You have to share those stories," Ebony said, her smile wide. Obvious surprise was all over her face.

"Let's exchange numbers," Tierra suggested.

Brad and I stood side-by-side and watched our ladies walk off. It didn't take a rocket scientist to know what they had in common or what they'd want to talk about: interracial dating and marriage. I had plenty of questions for Brad.

Before the night had ended, we were definitely making plans to double date while they were in town.

CHAPTER 31

Brian

"Yasmine is going to hate us," I said.

"Yeah, but we've been out with them before. Your cousin is only in town for a few more days," Ebony murmured against my mouth and slipped her lips over mine. Her fingers caressed the nape of my neck.

Instead of replying, I kissed her back. We were standing in the doorway of my house. Our scheduled dinner date with Brad and Tierra was only minutes away from where I lived.

My hands were on her hips, my fingers slowly inched up the hem of her dress. "They'd understand if we were a few minutes late."

The logistics of making love against the wall in the foyer wouldn't be hard. I had a condom in my pocket, and Ebony's clothing allowed easy access ...

"No, we should go."

I didn't miss the change of inflection in her voice. I pulled back and watched her regard the hallway behind me. "You'd rather wait until later? Even better, then I can get you completely naked." I shut the door behind me and followed her down the driveway.

Her laugh sounded forced.

"Why don't you drive?" She handed me the keys to her car.

"Is there something wrong with my truck?" I cocked an eyebrow.

"No, we always drive your truck. We can look a little classier this time." She joked, but her heart wasn't in it.

I palmed her keys, walked to the Nissan Maxima, and opened the door for her. We had all night to discuss whatever issues bothered her at my place after dinner.

Brad and Tierra were waiting when we arrived at the Mexican restaurant. The women exchanged hugs while Brad and I shook hands. We sat at the bar, ordered a round of drinks, and waited until a table became available. Ebony and Tierra sat on the only available stools at a small round table while we stood behind them in the crowded space. I contemplated sitting on the stool with Ebony in my lap after repeatedly being bumped into by the servers that rushed by.

Appraising our surroundings, it didn't take long to notice the amount of attention we were getting from the restaurant patrons. People always watched us. I usually paid it no attention, not giving a damn about anyone's opinions. But after Javan's remarks, it was hard not to notice the narrow-minded people around us. What they thought wasn't my concern. I only cared about Ebony's well-being. She fidgeted in front of me.

Apparently the sight of two white men with two beautiful black women was more than most people could handle.

It impressed me that Brad and Tierra were snuggled together ignoring the stares.

That's how I wanted our relationship to be. No matter where we were, it would be about us. My gaze fell upon a table of black men, their eyes riveted on Brad and me. I stepped closer to Ebony, put my arm around her waist, and held her possessively, daring anyone to come over and say something about it.

"How do you guys do it?" Ebony asked.

Tierra responded first. "How do we ignore the stares?"

Ebony nodded.

"By entertaining them." She signaled Brad with a finger. He laughed and leaned down for a kiss.

The kiss wasn't graphic or X-rated, just not rushed. A glance at the men who'd been watching, revealed brazen disgust plastered on their faces as they went back to their drinks.

Brad smiled down at his wife. I could feel the love radiating from them as he ran a finger over her cheek. "I love you."

"I love you more," Tierra replied, gazing back at him. It was as if no one, including Ebony and I, existed. "Do you guys kiss in public?" Her attention turned back to us.

Ebony laughed nervously. "Well, our first kiss was in public. We hold hands all the time but don't kiss very often... in places like this."

"If I kiss her, we're liable to be arrested for indecent exposure."

"Brian." Ebony swatted my arm.

"I'm serious. Every time I kiss you, I want to get you naked, not arrested."

Brad chuckled. "How long have you been together?"

"Five months," Ebony answered. "How about you guys?"

"A year and a half. We've been married for two months," Tierra replied.

Realization dawned on me. "No wonder I didn't get an invite to the wedding. I'd been out of town."

Brad shook his head. "We didn't do the big wedding thing. We kept it simple."

"What he means is, we got married in Vegas," Tierra corrected.

"It wasn't what we'd planned." Brad sipped his beer. "It wasn't spontaneous either. We were already engaged."

"Then, why Vegas?" Ebony sat in rapt attention.

Tierra sighed. "Because of my family." She shot Ebony a knowing glance. "When my parents heard about Brad, about his job, and how well he treated me, they couldn't wait to meet him. But then they found out he wasn't black ..." Her voice faltered.

Brad rubbed her shoulders. "I couldn't win them over. They cut her off from family gatherings ..." He shook his head in disgust.

"They call us if it's an emergency or to find out if I'm still with the *white boy*." She huffed. "It pisses me off that my family is so narrow-mined."

"It hurt to watch her deal with that kind of rejection; she comes from such a close-knit family. I tried to break things off, but she wouldn't let me. Instead, she asked me to marry her."

Tierra laughed and wiped the corner of her eyes. "I surprised the hell out of him."

"You can say that again. Here I am breaking up with her and she says, *marry me*. I realized it should have been me asking the question instead of trying to let her go."

"That's amazing." Ebony's eyes were wide with awe. "How did you guys end up in Vegas?"

"My company sent me on a business trip. A few days later, Tierra showed up to surprise me. We decided to avoid the wedding planning and family drama and got married there."

"We were marrying each other, not our families. No one needed to be there except us," Tierra added.

Brad turned his gaze on me. "Is her family giving you any problems?"

"My brother and sister are the only ones who know. I haven't told my parents," Ebony spoke up.

"Why not?" Tierra spoke directly to her.

"Timing. Right now they're trying to hook me up with sons of their friends. Their minds are set on the type of man they think I should marry. I don't want to just blurt out I'm dating Brian right after they tell me about yet another eligible black bachelor."

Tierra reached across the table and patted Ebony's hand. "Look, sweetie, I hate to tell you this, but their opinion of Brian isn't going to change based on when you tell them. It's not going to change how they feel. What you need is to be prepared to deal with it."

"I know, it's just —"

"Do you love him?"

"With all my heart," Ebony said.

Hearing her say it aloud to someone else touched me

to the depth of my soul.

"Then don't waste time telling your family. Either they'll accept the man you love or they won't. In the end, it's about the person you want to be with. Brad and Brian come from a supportive family. You'll never have to worry about being alone. And you'll have me, too." She smiled.

Ebony nodded, her hand rested on top of mine as I held her. Everyone sat silent for a moment.

"What does your family say now?" Ebony broke the silence.

Tierra and Brad gazed at each other and shared a secret smile. His hand slid down to her belly. "They're taking it in stride. They have to if they want to get to know their first grandchild." Tierra glowed.

"Hold up, you guys are having a baby?" My eyes widened in surprise.

"Yeah, can you believe it?" Brad followed his grin with a healthy swig of beer. I watched his cheeks redden; he appeared nervous about fatherhood. "Don't tell anyone yet. We wanted to make an announcement last night, but my mom couldn't make it. We're going to tell her tomorrow when we meet for lunch."

I walked around the table and gave Brad a one-armed man-hug, then patted him on the back. "Congratulations, both of you."

"Congratulations," Ebony echoed and leaned across the table to hug Tierra, her eyes glistening.

Believing her tears were just a girl thing was out of the question. Her tears solidified my desire to get to the bottom of things tonight.

"Young, party of four," called the hostess.

We stood to follow her to our table. I reached for

Ebony's hand and stopped her.

Listening to their story had opened my eyes. We were not the first interracial couple in the history of the world, but we were the only couple I knew of until now.

The time spent with Trina had been brief, but my feelings were not as deep as they were for Ebony. I'd thought long and hard about interracial dating after the run in with her brothers. I was aware there would be obstacles in our path. Tonight confirmed it. I'd never fully considered what Ebony's life could be like without the support and love of her family. Tierra's tale of hurt was the last thing I wanted my love to deal with.

In the middle of the restaurant, I placed my hands on either side of her face and kissed her long and slowly.

Ebony laughed her surprise at the few claps from patrons.

"Wow, I'm still dressed."

"Yeah, but tonight, it's about us, okay?"

She reached up to wipe lip-gloss from my mouth. "Okay."

We headed for our table.

CHAPTER 32

Ebony

Brian closed the passenger door, then walked around and climbed into the driver's seat. We'd been driving for a few minutes when I glanced over. He was unusually quiet. An overhead street light illuminated the car, showing him deep in thought. His eyebrows furrowed, his deep blue eyes focused on the road, and both hands clenched the wheel. Whatever was on his mind must have been serious. He didn't even acknowledge the radio when his favorite song came on.

Maybe we mused about the same thing.

Thank God my family wasn't giving me the same kind of grief Tierra's family gave her. Then again, everyone in my family didn't know about Brian. My parents' thoughts on the situation worried me more than Lashana's or Trevon's opinions.

I had imagined what my parents would say once they found out. My father, a man of few words, would probably give me the same stern look he'd given me as a child. The look that said I should rethink my decision and find another option.

My mother would ignore what I said and tell me about eligible bachelors number thirty-five and thirty-six ... tall, dark, and blah, blah, blah. She would pretend to listen and then insist a relationship with a black man would be easier than an interracial one.

That wasn't true. Relationships, no matter what race, were difficult. It took work on both people's parts to make it work. Happiness and satisfaction had nothing to do with the color of someone's skin.

Okay, maybe that wasn't the complete truth.

The difference in skin color could make it harder to relate to each other on a certain level. In the end, it all came down to how much emphasis we put on the differences.

But those differences, no matter how small or great, could make you become an open-minded person. Those differences could keep your relationship alive and interesting as time went on.

The time spent with Patrick had taught me that being goal-oriented hard workers and the same race were the only things we had in common. Our relationship lacked the most important things, such as support, genuine love, and understanding. He'd never approved of my job but wanted me to support him.

Brian was different; he wanted me to succeed. He loved and supported me, even when I turned away his help. His feelings for me were genuine, not forced, not faked.

The only difference was the color of our skin. What we looked like on the outside didn't change what was inside, in our hearts. I embraced our differences. The texture of his hair, the color of his eyes, the firmness of his narrow lips …

Being with someone else would never be an option, black, white, or any other race.

I loved the man, the person, the human being.

I had to admit, Tierra made some valid points. Telling my parents now or months from now would not change how they felt. In the end, what mattered most was what I wanted.

I wanted Brian.

The illuminated lights on the dashboard read nine o'clock, which meant it would be midnight in Charlotte. It was too late to call, but first thing in the morning, I would.

Wouldn't they be shocked when the phone rang with Brian and me on the other end?

"Baby, wake up."

Startled, I opened my eyes to find his hand extended to help me out of the car.

"Thinking with your eyes closed is a dangerous thing to do." I yawned.

His smile hid his thoughts. "It's been a busy week for both of us. Come on."

I reached for his hand, holding tight as he drew me out of the car. He locked our fingers together and guided me to the front door. My heart raced as he dug in his pocket for his key.

Brian expected me to go inside. My feet froze in place. I could not think of a valid excuse to avoid going in.

"What's wrong?" He stopped at the top step.

"Nothing … I'm just … waking up." *Damn. Another lie.*

"I can take care of that." His grip tightened as we continued up the steps and he unlocked the door.

Everything is going to be okay.

Brian led us into the living room.

My legs were like one-hundred-pound weights glued to the floor.

"I know you're tired, Ebony. This will only take a moment."

My hesitation was misinterpreted.

Brian let go of my hand and walked to the CD shelf.

The loss of his hand in mine left me feeling abandoned. Everything seemed to go into a tunnel as the memory of what happened at that very spot flashed before me, blocking Brian from my view. It felt as if I watched a movie.

Javan's massive frame towering above me, pinning me to the very shelf Brian stood before. A whimper built in my throat. "Don't do this, Javan … please …"

A piercing scream echoed in my head, causing me to jump. Javan's laughter was vicious after he slammed me against the solid wooden case when I tried to run. CDs rained down to the floor, dislodged from their resting place. The chilling sound did nothing to mask my cries or his grunts as he took what he wanted, stripping me of my will.

I could feel an echo of pain radiate down my back and arms while my knees grew weak from fear. Tears stung my eyes as my lips quivered. I forced my hand to my mouth before any sound escaped.

"Ebony, did you hear me?"

Brian's voice brought me back. I wiped my eyes before gripping my shoulders in an effort to keep my shaking limbs hidden. His attention was on the discs in front of him.

"What did you say?" I managed after clearing my throat.

"The *Sade* CD, the one we listened to the night we first made love. I can't find it." He continued to search. "*Hmm*," he muttered. "I could have sworn it was here before I left town. Did you take any of the discs the night you got your ID? There're a few missing."

My heart raced so fast I could hardly breathe. "Um, no. Brian, I'm going to the bathroom."

He nodded, still focused on the task at hand.

My escape managed, I closed the door as quietly as possible and locked it behind me. At least Yasmine would have Javan away from the house for the night. She'd mentioned their plans to spend the night at the hotel instead of going back to either of their homes.

I had to pull myself together. What happened to me had happened months ago to someone else. A rueful chuckle escaped. Why was I kidding myself? After I'd tried to convince myself for three months that what happened was all a nightmare, why would it suddenly become true?

"Brian will protect me. He won't hurt me. It's okay. It's going to be okay."

I leaning against the countertop and repeated the mantra. My head hung low and tears ran silently down my face. Deep breathing helped me focus on the present and push the ghost of the past behind me.

My composure regained, I splashed water on my face and stepped into the hallway. I walked with closed eyes past Javan's room, the scene of the worst night of my life.

Javan pinned me to his bed. Stripped of my dignity and invaded, I was unable to stop him. Unable to cry out for help.

Unable to have Brian come to my rescue.

When it was over, he'd tossed what was left of my tattered clothing at me. He'd thrown the words *whore* and *cunt* at me as if I were nothing. He'd warned me to keep my mouth shut by threatening my future with Brian and my friendship with Yasmine.

And when he'd dressed, he walked away and told me to get out, as if everything was my fault.

I'd left as quickly as I could. The short distance to Brian's room had felt like miles.

Brian stood next to the CD player. "I couldn't find it, but I have a suitable replacement."

"Okay." I forced myself to ignore the memory of Javan standing in this very doorway, tracking my every move. Instead, I closed the door and watched Brian kick off his shoes and strip down to his briefs. He dug into a drawer for a pair of gym shorts and placed my favorite sleeping shirt on the bed.

I closed my eyes tight. The shirt I'd wanted the night I'd come here — alone. It was the number-one reason I'd decided against buying a new ID. I reached for the fabric and held it to my chest.

Brian pulled the covers back on the bed and slid in between the sheets and waited for me.

I can do this. I can stay with Brian, in his arms ...

Praying he wouldn't register the fear in my eyes, I stripped down. His shirt felt like an extra layer of protection as it slid over my body.

Brian was here; Javan was not. Nothing could go wrong. Nothing bad would happen.

I slid into Brian's waiting arms, rested my head on his bare chest, and listened to his beating heart. The cadence of its rhythm reminded me that I was exactly where I needed to be.

"Brad and Tierra had one hell of a story, didn't they?" His fingers slid over my shoulder while he stared up at the ceiling. The lamp by his side of the bed illuminated the room.

"They are brave to push her family's feelings aside and consider their own happiness." I paused. "I learned a lot from them."

"That's good to know. So did I."

"Good, because —"

Brian shifted in bed, pulling his arm from around me. He rested on an elbow and faced me. I leaned back on the pillow and focused on him. I couldn't remember the last time he'd looked so serious. "Ebony, since we've been together, I've had no interest in meeting other women. You know I want to marry you."

My heart nearly stopped at the somber expression on his face and his intense gaze.

"I'm not ignorant to the way black men regard you when we're out. I'm not talking about the ones who have a problem with me being with you. I'm talking about the ones who want you. You told me when we first met that I wasn't what you wanted, physically ..."

My eyebrows narrowed. "Brian ..." I pushed up from the pillow. Where was this coming from? I made those remarks as an excuse not to be with him, hoping they would push him away. Then I got to know him, before my heart broke the rules and fell in love with him. I didn't give a damn about his physique. I loved his body; I loved his skin. I loved him.

"Let me finish," he said, cutting me off. "Listening to Brad talk about his love for his wife and being willing to let go of her made me think." He reached over and ran a finger over my cheek. "Because I love you, I'm willing to step back and let you find the man you're looking for."

"What?"

Brian didn't break at my outburst. "I know you love me, but I want you to be sure, without a doubt, it's me you want. When you decide to talk to your parents ... if they give you a hard time —"

I steeled my voice. "Brian, baby, I know what I want, it's you, and there is no doubt." My heart ached. He couldn't possibly be serious. Had he lost his damn mind? How many shots of tequila had he consumed at dinner?

"You say that now, but what if they threaten to dis-own you? I see how you feel about your family when you talk about them. If they threatened to push you away for being with me, are you sure you wouldn't lis-ten to them? Are you sure you won't want to be with someone else? He paused briefly. "Are you sure you wouldn't rather be with someone like Javan?" His voice was barely a murmur.

My mouth dropped open, and I felt the blood drain from my face. Breathing became difficult. My throat went dry and my voice was completely lost.

Where the hell had that come from? I was still try-ing to wrap my head around his statement when my cell phone rang. I ignored it. The ring tone eventually ended and silence permeated the room; neither of us moved.

It rang again. On the third ring, Brian got out of bed, retrieved it from my purse, and looked at the screen.

"It's Yasmine." He hit the answer button. "Yeah, she's right here, hold on." He handed me the phone.

The expression on his face read as if we were discussing the weather. But his eyes said differently. I could perceive the pain and resolve hidden deep within the blue.

"Hello?" my voice cracked. Yasmine yelled in my ear, laughing with extreme enthusiasm as she shared her news.

News that made my blood run cold. So cold my fingers went numb and the phone slipped from my grasp.

"Ebony, what's wrong?" Brian's voice seemed far away.

Just when I fooled myself into thinking things were getting better, my entire world collapsed around me. All the strain I'd endured to protect the ones I loved was going to hell.

Brian picked up the phone. "Yasmine? Hello? Damn, she hung up." From a distance, I could hear the frustration in his voice.

Oh, God, oh no ...

"Baby, is everything okay? Did someone get hurt?" Brian sat back on the bed next to me, rubbing my hand.

I couldn't face him. Bile from my stomach neared my throat.

"Worse. Yasmine's going to marry Javan."

CHAPTER 33

Yasmine

In my opinion, engagement sex was much better than dating sex.

Javan was beside me, panting, his eyes closed. The man knew how to please. And to think, I would be waking up next to him for the rest of my life.

When we started sleeping together, commitment of any kind was not the plan. We'd have dinner, maybe some pillow talk. But mostly it was all about sexual satisfaction.

Then one day, Javan decided to take things to a different level. Or had it been me who instigated the change?

It really didn't matter, because in the end, we both followed the other's lead. Somehow, he'd managed to put up with my ridiculous desire to put on a show about being together. I planned mini anniversary dates where he'd show up dressed to impress. His long flowing dreads would be shiny and well maintained. He'd wear a tailored suit that fit his football frame to a *T*. A bottle of wine and roses would always be present.

And his sexy, wide-mouthed smile. The same smile he wore when I took my time pleasing him. The smile he wore now as he drifted off to sleep.

A small squeak escaped my smiling lips. He'd put in his share of work, but I'd rocked his world thoroughly.

My heart could explode from the unfounded joy.

I'm getting married!

So much to do, so little time. Or was it? It all happened so fast we hadn't set a wedding date yet.

Javan surprised me by arriving before I got off work with a box of chocolates and a dozen yellow roses. Our plans were to have dinner, of course. It didn't surprise me when Ebony and Brian opted not to hang with us. Ordinarily I would have been mad, but not tonight. At least one of them broke away from whatever kinky sex they were having and answered when I called to share my happy news. Even though the call had ended abruptly, I knew deep down, she would be excited for me.

Ebony and I didn't see eye-to-eye when it came to relationships. I was happy she'd finally found the right man for her. Brian definitely knew how to take care of my girl. I wished them happiness.

A smile spread across my face as Javan snored in his sleep. I definitely had found mine.

Now that my life and relationship seemed to mirror hers, I hoped my dedication to the career I wanted would be the same. Like Ebony, I would do whatever it took to see my dream come true. Over the past few weeks, she'd inspired me to make plans to transition to my dream job as a fashion consultant. I'd always had a passion for fashion, hell after growing up near Hollywood and Rodeo Drive, who wouldn't?

For the past two months, I'd been toying with the idea to make my business official. My parents didn't know I had offered my services to hotel guests as a test study. Since they worked primarily at the original hotel's location, I had unrestricted say over what happened here. The only thing my father expected was paperwork and reports turned in on time, along with increased profits. As long as I produced, he didn't keep an eye on the day-to-day activities.

So far, I'd averaged at least two clients a week. I could only imagine what would happen once I advertised my services outside the hotel. I'd just started on my business plan. When it was complete, I would present it to my father, and if all went well, they'd not only give me their blessing, but financial backing as well. If they agreed to let me rent out an unused room in the hotel, I would have an affordable storefront, and draw business to the hotel as well. It would be a win-win for all.

If everything went according to plan, *Dreams* would be up and running in three months. But first, I had a wedding to plan.

For once, everything in my life had found a balance. My only wish was that both of my friends would know happiness the way I did now.

I studied Javan's sleeping face. He looked so peaceful. We'd failed to pull the sheets over us, so I took advantage and studied his delectable brown skin from head to toe. Well, mostly the wonderful part between his powerful thighs.

Wicked thoughts came to mind. How long would it take him to wake up if I ... Only one way to find out.

CHAPTER 34

Brian

"Ebony, what's wrong?"

The stress in Brian's voice was audible. How many times had he asked me this week?

His fingers were warm when he brushed them over my skin and pulled my hair from my face while I threw up.

Yasmine is going to marry Javan. What happened? They weren't supposed to be together this long. This was my fault. I should have told her; now it was too late. Protecting her emotions had been one of the reasons for keeping what happened a secret. Now, things were ten times worse. She'd done the one thing I never dreamed she'd do.

She'd let her heart get involved.

I couldn't let her go through with it. I had to tell her

about Javan.

"Ebony, talk to me."

Oh, God, telling her meant Brian would find out, too. What choice did I have? Continuing to keep this secret would only ruin Yasmine's life. Hadn't I done enough already?

I rose from the toilet's edge, moved to the sink, and rinsed the taste of bile from my mouth.

"There's something you're not telling me. You've been acting strange lately, crying, and now you're throwing up? What is really going on?" Brian grabbed my shoulders and spun me around to face him. "Are you sure you're not pregnant?"

Confusion and fear lined Brian's brow. I could no longer continue to live this lie. I had to have faith in our love. I had to trust Brian would believe me. I opened my mouth to speak, but the words I needed to say stuck in my throat.

"No, I'm not." I pulled away and turned back to the sink.

"Then what is it? Why do you cry all the time? You've been shedding tears as though, I don't know ... as if you're not happy with me. Damn it, Ebony, you even cry when we make love. Is it me? Am I right? Would you rather be with someone else?"

I turned to face him, leaning against the counter's edge for support. I had to find my voice. "No, Brian, it's not that. I want to be with you ... it's just ..."

He eyed me suspiciously. "It's just what?" He huffed. "Ebony, you've changed. We used to get together any chance we could and it didn't matter where we were. Now we only spend time together on your terms. At your place, or anywhere but here. I damn near dragged you inside tonight! You've never acted that way be-fore. And now the moment Yasmine says she's marry-ing Javan, you run in here and ..." His eyes narrowed. "That's it ... shit!" He spun and punched a hole in the bathroom wall.

I shrunk back, my heart pounding at his outburst. I'd never seen him angry before. Fear crept into my veins. "Baby, what are you talking about?"

"You'd rather be with Javan," Brian said through tight lips. "He warned me, he flat out told me you'd been with someone else, but I didn't believe him. I didn't want to believe him. What he really meant is you'd been with him." He shook his head in disgust. "Why? Ebony, you said you loved me. And Yasmine ... your best friend?"

"He told you I slept with him?" That arrogant son of a bitch. He wasn't sure I wouldn't tell Brian what he'd done and covered his ass. "I didn't sleep with Javan. He raped me!"

The moment the words left my mouth, my eyes widened. The ugly truth was out on the table.

"That's a lie," Brian spat out.

I was speechless. That's not how he was supposed to react. Angry, yes, but not at me. The man who loved me was supposed to pull me into his arms, tell me every-thing would be okay.

He was supposed to go find Javan and beat his ass.

Brian stalked the small space in the bathroom. "How could you lie? Rape? That's the one thing a woman can say to ruin a man's reputation for the rest of his life." He faced me, his blue eyes ice cold. "You're a grown-ass woman, Ebony. I'm a grown-ass man who," he chuckled darkly, "loves you so much I was ready to step aside and let you decide if you wanted to be with someone else." The tone of his voice went frigid as he squeezed his eyes shut and inhaled deeply. "Apparently I waited too long. Since you've made up your mind, we don't have to waste any more time. Who do you want, me, him, or someone else?" His eyes flashed opened and zeroed on me.

I was in complete shock. Did he not hear a word I'd said? How could the man I love not believe me? What reason did he have to accuse me of defamation of character?

I breathed deeply. I had to make Brian believe me.

"I would never lie about something like this." My body shook. It took everything within me to project my voice.

His expression continued to show disbelief. My word against Javan's strategic lie was not enough.

"Do you remember the day after you left? You called ... I told you about my lost ID?" He glared but didn't answer. "You told Javan to let me in. He did. He followed me to your room and questioned me about our relationship. He cornered me, Brian. I made it to the living room." My throat tightened, my breathing became rapid, making me lightheaded. I shut my eyes, unable to avoid visualizing the scene once again.

"He told me I should give him a try ..." My voice faltered. "He backed me into the bookcase ... your CDs fell ..." Javan's ragged breathing flooded my ears. "I begged him to let me leave. He laughed ... he laughed." Tears fell as the pain of the past few months forced its way out. "Oh, God, Brian, I ran and fell ... I fought, but he slammed me into the wall ..." My rapid breathing made it impossible to articulate. "He dragged me to his room

… and raped me."

Brian stared, his jaw clenched and he drew his lips into a tight line. "If he raped you, why didn't you tell me? Why wasn't he arrested?"

"Because, I didn't want to hurt you! I didn't want you to stop what you were doing to see about me, I didn't —"

His hand flew up and stopped me in mid-sentence. "You know, I thought we could work through this. I want you to be honest and just admit you slept with him. I can deal with that. But I can't deal with the lies. I've never lied to you, Ebony. Never about my feelings, my family … nothing. I expect the same from you." His eyes held pain and disbelief. "If all you can do is lie to me, then it's best if you leave." Brian punched the door and stormed out of the bathroom.

Unable to stand on weak legs, I slid soundlessly to the floor.

What the hell had happened? I had been honest. I'd told the truth. And now he no longer wanted me.

Javan's cynical laughter replayed in my head. *"You cheated on him. That's what he'll say. Why would he believe you?"*

He was right.

Brian believed the liar, convinced the person who told the truth was the one being deceitful.

Javan had won.

I lost everything that mattered most.

The man I loved had walked away from me.

The moment Yasmine learned the truth; I would lose my best friend.

And I might have lost our baby …

My heart broke into pieces on his bathroom floor. I

did the only thing I could, pulled myself together and went to his room. He wasn't there. I dressed quickly and gathered my things.

Brian sat on the sofa in the living room with his head in his hands. Disheveled blond curls and blue eyes rimmed in red regarded me. His lips parted to speak, but nothing came out.

So I spoke instead. "You're right, Brian. I have lied, and I'm sorry. But I would never lie about something like this." My voice remained unbelievably controlled despite the whirlwind of emotions that flooded me as I died inside. "You asked about me being pregnant. No, I'm not, but I could have been. Now I'll never know. Javan didn't use a condom. I took a morning-after pill to protect myself, to protect you. I couldn't stand what would have happened if I was pregnant, not knowing whose child I carried. What would have happened if I gave birth to a child that wasn't yours? Could you live with that? I never wanted you to find out about this, Brian. I wanted to have your baby. Now, because of what Javan did to me, I may have very well killed it. You have no idea how much that hurts me." My balled fist went to my stomach and my heart; my breaths emerged ragged. I took a deep breath to steady myself.

Brian's eyes widened.

"Now I have to live with the consequences of my decisions. You wanted honesty, there it is. I swear to you, I've never lied about my feelings for you. I wish you would believe me, but if you don't …" Unable to continue, I took one last long look at him, praying he'd say something.

He didn't.

I turned and walked out the door.

I managed to hold my emotions in check as I backed out of his driveway.

Two miles down the road, I pulled into a gas station and succumbed to tears.

CHAPTER 35

Brian

The woman I loved just walked out of my life without slamming the door.

What the fuck had happened?

Twenty minutes ago, we were in bed while I said the stupidest shit in my life.

"I love you. I want you to be happy. I want you to be sure."

It was all true.

I loved her deeply. I wanted her to be happy with me. I needed her to be sure.

Listening to Brad talk about how his willingness to give the love of his life up solidified their happy ending was admirable. Was I wrong for wanting the same?

Ebony made it known the night we met I was not her type. But I wanted her. My persistence eventually broke down her walls and let me in. Not just as a friend, not just as a lover, but into her heart.

At least that's what I'd thought.

Ebony was mine when I'd left town. She promised to wait for me. I promised her I'd be faithful, and I had been. No matter how many times temptation to relieve the sexual frustration building inside waved itself in my face.

I never questioned her whereabouts nor speculated what she was doing the times she didn't answer her phone. Ebony never gave me a reason not to trust her with my heart.

I remembered the day she changed. Things were fine the first day I was gone. We talked, sent text messages, flirted on the phone, taunting and teasing late into the night.

Until day two.

It was the night of our first show and the stadium was filled to capacity. Anxious to tell her about it, I called after two a.m., even though she would be going to class early the next morning. When there was no answer, I assumed she was asleep. We hadn't missed a call the same time the night before. I was disappointed, but understood.

That was the night Ebony had gone back to my house for the ID she claimed to have lost.

I closed my eyes. Then it dawned on me. She hadn't answered because she'd been with Javan. The image of her caramel legs spread wide for him, mocking me as he pumped inside of her pushed itself into my head.

He hadn't answered his cell either.

Dammit!

We talked the next day. I asked about the missing card and it took a minute before she answered my question. With all the problems she'd endured because of losing the thing, it surprised me she hadn't been excited about getting her book.

I'd sent her the money she needed and extra for anything else she hadn't mentioned.

Now I understood.

She used the lost ID as a ruse, a convenient excuse for her to slip in and fuck Javan's brains out.

Ebony was that damn good in bed.

I rubbed the aching spot in my chest, the place where my heart had been before she ripped it out.

No wonder he'd been smug about the possibility of her cheating. He'd been joking about sleeping with her since the first time I mentioned her name. If Ebony had given him a hint of wanting to fuck him, he would have jumped at the opportunity without thinking twice.

The sick bastard.

What happened to the Ebony I knew? The beautiful, caring, hard-working woman I'd fallen in love with? That woman would never lie about her feelings for me, then sleep with my so-called friend. My Ebony would never sleep with her best friend's boyfriend.

I rose from the sofa to pace the living room.

The last night we'd spent in my bed before I left town blew my mind. She declared her love for me. She promised to wait for me. She promised to love our baby if she'd gotten pregnant.

The love we'd made that night had been like nothing we'd ever done before. I knew without a doubt she wanted to be with me.

When I boarded the bus, she kissed me with such passion everyone within viewing distance knew the depth of our relationship.

If Ebony truly meant it, why in the hell would she

cheat on me less than two days later?

I couldn't wrap my head around it.

"Javan raped me."

Why allege the assault? I stopped in the middle of the living room and dug the heels of my palms into my eyes to wipe the memory of the conversation away. It didn't work. Ebony's pained expression planted itself firmly in my mind.

Her face appeared to be a mixture of pain, sorrow, and relief. Why would her telling me she'd been raped —not made love to or even fucked—be a relief?

If she cheated on me and I addressed it, wouldn't she look guilty?

There was no evidence of embarrassment or regret in her voice or her eyes.

My pace brought me to the CD shelf and blocked my path.

Ebony claimed Javan trapped her between the sofa and the door.

I tried to picture it in my mind. Javan and I were the same height. At six-two, Ebony's head stopped at my shoulder, making her the perfect height to lean down and kiss. The difference in our height made me feel the need to protect her like a fragile vase in need of care so that it wasn't broken.

To Javan, she would be the perfect target for intimidation.

What had she said?

"He slammed me into the wall ... CDs hit the floor ..."

My attention went directly to the shelf and the empty spaces of the missing discs. When I had gotten home, the shelf had been out of order. Javan very rarely borrowed any of the discs. He preferred hi-tech equipment instead of old school CDs. He'd given me his entire collection after moving his music to MP3s.

Ebony hadn't borrowed any discs.

On a hunch, I pulled the shelf away from the wall. Despite wishing I were wrong, the evidence didn't lie.

The four-inch-wide dent in the wall had not been there when I left. When I looked down, I spied the missing CDs half hidden beneath the corner of the shelf. A thick layer of dust collected on them.

And there was Ebony's ID, covered in the same layer of dust.

My heart dropped to the floor, the same time my knees hit. I wrapped my fingers tightly around the plastic. My grip snapped it in half.

Ebony had been telling the truth.

Javan did rape her.

I am going to kill ... that sick son of a bitch.

CHAPTER 36

Ebony

"A re you sure you're okay?" Kaitlyn sat on the edge of my bed and handed me two aspirin and a cup of water.

She'd been by my side since the moment I'd walked in the door with red eyes and tear-stained cheeks.

"Is it about Brian?" The angrier she got, the more pronounced her country twang emerged. "Did he hit you?"

I swallowed the aspirin and chased it with the water. "Yes it's about Brian, but it's not what you think. He'd never lay a finger on me." I drank more water. Despite the cool liquid, my throat felt as dry as the Sahara desert.

"I don't believe you." Her suspicious eyes traveled over my body.

I glanced down at my disheveled clothing hastily

thrown back on before leaving Brian's house. "Believe me." I sat wearily, kicked off my heels, and pushed up from the bed to change my clothes.

The reflection in the mirror told it all. My appearance had changed drastically from the time I'd left earlier in the evening. Every hair had been in place, make-up lightly applied, and a look of pure love and happiness had been on my face.

Now I looked like the emotional hell I'd been through.

The look of hate on Brian's face when he accused me of lying would forever haunt me.

I would forever be *the other black woman* who'd broken his heart.

How had things gone so horribly wrong?

From the beginning, Brian was vigilant, despite my attempts to discourage his advances. He'd done what I didn't expect. He'd boldly declared his intentions for a relationship before getting me in his bed. He'd been honest about not wanting a quick lay; he wanted me. And true to his word, he'd used every trick he could muster.

He'd gotten inside my head before my pants.

Despite what had happened, I knew he still loved me, because God knew how much I loved him.

He had to still love me ... he just had to.

It was hard to process the evening's events. First, he'd acted like a complete moron and suggested I leave him to be with someone else. It would never happen, not even for a short period of time. Just because his cousin's story had romantic elements mixed with a heroic gesture, which had led to a happy ending didn't mean our relationship was in need of the same.

Why couldn't he understand it would never work for us? I would never see anyone else. We would be two miserable people trying out a stupid trial separation that wouldn't lead to anything.

I never got to address the matter.

Brian believed I cheated on him, not just with anyone, but with his so-called friend. Nothing else that I said mattered. Not the rape ... not the possibility of a lost pregnancy. All Brian saw was my supposed infidelity.

Javan had planted a diseased seed in Brian's head that sprouted into a tree of deceit.

I suspected Brian had been plagued with the fact he wasn't black. Even though he hid it, I knew it messed with his ego. I knew, because there were times when we had been together in public and I wished I could be white. Not because I didn't love my heritage, but because for once it would be nice to blend into the background and not feel like every whisper was about us.

My love and commitment to Brian and our relationship helped me ignore the negative and focus on the positive things between us.

Being with him was all I wanted.

Javan's lie was kindling onto an already smoldering fire.

I should have told my parents about us months ago. If I had, maybe Brian wouldn't have been so quick to believe what he'd been told. Now I knew why he'd questioned me about my family. He was worried I'd leave him for someone my family would approve of.

I knew that would never happen; he didn't.

It shouldn't have taken hearing Tierra talk about her family's negative opinions to convince me to shout my love for him from the rooftops. Telling my siblings was not enough. In the end, I should have known he'd be concerned about my parents' opinions. Especially since he intended to marry me.

Now it would never happen.

But Yasmine was going to marry Javan.

My head ached.

Hearing about their impending union had left me speechless.

Caught up in my own personal drama had made me blind to everything going on around me. Trying to pretend Javan hadn't attacked me had not been wise. I should have opened up and told Yasmine. She should have known the man she was dealing with before her heart came out of its enclosed shell. And now, because of me, it would be broken again.

Just like I'd broken Brian's. Although I hadn't physically done anything to hurt him, my lack of faith in our relationship was just as bad.

Despite my best intentions, what I thought of as my burden alone to bear had affected everyone around me. Even Kaitlyn.

Emotionally exhausted, I slipped out of my dress and into jogging pants and an oversized T-shirt.

"Did Yasmine say when she'd be back?"

Kaitlyn continued to watch me. "I believe they're stayin' the night at the hotel. Guess she'll be back in the mornin'."

It was nearly midnight. The only option would be to wait it out until morning.

The shrill sound of the doorbell followed by pounding on the door made us both jump.

"Who the hell is it at this time of night?" Kaitlyn

walked to my bedroom window. "It's Brian."

I gasped. What was he doing here? Had he come to accuse me of more lies?

The knocking and ringing continued with no signs of letting up. "Ebony, we need to talk!" His voice drifted up to my bedroom window.

I sat rooted to my bed unsure how to react.

"I take it you want me to answer the door," Kaitlyn said. "Do you want him to go away?"

Unable to articulate, I couldn't even shake my head. Kaitlyn didn't wait around.

Somehow, I managed to get on my feet and walk to my desk. I rested my hands on the back of my chair and strained to hear the raised voices from downstairs.

"Brian, no!" Kaitlyn yelled. "She doesn't want to see you."

Heavy footsteps resounded on the stairs then stopped abruptly when Brian reached the threshold of my door.

"Ebony ..." he said softly. "Baby, I'm so sorry ..."

I forced myself to look at him. His intense gaze focused on me, yet he made no move to come closer.

Pain, worse than what I'd experienced from Javan's hand, racked my body. My grip on the chair tightened. I made no attempt to hide my tears. I didn't know why he'd come here, and I didn't care. The fact the word *baby* had left his lips told me what I needed to know.

He still loved me.

Kaitlyn appeared in the doorway behind him. "Ebony, I tried to make him leave ..." Brian's body blocked my view, but her voice carried over his shoulder.

"It's okay," I managed.

Brian continued to watch me. Pain, sorrow, and apology were in his eyes.

"I'm an asshole, Ebony. I never should have doubted you. I should have listened. Baby, I am so sorry." The corners of his eyes glistened over bloodshot eyes. He hesitated before taking another step toward me.

"Why would you believe me now?" Hearing him apologize wasn't enough.

"Because of this," He held out broken pieces of my ID, the one I'd lost, the catalyst of my nightmare. "I found it behind the CD shelf after moving it and found the gash in the wall. Ebony ..."

My knees went weak from relief. Brian caught me in mid-fall and held me tight against his body. He carried me to the bed, sat down, and pulled me into his lap.

For the first time in months, I truly cried. Tears of joy, tears of pain, and tears of sorrow. Every unwept tear held inside of me found its way out.

I held onto Brian as tightly as he held onto me. Although he didn't make a sound, his quivering body told of silent tears as much as the wetness on his cheeks.

I pulled back, cupped his face in my hands, and waited for him to lift his sorrow-filled eyes to meet mine.

"It's my fault. I never should have left you." His voice was rough with despair. His hands no longer held my waist. Instead, he'd balled them into fists as his lips pulled in a grim line.

"No, Brian, it's my fault. I should have listened to you. If I had, I never would have been there."

Kaitlyn cleared her throat. "Uh, excuse me. I don't know what this tearful reunion is about. Can somebody tell me somethin'? Is this any of my business, or should

I leave you alone so you can stop cryin' and have hot make-up sex?"

Kaitlyn's comment obviously meant to lighten the mood didn't work.

Brian looked at her briefly. "She doesn't know?"

"Know what?" Kaitlyn watched both of us. Worry replaced curious humor.

I shook my head.

Brian's eyes stayed on mine. "Javan raped her while I was away," he said through clenched teeth.

"What?" Kaitlyn leaned against the door. "Are you okay? There was a pause as her hand went to her mouth. "Yasmine doesn't know, does she?"

"No," I said.

"Oh. My. God." She stared at both of us in disbelief.

Brian focused on Kaitlyn. "Where are they?" His voice went hard.

"Uh, at the hotel where she works." she stuttered, her gaze flipping back and forth between us.

Brian kissed me gently, then firmly pushed me off his lap and stood. "Which room?"

"The Honeymoon Suite, I think ..." The moment it dawned on her why he'd asked, her green eyes nearly bulged out of her head.

Brian stalked to the doorway where Kaitlyn stood. "Move, Kaitlyn."

"What are ya gonna do?" she asked, standing toe-to-toe, her green eyes never wavering.

"I'm going to kill him." His voice was devoid of all emotion as he moved her effortlessly out of the way.

"Brian, baby, no ..." I rushed the door and stopped in my tracks when he turned on the top step and faced me.

"He raped you, Ebony. He forced himself on you and

took what was mine. He forced you to kill what could have been our child." His voice dropped low, full of rage. "He nearly caused me to lose you."

Our eyes connected. I could feel his anger and pain seep into my very skin.

"We can call the police ... find another way to handle this," I pleaded, hoping being rational would calm him down long enough to rethink his decision.

"Call them and pray they get there first."

He disappeared down the steps in a flash. The door to his truck slammed before his tires screamed as he peeled out of the driveway.

CHAPTER 37

Yasmine

"Mmm, that feels good, don't stop."

Javan's large hand moved slowly, massaging my back. Even though we'd made love twice, the feel of his hands on my body ignited me like the first time. "So what do you think about June?"

His fingers froze. "For what?"

I rolled over on my back. He looked delicious. His thick dreads hung loosely, masking his face. My eyes tracked to parted lips that waited for action, his deep penetrating gaze heavy with desire. I bit my lip as my thigh brushed over his arousal.

I glided my fingers over a handful of locks as he leaned down and kissed me deeply. I loved the way our lips locked together. They felt like heaven and sin as his kiss moved down and worked my chin, my throat, and my breasts.

"Oh, no," I giggled. "You're not avoiding this conversation. What do you think about a June wedding?"

Javan regarded me with eyes so filled with desire he looked confused at the topic at hand. His head — actually, both of them — focused on one thing.

His eyebrows furrowed. "That soon, Yasmine?"

"June is nine months away. There's so much to do. I've got to find a place for the wedding and reception. We've got to come up with a guest list. I've got to find a dress for the girls and for me. And we've got to find someplace to live. Both of us have roommates so moving in together is not an option. And, oh, God, we haven't met each other's parents yet."

The expression on his face was comical. "I didn't think about that."

"Yeah, baby, it's work to get married. But once we are, the benefits are ..." I grinned wickedly. "Let me show you." I pushed him onto his back and straddled him.

"I like this part." His voice went deep as he grabbed hold of my hips.

Our tongues were fighting their private war when heavy banging on the door startled us.

"Didn't you put the DO NOT DISTURB sign on the door?" His annoyance mirrored my own.

"Yes." My employees knew not to disturb me unless it was an emergency. Such as the hotel being on fire. "This better not be about the computers," I mumbled and climbed off Javan to grab the guest robe from the bathroom.

Javan stayed in bed, smiling. His thick biceps were pronounced as he shifted his arms behind his head.

The banging continued.

"Go get 'em, baby." He chuckled.

I reached the door, twisted the lock, and yanked it open. "What the hell do you — Brian?" He had a murderous expression on his face. "What's wrong? Is Ebony okay?" I pulled the lapels of my robe tightly across my chest.

"No, she isn't." His lips were drawn tight, his brows dropped low. "Where is he?"

I was really confused. Brian should have been with Ebony, but she didn't seem to be around.

"Why do you —"

"Move."

I stood firm. "Not until you —" Brian shoved past me and headed for the bed where Javan lay.

"Your ass is mine," he growled.

Ebony

"Do you want me to call the cops?" Kaitlyn asked. She held her cell phone in one hand and gripped the door handle with the other.

I drove wildly, trying my best to catch Brian at the hotel before someone got hurt. I struggled to keep from running red lights.

"Come on, come on …" My palm ached from pounding the steering wheel.

"Never mind. The way you're drivin' the police will just follow us in."

"Kaity, I don't know what to do. This is all my fault. I should have said something as soon as it happened."

"Why didn't you?" I saw her turn to face me in my peripheral vision.

I glanced at her, then burned rubber the moment the light turned green.

"Honestly, I didn't think she'd stay with him this long. You know how Yasmine is, always with a new guy every few months. Brian didn't need the distraction while he was on the road. He would have dropped everything and come home. It would have ruined his career. Plus, I was scared he wouldn't want me anymore."

"That's just plain stupid," she said. "Why didn't you tell me?" Another quick glance revealed hurt feelings on her face. "We're friends, Ebony. I could have helped you. You shouldn't have dealt with this by yourself."

Another wave of guilt hit me. "Honestly, Kaity, I didn't want you to keep it from Yasmine. It wouldn't have been fair to you. I'm sorry."

She reached over and gripped my hand. "And you were pregnant?"

I shrugged. "I don't know. I could have been. Before Brian left, we'd had a moment ... and well, both of us were willing to accept the consequences. The next night, Javan raped me and didn't use protection. It scared me. I thought about what would happen if I ended up pregnant and the baby was his instead of Brian's. I couldn't live with that, so I did what I had to do. And I hate myself for it."

Her grip tightened. "God, Ebony, I am so sorry. Whatever you need, I'm here for you."

"What I need is to stop Brian from doing something stupid and destroying his career. I've got to get to him. I need him."

"I'm gonna call the police." She placed the call with her free hand.

The lights of the hotel loomed in the distance. I released her hand to grip the wheel and pushed the pedal to the floor.

Brian

"What the fuck, man!" Javan grumbled as he scrambled naked from the bed and reached for his pants. He hopped around on one leg to get them on. Only the king-sized bed separated us.

My mind went all over the place taking everything in. The fact Yasmine gripped my arm and shouted at me was insignificant to the hum of anger that buzzed in my ear.

I took one look at the bed and felt sick to my stomach.

This was the same room where Ebony and I'd spent the weekend. The room she cried in the moment I opened the door.

And then it hit me, a full shot to the chest.

She'd made love to me after he'd raped her.

How was that even possible? How could she want to be with me after that violent act? After having her will of what happened to her body stripped from her?

The hatred for the man I considered my friend for the past ten years blazed out of control. The logical part of my brain clicked off and went primal.

I vaulted the bed, grabbed him, and threw him against the wall with force I prayed felt twenty times worse than what he'd done to Ebony. I held him in place and, with my free arm, reached back as far as I could, and pounded his face.

"Brian! Oh, my God! Stop, you're hurting him!"

Yasmine grabbed my fisted arm and put her full weight on it, slowing me down.

"You, son of a bitch! How could you do that to her? Why?" I got a few more licks in and a kick to his groin before Yasmine managed to knock me off balance.

Javan slipped out of my grasp and slid down the wall, groaning and holding his sack. It wouldn't be long before his jaw, eye, and lips were black and blue. The sight of blood pouring from his nose and cut lip gave me a small amount of satisfaction, but it wasn't even close to what I wanted him to feel.

"Oh, no, Javan, baby ..." Yasmine pushed past me, ripping the sheet from the bed to blot the blood running down his face. "Brian, what the hell is wrong with you?"

"Whatever she said, the bitch is lying," he spat out along with blood.

"Call her a bitch one more time, and you'll be picking teeth off the floor," I growled while pacing the room. I wanted to push Yasmine out of the way and get to him again, but there was no way I'd put my hands on her.

"What the hell is going on?" she shouted.

Javan struggled to get up. "Brian's woman is a liar."

Yasmine looked at both of us in confusion. "Ebony? What are you talking about?" When Javan didn't supply an answer, she turned to me.

"He raped her." Saying the words again shot a pain to my stomach and chest. Anger like I never felt before flared before my eyes. I wanted to grab Javan's throat and keep him from breathing.

Yasmine's eyes flashed in disbelief.

Javan moved to get up again.

"Sit your ass back down before I put it down for good," I warned.

Yasmine turned to him, an expression of confusion on her face.

"Your girl is a *ho*. She wanted me to —"

I stepped over to give him another helping of personal justice, but Yasmine beat me to it by giving him something akin to a bitch slap. His head spun around, dreads swinging through the air as his head hit the wall. I wanted to punch his teeth in, but her slap sufficed for now.

"Don't talk about her like that! And ... *she wanted you to?* Brian never said Ebony's name. Did you rape her?" she asked.

I couldn't see her face, but her voice sounded pained.

"Because the bitch —"

Yasmine's hand shot out again, but this time he caught it and twisted her wrist. She yelled in pain.

"Don't ever hit me again, bitch," Javan growled.

I got in his face in two strides. "Let her go," I said through gritted teeth.

My hands fisted in a handful of his dreads as I snatched him up off the ground, thankful for the excuse to exact my revenge. He released her, shoving her away. She stumbled to the floor. Javan swung at me, his fist connected with my face and doubled back for my gut. Adrenaline pumped through my veins; I didn't feel a thing.

His next swing missed as I dodged, leaned down, and rammed my head into his chest. I wrapped my hands around his waist and slammed him back into the wall. He pounded my back while I retaliated, throwing punch after punch into his gut.

"Brian!"

In the midst of the yelling, grunting, and crashing of hotel furniture as we fought, Ebony's voice rang crystal clear in the room. I managed to turn my head enough to see her standing horrified in the doorway with Kaitlyn on her heels.

CHAPTER 38

Ebony

The sight before me made my heart stop.

Brian grappled in what looked like a fight to the death. Javan pounded his fist into Brian's back while he punched him repeatedly. Blood smeared them, the sheets, and the wall.

Yasmine was slumped a few feet away, shock, horror, and confusion in her eyes. She rubbed her wrist, tears running down her face.

"Brian, stop, baby, please! The police are on the way!" I wrapped my arms around his waist and pulled while trying to avoid Javan's flying fist. I succeeded with Kaitlyn's help.

Brian panted heavily as I guided him to the other side of the room, anxious to put as much space between them before someone got seriously injured.

"Brian, look at me, please, you've got to calm down," I pleaded.

"Let me go," he ground out through clenched teeth as he pulled roughly at my hands.

His eyes remained focused on his target. Blood ran from his cut lip.

"Stop, baby, please. You've done it, you beat his ass, now please stop ..." Tears were in my eyes and voice. I held on tightly, refusing to let him go.

His eyes dropped down and focused on me. I could tell the moment reason clicked back in because his eyes softened. He pulled me close, and held tight.

"Ebony, what the hell is going on? I don't understand." Yasmine managed to stand, clutching at the robe she wore. Her eyes shifted wildly around the room as she put distance between herself and everyone else in the room.

Kaitlyn went to her side and put her arms around her shoulders in support.

My heart ached more than I'd ever imagined possible. The next words uttered from my mouth were going to devastate her already damaged heart.

"It's true. Javan raped me."

Yasmine's eyes closed, her jaw clenched and unclenched in time with her fist. "When?"

"The bitch is —" Javan spat out, but stopped short the moment Brian pushed me aside to get to him.

"No, Brian, that's enough," I begged. He looked down at me and resumed his hold. Satisfied he would stay put, I turned and faced her. I looked her directly in the eye so she knew what I said to be true.

"It happened after Brian left town. I left my badge in his room. Brian knew I was going over to get it because he called Javan and told him to let me in. When I tried to leave, he dragged me into his room and —"

"Enough," Yasmine said through gritted teeth. She opened her eyes and tears poured down her face.

"She's tellin' the truth, Yaz. Brian didn't believe her either," Kaitlyn confirmed.

"I didn't believe her until I found evidence that proved what she said." His voice was heavy with regret. "He tried to cover his ass by suggesting Ebony cheated on me."

Yasmine looked away and shook her head. "I know he's lying," her voice waivered. "I remember the night she came home different. I thought she was upset because you left ..." Tear-stained eyes zeroed in on me. "Why didn't you tell me?"

The ache in her eyes broke my heart. Why did I let things get this bad? She would not have to deal with this pain and betrayal if it wasn't for me. I wasn't the only one affected by Javan's actions. I may have taken the physical brunt, but it was impossible to protect Yasmine from emotional rape.

The realization of my decision shook me to the core. If it wasn't for Brian's physical support, I would have dropped to my knees.

"Ebony didn't tell anyone. She didn't want you to get hurt," Kaitlyn said.

The room remained silent until Yasmine's outburst.

"Why?" She directed her rage at Javan. "Wasn't I enough for you? I thought you were happy with me! You said ... you said ..." Yasmine stopped speaking, her voice gone to tears.

Javan didn't say a word, only stared past her and everyone else in the room.

"He's a manipulative son of a bitch, that's why. He played the same crap on women he dated in college. He played all of us. I should have known." Brian shook his head in disappointment. "That's why he's such a great head doctor."

I'd forgotten Javan was a psychologist. He knew exactly how to convince me to stay silent and make Brian believe him. And how to keep Yasmine preoccupied.

We were still speculating this fact when the police arrived. They took my statement before arresting Javan.

The police cuffed Brian for assault, then told me I would be able to bail him out of jail the next day. I dreaded having to call his parents to get help raising bail money.

Brian stared at me. "I'm sorry I didn't believe you before. I promise I'll never doubt you again."

"It's okay. I should have told you. I'll never keep a secret from you again."

When Javan and Brian disappeared around the corner, I faced my friends.

"Guys, I don't know how to say I'm sorry ... Yasmine ..."

Yasmine stared at me for a moment, her arms still tightly wrapped around her body as if trying to hold herself together. The pain on her face was too much to bear.

After a moment, she turned, gathered her clothes from the floor, and walked to the bathroom. The door shut silently behind her.

Kaitlyn stepped over and reached to dry the tears falling down my face. "Just give her some time."

I nodded and stared at the closed door.

Despite the fact my relationship with Brian was still

intact, my best friend had found nothing but more heartache.

Because of me.

Would she ever be able to forgive me for keeping the truth from her?

Nothing Javan told her had been real. I'd known Yasmine long enough to know the lock Javan had loosened would only be tighter now. The next man who found his way into her life, the one meant to be with her, would have to work hard to win her jaded heart.

Kaitlyn and I turned and watched as the bathroom door opened and Yasmine emerged. Her light-skinned complexion had paled. The edges of her long hair were wet, along with her face as if she'd doused herself with water. Her gray eyes were heavy, rimmed in red. Her attention strayed to the bed and wall before her eyes closed.

"Yasmine …" I paused, unsure of what to say.

She held up a hand. After a moment, her eyes opened and locked on me.

"Ebony, there is nothing you can say to explain why he did what he did. I should have known something was wrong." She sighed. "I think I did know, but I was too wrapped up in my relationship to be the friend you needed. You should have come to me, Ebony. I may not have liked what you said, but I would have believed you."

I nodded as a fresh wave of tears fell. "You're right, I should have said something. All of this," I waived my hands around the room absently, "is my fault. I'll find a way to pay for this."

Yasmine shook her head, a small hint of a smile emerged as she wiped a tear. "The hotel has insurance.

Just promise me one thing?"

"What?"

"Never lie to me," she pointed at Kaitlyn, "us, ever again. If there's a problem, you tell us. That's what friends are for."

"Never," I said, my voice sure. Never would I allow something like this to tear apart my friendship with the ones I loved. It wasn't worth the cost.

"Come on, guys, let's go home," Kaitlyn said.

Yasmine and I stood staring at each other for a moment longer before she opened her arms. I willingly accepted the gesture.

She hugged me tightly. "You're still my girl."

"So are you," I said, hugging her back.

"Oh great, leave out the white girl." Kaitlyn threw up her hands in mock exasperation.

"Get over here," Yasmine and I said in unison.

A group hug brought us together.

I peered over their shoulders at the room that had once been filled with love and roses, but now boasted devastation.

And yet, another love remained.

The man who loved me had stood up for me here.

The love of my friends withstood what I felt would end our relationship.

I would never test the extent of the relationships of the ones I loved again. Love and trust were what would protect the ones I held dear. And honesty. Honesty was just as important.

Secrets should be avoided at all cost.

I gathered my friends and held them close to my heart.

Arm in arm, we went home.

EPILOGUE

Ebony

December – One month later

"**W**hat time did your parents say their flight would land?" Brian asked as we drove to our destination.

"They'll be here at seven." I still couldn't believe my parents were flying to California. Over the years, I'd gone back home to visit my entire family. My parents, on the other hand, hadn't been out here since the day they dropped me off at college, seven and a half years ago. "I can't wait for you guys to meet in person. A picture and talking over the phone doesn't do you justice."

Brian laughed. "Yeah, your mother says she owes me a big hug and your father promised a hearty hand shake. I plan to make sure they live up to their words."

After everything went down, I not only told my parents about our relationship, I told them about my rape. Hearing how Brian fought Javan in retaliation had won them over, especially my father. Now, a month later, they were flying in to spend Christmas in California, breaking my mother's long-standing tradition of having the entire family home for the holidays.

"I still can't get over the fact they agreed to stay at my parents' house," he said. "My mother is working my father like a drill sergeant to get things ready for them. You'd think the president was coming."

I laughed. When it came to entertaining guest, Mrs. Young had no problem making Mr. Young get things done. She did bark orders like a drill sergeant.

"It's not every day you meet your future in-laws," I reminded him.

I appraised the 14-karat white-gold band that boasted three princess-cut diamonds. The two smaller stones represented our lives before we met. The center half-karat stone represented the life we were building together. Brian found symbolic meaning in everything significant in our life. In fact, he found another charm for my bracelet. I already owned one heart, but this one was different.

This heart was broken in half and meticulously put back together: a healed heart.

He told me it symbolized what we had gone through. It served as a reminder that with love, constant communication, and work, our relationship could stand whatever threatened to tear us apart.

No matter how many more charms he gave me, this would forever be my favorite.

"Have you finished packing? Peter and Dylan are free on Saturday. Between the four of us, we should have you moved in within a few hours."

"Don't forget Yasmine and Kaitlyn. They'll be help-ing, too."

"How's Yasmine holding up? We haven't talked much since that night." Brian's eyebrows furrowed in genuine concern. He was aware of the emotional trauma Javan had heaped on her.

"She puts on a brave face, but she's hurting more than she lets on. Her reasoning is at least it was a short engagement. In her mind, four hours didn't count." I laughed lightly. "Now as far as me moving out, she's counting down. My old room is across the hall from hers. She's turning it into her home office."

"Home office?"

"For her business, *Dreams*. She's been playing around with the idea for a while now. Since she has free time, she's decided to keep busy by focusing on getting it up and running. Her parents don't know about it though. Oh and get this, Kaity is planning to be her assistant."

Brian's eyebrows shot up. "Wow. You sure you're not going to feel left out of the loop, you know, not being with your girls?"

I studied the handsome profile of the man I loved with all of my mind, body, heart, and soul. His blue eyes still made my heart race whenever he looked at me.

"Let me think about it." I feigned serious thought while ticking off fingers. "We're engaged. I'm five months away from graduating with a D.V.M. behind my name. If all continues to go well, I'm a shoo-in for the job I've worked eight years to get. Nala, my dear sweet orangutan, is slowly regaining her health. Um ... let me see if I've missed anything." I tapped my finger sarcas-tically on my chin. "Oh, yeah, my gorgeous fiancé has a job making mad money at a major recording studio. And to top it all off, we've just rented a house and are moving in together in less than a week. What is there to miss?"

Brian laughed heartily. "Okay, okay. You're happy with me. Thanks, my ego needed that."

"Oh, don't get it twisted, lover. There'll still be girls' night out."

"And I'll be waiting, keeping our bed warm until you return."

Our bed. I loved the way that sounded. "You'd better." I leaned over to kiss him once we parked.

We emerged from the car. I stood by the door and waited for Brian to walk around and take hold of my hand and intertwine our fingers. We both stared at the brick building.

So many things had changed in the past month, yet our relationship had only gotten stronger.

The moment he was released from jail, Brian had moved out of the house he and Javan had shared. He had a great attorney who got him out on bail the next morning. Because it was a first offense and he had no record, he received probation, community service, and couples' counseling for rape victims, which we attended together.

Javan, on the other hand, had a different outcome. Because I had not reported the rape after it happened, there was no evidence. I'd thrown my torn clothes away and showered the moment I got home. With no rape kit, or visible physical damage, the District Attorney couldn't build a strong enough case to prosecute. It became a matter of my word against his. In the end, Javan got out on bail and the charges were dismissed.

He lost his job as a psychologist, which was a good thing, and moved back to Georgia, his hometown. I could only imagine how many women he'd taken advantage of over the years.

My journey to healing began the moment I started seeing a rape counselor. My doctor had been right. Being able to confide in my counselor, cry, and express my anger allowed me to understand the events of that night were a matter of uncontrollable circumstances and not because of the bad decisions I'd made.

It wasn't my fault. It wasn't my fault.

No matter how many times I repeated the mantra; there were times when I didn't see it that way. Regardless, it was true. My determination to remain financially independent of the man who loved me didn't cause the rape. Javan's malicious intentions did.

"Are you ready?" Brian asked.

I squeezed his hand. "Yes."

Our weekly sessions with the counselor were exactly what we'd needed. If it wasn't for these meetings, I never would have known the depth of guilt Brian felt about what happened. He was slowly beginning to forgive himself for not seeing the signs suggesting Javan would become a threat.

One month down. We would continue to take these classes for as long as it took.

I peered up at Brian. The love I felt reflected back at me in his ocean-blue eyes. He raised our linked fingers to his lips, kissing the back of my hand.

Together we walked in, ready to take another step in building our future.

Thank you for reading *A Heart Not Easily Broken*, the Butterfly Memoirs – Book 1. We hope you enjoyed it.

Find links to all of M.J.'s bestsellers and stay up-to-date with her new releases and specials on her author page: www.WrittenMusings.com/MJKane

MEET THE AUTHOR

M.J. Kane stumbled into writing. An avid reader, she never lost the overactive imagination that comes from being an only child. As an adult, she made up stories — though never shared them — to keep herself entertained. It wasn't until surviving a traumatic medical incident in 2006 that she found a reason to set free the characters inhabiting her imagination. Upon her husband's suggestion, she commandeered his laptop and allowed the characters to take life. It was either that, or look over her shoulder for men carrying a purple straitjacket. And the rest, as they say, is history.

No longer a television addict, if M.J. isn't reading a book by one of her favorite authors, she's battling with her creative muse to balance writing, working as a librarian, and being a wife and mother. She resides in the suburbs of Atlanta, Georgia with her high-school sweetheart, four wonderful children, and three pit bulls. You can find MJ on social-media sites sharing writing tips, talking about music, life, and family. She's always excited to meet new friends.

Instagram: @MJKaneMedia

Twitter: @MJKaneBooks

Facebook: @MJButterflyBooks

NOVELS BY M.J. KANE

<u>The Butterfly Memoirs</u>

A Heart Not Easily Broken

Jaded

Lonely Heart

Nobody's Business

Alone

<u>Short Stories on WrittenMusings.com/MJKane</u>

The Photoshoot

Crossroads (A Butterfly Memoir Novella, Book 3.5)

Family for the Holidays (Ebony & Brian Mini Memoir)

ACKNOWLEDGMENTS

I'd like to thank my family who has been so supportive of my writing career. To my amazing husband, K.C., I would never have picked up a laptop (well, your laptop!) and started writing, much less learned the business side of things (a work that is still in progress). Words can never express how much I appreciate your time and patience, even when it seems I don't. I promise, one day it will stick! To S.C., my manager, number-one beta reader, best friend, listener, and sounding board for my crazy ideas, if it wasn't for your opinions and suggestions, I never would have taken the time to delve deeper into my characters and find their real stories. Knowing that if you liked it, someone else would too, has been my motivation! To my wonderful kids, K.C., J.C., X.C., and E.C., although you've driven me crazy along the way, you've been an inspiration and support in your own ways. Thanks for your hugs and kisses and undying support, and above all, thanks for letting Mommy find herself again!

A heartfelt thank you goes to the many authors I've met along the way. Sandra C., an amazing playwright, who became my first writing mentor. Thanks for taking me under your wing and sharing your knowledge. To the talented women of the Critter Yard: Chicki Brown, Erin Kern, and Zee Monodee, you have paved the way and helped me find my true writing voice. Remember what the first draft of this story looked like? LOL! It took four years to get it right.

Thank you to Sherry Turner, an amazing librarian who is always there to show support to the talented people of Clayton County. She never hesitates to go above and beyond to make the programs offered stay alive. Without you, the opportunities to showcase our talents, (authors, poets, artist, and musicians) would not exist. Thanks for the advice you've offered me along the way.

To my beta reader, A. S., my longtime friend and classmate, thank you for reaching across cyberspace to read my work when it was still in its raw stages. I'm sure you'll love the edited version. Special thanks to fellow author Carmen DeSousa for reaching out to hold my hand through the process of becoming a published author.

And deepest thanks to each and every one of you who have followed my writing journey online and have bought a copy of this book. Enjoy!

Oh yeah, can't forget about my two most loyal followers: my dogs, Vader and Ivy, who were always there to lick my feet, trip me up when I tried to get up from my desk, and begged for special attention. Now we can go outside and play. Well, until the next deadline draws near.

MJ

Made in the USA
Columbia, SC
17 February 2020